The Se[...]
From Aldura

Copyright 2024 by Amye Francis

All Rights Reserved. No part of The Senator from Aldura may be reproduced, stored in a retrieval system, or transmitted in any form or by any means—by electronic, mechanical, photocopying, recording, or otherwise—in any form without permission. Thank you for buying this book's authorized edition and complying with copyright laws.

For wholesale inquiries, please reach out to amyefrancis6060@gmail.com

Published by Radiant Publishing

Paperback ISBN 978-1-963922-09-7

First Edition
Printed in the United States

Acknowledgments

To my cousin by marriage, Abigale Francis,
Thank you for your help in proofreading my manuscript all the way through to the end, and for pointing out the areas that could be improved upon. Your help and insight were invaluable and made this final story a better one.

To Colleen De Silva,
Thank you for helping me fearlessly pursue my creative dreams, and for your help in finally getting this book published!

To my music college mentors, Tanner Erickson and Antonio Marin,
Thank you so much for pouring into me during my days as a student. Your leadership, encouragement, and submission to the Spirit of God have changed my life and given me everything I needed to see the calling on my life and to step out and pursue all my creative dreams.

Table of Contents

The Senator from Aldura 1

Ariella's Choice 43

Vala's Choice 97

The New Year 135

Sunshine and the Darkness 171

Chemical Weapons and a Mystery Girl 213

Flames 257

The Return Home 283

The Battle for Aldura 307

Tears of the Past 327

Epilogue 359

The Senator from Aldura

In a small remote palace on the planet of Steelar-Romlin, an early middle-aged man was sitting at an ornately carved and decorated desk. It was made of a rare dark wood and inlaid with other precious materials. He was dressed in fine robes that showed his taste for luxury. The room he was in was his office space, and as you would expect from his appearance, the room was decorated with fine carpets, curtains, statues, artwork, and many trophies and tokens from his achievements and adventures. He had an appreciation for rare and beautiful things. This man was Casimir Blade, who had just been re-elected as Steelar Romlin's senator to the Galactic Union. Casimir was caught in thought, and dreaming a bit, when his butler announced the arrival of his friend and political colleague, Verdell Andres.

"Verdell, welcome back from your travels. I'm delighted to see you again," said Casimir as he got up to greet his friend.

"Thank you for the warm welcome. It was a very refreshing time but I am glad to be back…and I am honored to be one of the first to congratulate you on another four years of service to the Galactic Union. Another great success or you."

"Yes. I am proud of this victory. I believe it's going to be a good year, and there is much I plan to achieve."

"And I am sure you will achieve it."

"Yes. I intend for our union to become something new. Something that will be big, powerful, and glorious. And to bring much more unity to our people and our government. There are so many opposing views out there right now and I'm afraid the diversity and division will only cause us to fall apart. I aim to bring everyone together in unity, all working together under a single vision. Then, we will become greater than we ever have before…unstoppable, even, in pursuing the vision. Perhaps the greatest civilization in all of history. At least, that is my goal." Casimir paused and began to dream on. "Imagine if time travel was possible, then I could truly learn how to make this the greatest civilization of all time. Maybe someday I will figure it out…"

The Senator from Aldura

Verdell said nothing in response. He was trying to imagine what things would look like if Casimir's dream became a reality. As Verdell was contemplating Casimir's words, Casimir came out of his thoughts and suddenly changed the subject with a question. "Remind me again where you visited."

"Oh, I stopped by Karbalenda and Ontaero... but my last stop was particularly interesting. I visited Aldura. You know, not many people even consider Aldura or have it on their radar. Aldura seems to stay pretty quiet and hidden, but it really is an extraordinary place. Very beautiful, very exotic, and very well educated. It turns out they are way more advanced than I thought. Some of the tech they're working on exceeds that of most planets in the galaxy, in fact. Seeing your taste for beautiful things," Verdell was gazing around Casimir's office space at his many trophies and decorations, "I think you would enjoy a visit there."

"Aldura...interesting." Casimir's interest seemed to grow as he gazed around the room, lost in thought. Then he broke the silence. "You know, Verdell, one thing I have yet to achieve is to find a wife. But she must be no ordinary woman. Fair and beautiful, and a rare treasure among womankind. What would you say of the women of Aldura?"

"Well, like most other women, I would say. Though their culture does produce elegance and beauty. You can find some beautiful and well cultured ones there.

They are rather diverse too. There are people of a rare kind that can be exceptionally beautiful, and some in colors I've rarely seen anywhere else. Of course, then there is the darling of the capitol who has gained quite the reputation as of late. They claim she's one of the most beautiful women alive, and she has the charm and grace to go with it. She is however, a great challenge for anyone who dares to attempt to win her heart. I don't know the details of her story, but she has the reputation of being uncatchable by men, nor does she allow them to control her or sway her. No one has succeeded in winning her heart and not everyone has the honor of earning her favor. She is a proud, single, woman. Interestingly enough, she is only eighteen years of age."

Casimir's interest was piqued.

"In fact, you will have the chance to meet her. She was elected to represent Aldura in the Galactic Union."

"I'm intrigued. Perhaps I will arrange to visit Aldura before the term starts. She could be a challenge worth taking on; and perhaps there are other treasures that remain to be discovered on Aldura."

"You mean…you're going to try to win her affections?"

"If she's worth it…why not?"

"But you are quite a bit older than her…"

"Age means nothing to me. And I think younger will be better, and more lively."

"I don't want to put down your ability to accomplish anything you desire, but this is a woman's heart you're dealing with. Do you really think you can win her over when the younger, more attractive men cannot? I hope your conquest for significance doesn't drive you too far. This is a pretty serious issue to mess with."

"Well...I'm confident there is a way I can make it work out in my favor..." said Casimir thoughtfully. He seemed to know something that Verdell didn't.

Verdell stared at him in awe, not sure how to respond. "Well...if that's what you want..."

"We will see. I think I am going to prepare a visit to Aldura. What's her name?"

"Ariella Callista."

A week later, Casimir did follow through with his plans and arranged to visit the high officials and leaders of Aldura. On his trip, he made it a point to carefully study Aldura and learn all he could about the people and the planet, especially desiring their knowledge of science, technology, and architecture. On his last day, he was invited to attended a reception in the palace, arranged by Aldura's queen and her office to send off Senator Callista. While the celebration was going on, a young Alduran woman named Vala was in the palace servant's quarters packing and getting herself together. Her future would change from here on. Although her prospects looked bright, she could never escape the past. It was about five years ago now. She had lost her family and those closest to her. He had done it; a dark figure who, try as she could, Vala could never recall how he looked except that he was arrayed fully in black, and the voice made her tremble. It said, "May this scene always haunt you in the future. This is my revenge for your doings, all that you cost me. Maybe you will even think twice next time you have the chance to start a strong relationship, hated child!" What she had done to incur this hateful wrath, especially at the age of fifteen, she had not even a faint idea. She had been a normal Alduran girl and lived a normal life learning about fashion, fabrics, sewing and hair styling. Now she was a young woman with a dark past and she had never made a close friend since. She was done. The loss was too painful, and she could never be close to someone again. After it had happened, she had no reason to continue on with life, but she eventually got past her grief and moved forward. Now, her purpose was to protect others and make sure they never had to experience the same fate she had. At sixteen, she decided to change her career path and train to become a police officer, or someone of a similar occupation. It was the custom for Aldurans like herself to choose at the age of thirteen and fourteen whether to stay in school and study more or find a mentor in a certain occupation to apprentice with. When a mentor was found for her, she began rigorous training to become an officer but when her other skills in fashion were discovered, she was selected to begin training for a special assignment. One that must be kept secret. She agreed, and that was why she was now here, packing. She was to be the new handmaid but also a secret bodyguard for Aldura's new senator who would represent her planet in the Galactic Union's senate. While preparing herself, she was remembering again the horrible slaying that brought her here. She didn't feel safe to share it with anyone, so she kept it locked inside her and it hardened her. Soon, she would have to find the packed belongings of the senator and load them on the senator's ship which would fly them to the capital. Then she would have to meet this senator whom she was to serve and protect since she had not yet had the chance. She gazed around her little room, this could be the last time she saw it. She had spent the last year living on the palace grounds during her training. It was a grand and beautiful place.

The palace was a campus of mostly government buildings and living quarters. The most grand and central residential building was the residence of Aldura's elected sovereign. The upper rooms of this "main palace" were private as was typical for Alduran homes, but the ground level was open to approved government officials and sometimes the general public. In the main palace, government officials and the media were gathered to converse with the galactic senator who would represent them, and the few councilors who would work alongside her. The senator was a young lady of only eighteen - almost nineteen - years of age who had won the favor of the majority of both the people and Aldura's politicians. As the senator was speaking with a few Alduran officials, the queen, Aldura's current sovereign, approached her with a man in his middle age.

"Senator Callista," she said to the young senator, "this is Senator Blade from Steelar-Romlin. He has come to visit us, and you in particular. I expect you will see a lot of him during your term."

"I've heard there is something about Aldura that makes their women very beautiful, but I never believed I would find the most beautiful lady in the galaxy here," said Senator Blade, who was truly impressed that Ariella's beauty lived up to what he had heard and imagined.

Ariella Callista was indeed beautiful. She had long golden hair, sapphire eyes and often wore two curls on both sides of her face which added a feminine touch. To Blade's remark, she subtly rolled her eyes and made it apparent that she could care less.

Blade continued, "I am glad to make the acquaintance of such a charming, graceful, and beautiful young lady as yourself."

"Oh, another man to comment on my charm and beauty?" replied Ariella, hiding her contempt with a slight smile. Then her smile vanished into a sterner look. "Flattery has no effect on me, I'm only interested in my duties to my people."

The Senator from Aldura

Senator Blade raised an eyebrow with slight fascination. "So you're one of those politicians? Strictly business and no messing around?"

"You'd better believe it."

Blade briefly looked Ariella over as though he didn't believe she really was what she said she was. "You seem rather young to be taking on this job," said Senator Blade.

"I am, but I have lots of experience. I studied politics most of my life. I participated in youth government programs, held youth offices, paged for senators and representatives, and was an aid for our last senator. I was found to be a good candidate for this office even though I've never held an official one in Aldura's government."

Senator Blade's curiosity grew. He pressed on to see what more he could learn about her. "I understand your planet puts terms on all their offices."

"That's correct. Our government system is a federation with three branches of power and a bicameral legislature." Ariella continued on, with her passion aroused. "We are a capitalist society and our current economy is doing quite well. We even have certain rules that provide provision for the needy more so than many other governments. Our senators are chosen by the provinces' governments while the representatives are elected by the people. We galactic senators are different though, because the galactic senate is unicameral. The people choose two candidates via the representatives and Aldura's government chooses the senator from the two selected candidates."

"You seem to be proud of your planet's governmental system," said Blade.

"Yes, I am; and I could tell you a lot more about it. I believe our system is the best."

"It seems like a lot though, and quite complicated. Your queen is not really a queen, it is simply the title given to her by old tradition. She only has certain powers such as vetoing bills - which can be overridden with a large enough majority of the legislature - and commanding the military; and she doesn't even have the power to declare war? And she can only serve two five year terms." Casimir had clearly done his research.

"And your planet doesn't?" Ariella responded.

"No. We have one ruler whose power and position get passed on to the oldest child. We have only a senate, a unicameral system with an 'emperor' or 'empress'. Things get accomplished a lot quicker."

"Maybe, but is it in the best interest of the people? I think more complicated is good. It prevents tyranny, unless the whole government is occupied by people who are all scheming together; and if that were the case, that's where the people can rise up and overthrow them. If the government does become tyrannical, the people can still fight back."

"It sounds like your people are very difficult to control."

The Senator from Aldura

"That is exactly the point, senator. They are free..." Senator Callista briefly gazed off in the distance, then brought her focus back. "Well senator Blade, it was good to meet you and I hope we will work together for the good of the people of the union, but I don't have much time left to be here at home, so I would like to enjoy the rest of it with friends and family; and I still have to meet those who will be my constant companions for the next few years." With that, Senator Ariella Callista departed.

"Is everything ready to load?" Vala was at the royal hangar where the senator's spaceship was being prepared. The ship was sleek and stylish and colored a beautiful misty silver. The captain of the ship had just approached her.

"I'm Captain Camara, I'm the senator's bodyguard and the captain of this ship. You must be the new handmaid and yes..." he said in a lower voice, "I know you're also a bodyguard." He was just past middle age with plenty of experience.

"Yes, I am," said Vala. "My name is Vala Stella and yes, everything should be ready."

"Well then, let's load up. Amara, come meet the new maid and help us load the ship," said Camara, beckoning to a girl who was not yet eighteen. She wore a uniform similar to what Captain Camara wore but tailored to a women's fit. She had long dark hair that she typically kept in a braid, twists, or hair accessories to hold it back, or sometimes a braid bun. These hairstyles were not uncommon on Aldura. "This is Kaiya Kaida Amara. She's training under me, but I think she's competent enough to do this on her own now."

"You will call me Amara," the girl said. There was little warmth in her voice.

"She's not native to Aldura," said Captain Camara, "she's from the planet Kairah. She left when she was fourteen, but I'll leave it there. It's up to her whether she wants anyone else to know her story. She has no family here and no close friends so I'm the closest she has to family."

Sounds like me, thought Vala to herself.

"Kaiya, if I may use that name, is one of the best guards we have. You may have heard some about her aloof people. They are highly sensitive, able to sense small movements and sounds, and they can read body language rather well. They also have amazing reflexes, stamina and speed. And did I mention she's also a great pilot? I think she has a wonderful career ahead of her."

When everything was loaded, the senator arrived at the hangar where the ship and her companions were waiting. "Captain Adwin Camara," she said as she approached. "I was delighted to hear that we will be working together again this session."

"It certainly is nice milady - I suppose that's what I must call you now - only this time you're my highest priority as far as safety is concerned."

The Senator from Aldura

"Yes, but now you won't have to worry quite as much over the aid. Instead of a human, I have Seren here." Seren was a robotic AI companion with highly functioning software. She was very intelligent and was designed in the image of a woman. "Seren will do a lot of work for me, I'm sure she'll be very helpful."

"Welcome Seren," said Camara.

"Thank you, sir," replied Seren.

"I'm sure you remember Amara, Senator," said Captain Camara.

"I do. I'm glad you will be with us again Amara."

Amara was silent but gave a shy, pleasant smile in response.

"This is your handmaid, Vala Stella," continued Camara.

"Nice to finally meet you Vala," said Ariella as she gave her new red-haired companion a smile.

"I'm glad to have finally met you too milady," Vala replied.

"Well Captain, are we ready to go?" asked Ariella.

"Amara?" the captain said, turning to Amara.

"The ship is ready Captain."

"Well then, it looks like we're ready," said Camara and he escorted the passengers aboard while Amara went ahead to the cockpit.

"Have you ever flown into space before, Vala?" asked Ariella as they made themselves comfortable. There were white cushioned seats, a few tables, sleeping compartments, storage compartments, a kitchenette with food and drink, and just about everything needed to make the trips through space as comfortable and luxurious as possible.

"No, milady, I haven't."

"I think it's fun, especially the blast off," replied Ariella. The engines began starting up. "If you get sick, we have medical supplies and I have some basic first aid training. My father is a doctor, and my mother worked for several years as a horse doctor, so I've learned a lot from them. They would let me join them in their work and allowed me to help with simple tasks," said Ariella.

On Aldura, there were three things the people enjoyed most and put most of their time and education into: sports, arts, and science. The most popular sports were equestrian and archery. Just about every Alduran had either a horse or a bow and knew how to use it. Because horses were so common and well loved, and often considered members of the family, a veterinarian was just as important in their culture as a doctor. Aldurans enjoyed painting and other sorts of art too, and were especially known for their architecture, fashion design, and most of all, dance. Almost every Alduran knew how to dance – they began learning almost as soon as they could walk. Dance was a big part of social gatherings, parties, and events. Ariella loved dancing ever since she began and had learned just about every style of dance. She was one of the best dancers even on

Aldura. Dancing also included ice dancing, which was popular in the winter months but was also used as a cool pastime during the hot summers. Dancing was not only considered a fine art, but also a sport and a part of social life. As far as science went, Aldura had some of the most extensive knowledge and was very advanced in technology. In addition, Aldura was known for its fine drinks, perfumes, scents, and flowers. Aldurans loved flowers. All the cities and houses were decorated all year round with seasonal flowers. Flowers were a favorite decoration for celebrations and special events so when a celebration took place, whole cities would burst with the colors of hundreds or thousands or even millions of flowers. In the spring or late summer when most flowers bloomed, beautiful scents would flood cities, towns, and the country. Flowers were even farmed on many acres of land and bred specifically for scents, looks, and oil. Rose oil was especially loved by Aldurans – they used it for many products as well as their rose tanned leather. Ariella was remembering the beauty of the flowers and the lively dances, knowing that where she was going, these things would be harder to find. She would miss them, and she would miss Aldura. She would be living high up in a penthouse in a large city. She was drawn out of her thoughts when suddenly, she heard over the communicator the captain instructing them to fasten their safety belts until it was safe to move around. Everyone in the ship followed his instructions and

Ariella, excited about the takeoff, eagerly looked out the window while they went higher and higher out of the atmosphere into the peaceful, silent stars. Home was now behind.

A few days after their arrival at the capitol, Ariella, Vala, and the others began to settle in. It didn't take long, as everyone but Vala had lived here before.

As they walked through the capitol building to prepare for the new session that would begin the following week, Ariella came across a few familiar faces and also met many new ones. Previously, she had been hidden in the shadows as an aid and therefore, many people did not recognize her. She was a surprise to many, especially with her appearance. Several people wondered if this fresh, young, fragile looking girl was up to the task of representing an entire planet, and participating in the rulings and law-making of the union. Some chose to take little notice of her, while others desired to meet with this new senator - either because they were fascinated and wished to explore the possibility of becoming friends and allies, they held something against her (whether it be age, looks, or her strong determined will) and sought to know her as a potential enemy or someone to take advantage of, or they were simply curious about her. Ariella began receiving many invitations to meet and tasked Seren with arranging her schedule. As she was walking through a bustling hall, a familiar face approached her.

"Miss Callista."

The Senator from Aldura

"Senator Blade," greeted Ariella.

"I was wondering when I'd see you. I wanted to check in and offer you any assistance you might need in your transition to your new position as senator."

"I appreciate the offer, but so far I am doing just fine. This is not my first time at the capitol. I stayed here for two years as Senator Valencia's aid. I know my way around."

"Ah...but you should know that the life of a senator is very different than that of an aid. Your history will help you, I'm sure, but the life of a senator is a different game. It will take some getting used to. And I don't mean this remark as prejudice against your age..." he studied her carefully, "...but I am concerned you may not be up for the challenge. Or at the very least, it will be difficult for you to adapt and fit in. You are rather young...I would strongly advise you to befriend a senator who is stronger and more seasoned. Someone you can trust to receive advice and protection from. You are going to tread some dangerous waters in this occupation."

A fire had been building up inside Ariella as Casimir spoke each word. She erupted with confidence and a determination to handle things herself. "Senator Blade, I am fully aware of the games people play here. Yes, I am young, but I am not alone and I do have some experience here. I am aware that the politicians here make all kinds of deals and many of them involve relationships, favors, bribes, gifts, flattery, blackmail and even infidelity. I know that, unfortunately, far too often those are what drive the process of decision here. I am determined to come against that norm and show some integrity in this place, and hopefully inspire some others to do the same. That is one of the reasons for my being here and I hold firmly to it. I'm not interested in bargains and bribes, I'm insterested in representing my people well and through honor. I'm strictly here for business, not to find fame, riches, or to fool around. I am not for sale and I hope everyone here will take note of that." She gazed at him with her feisty, piercing blue eyes.

Casimir stared back at her with a calculating look, stifling his amusement with her. "I see. Then I look forward to seeing you hold fast to your integrity. If you can pull that off, and manage to draw a few others into doing the same, I will be impressed. Perhaps you are what this corrupt place needs...a change in the winds...yes, I do look forward to seeing you in action. I hope we can meet again, and soon."

Casimir gave Ariella a very slight bow and she gave him a slight nod, still holding eye contact, as they began to turn and go their own ways.

As time passed, Senator Callista proved to be a very powerful speaker and gained a lot of respect, but there were also those who began to despise her. Casimir Blade would check in with Ariella regularly, and increasingly seemed interested in learning more about Aldura. Ariella continued to remain steadfast in her convictions as the year progressed, amazing quite a few politicians in the senate and even inspiring change in a few. As the second half of the year came about, however, tensions began to arise in the union which then began to trickle into the senate. Soon, there was unrest everywhere. New ideas were rising up – new ideas of the government exerting more control and implementing stricter rules in order to keep the union safe from the rise of a new military threat that was developing outside the union in a remote part of the universe. Naturally, these ideas were resisted by many others who wanted to keep their freedoms. With the rise in tension and confusion, Ariella gained both friends and enemies. A new party had sprung up as well. It was called the Imperialist Party and Senator Blade was its chairman. This party shared the beliefs of bringing in a more militant structure of government. Although Ariella did not agree with the new party's ideas and views, which were very different from hers, she remained on good terms with its leader. As hostilities continued to grow with the completion of the year, Ariella and several other key speakers and leaders began to find themselves in danger on occasion - usually from assassins - and their security guards became extra wary. After the second year came about, Ariella and a number of other politicians who sided with her on many issues began to find themselves under increasing pressure.

By now, Ariella and Vala had become friends as they had spent a lot of time with each other. A close bond between these two would be important. Vala knew this when she began training for her job and at first, it was difficult for her to accept but after about a month, she gave in and began to find a wonderful friend in Ariella. "I'm feeling overwhelmed, Vala." said Ariella as Vala was helping her prepare her hair for a meeting with Casimir Blade. Alduran women wore their hair up for formal or semi formal occasions. Wearing hair down was considered a very informal or casual style. Hairdos often included braids, twists, beads, flowers, tiaras, ribbons, tassels, other accessories, and sometimes even elaborate headdresses. It took time and skill to do some of the hairstyles Ariella wore.

"I can't wait for the break when I'll have the chance to escape this place and spend some time on Aldura. I'm afraid that I'm going to crack under this environment - that I'm going to fail and become like everyone else around here. It's hard to find genuine people. So many of them won't even listen to me unless I offer them something. That's how politics work around here. I'm afraid I'm going to have to lose my integrity and become just like them in my attempts to make sure our people still have a voice. This year I've been bombarded with invitations to parties I'd rather not be a part of and offered money, positions, and all kinds of random gifts in exchange for taking a side I don't agree with. And people have tried to sell themselves to me in exchange for my vote, my time, or specific gifts and requests that I'm not comfortable with. Some have even been bold enough to invite me to sleep with them! The system is so corrupted. I'm strongly doubting there is any hope left. Yes, I've been in this environment before, but I did not fully realize the burdens I'd be facing as a young senator."

Ariella paused and kept silent for a bit, with thoughts still running through her head. Vala meditated over Ariella's words for a bit and then spoke up.

"I agree the system is very corrupt and needs reform. But don't give up hope. They need to see your example. If you can continue to walk in your integrity, it will send a powerful message. I think eventually, others will be inspired to change. Just keep spending time with the ones who are true. And you have Captain Camara, Amara and I, and all of Aldura to support you. We're here for you. I know its hard, but imagine how you would feel ending your term knowing you did a good job and were not swayed, versus having given in. Which one would you regret more?"

"Thank you for your helpful words, Vala. I'll take them to heart," said Ariella thoughtfully. She lost herself in her thoughts again as Vala silently finished her hair. "What do you think of Senator Blade?" she suddenly asked.

"I'm not sure," replied Vala, "I feel uncomfortable around him; especially when he speaks. There's something about his voice."

"I can't tell if he is genuinely a good ally who's looking out for us, or if he's up to something. Perhaps I'll be able to deduce more at this dinner," Ariella replied.

"I'm a bit uncomfortable with him insisting this dinner is private, and not letting anyone accompany you," said Vala.

"His personal security guards will be there. And you'll still be free to wait for me outside," Ariella assured.

"I know…but still…" Vala did not looked reassured despite Ariella's words.

Ariella stood up. "Well, it's time to go." She walked towards the door of her apartment and Vala followed behind. Amara also joined them to escort Ariella to Casimir's chambers in the senate building where he insisted they meet. Once they arrived at his door, Vala and Amara remained outside in the hall where they would wait, while Ariella went in to meet with Casimir. Most of the dinner conversation was around the latest events and bills being brought to the senate, the current state of the union, and small talk about other planets and their senators. As the dinner finished, however, and Ariella got up to leave, Casimir gently constrained her. "Ariella, "I have an important question."

"Go on," replied Ariella as she sat down, feeling a bit of tension rise in the atmosphere around her.

"I want to ask how things are going for you."

"Truthfully, it's been a bit hard today. I just had a conversation with my hand maid about the corruption here. Everyone seems to want to buy me or sell themselves to me. They're asking me for things I'm not comfortable giving. And if I refuse, they choose not to support me or my people. I'm sick of it. How can they be so heartless and numb to justice? It's all about them and satisfying their own selfish desires. I was hoping to inspire others to change, but I don't see that happening."

"Yes. Sadly, it's only getting worse over the years. I've witnessed it and I've also been thinking for a few years now about ways to bring reform. The whole system just needs to be over turned and replaced in my opinion. I have my ideas of how to bring more order and end all the little games they are playing. I don't believe one person can change an entire culture just by trying to set an example, though I do applaud you for trying. No, there needs to be a new system put in place through other means. They use laws and many forms of persuasion to get what they want, so I think perhaps it would work best to catch them in their own games, using their methods to bring about a reform. And this reform will sneak up on them because they'll be too busy focusing on the little victories they're winning for themselves that they won't see the big picture. I'm already working on a plan. And of course, using a little force may also be necessary." Casimir paused and then continued carefully with intention and focus, as if walking on a glass floor that must not be broken. "I have a proposal for you. You can join in my quest for reform. I propose that you become my wife, or at least, we get engaged. Then I can offer you my full support and protection and we can work freely together. It may even help our two parties unite, or even help them see that it is possible to support and work with each other despite our differences." He finished and looked her straight in the eye.

Ariella stared at him shock. "Marry you? Is that what you just said? It sounds like you're no different than the people who you just said you want to reform. And I don't understand how this would benefit us."

"Ah, yes, it does sound like a contradiction. But remember, this is just a game and as I said, I will use their games and their methods to bring them down. I already have a plan laid out. You can choose to play along, stay under my protection, and all will go well; or you can choose not to, and there's no telling what will happen then."

Ariella glared at him. She remained cool on the outside while internally, she wanted to escape. She hid her shock as she pondered what he had said.

"I know it's a bit of a shock to you, but I will warn you, if you refuse to play along, you may regret it in the end, knowing what these politicians are like. And I expect things are only going to get worse before they finally get better."

Ariella kept her game face on and matched Casimir's strong, cold stare. "It's very bold of you to ask. And it's a lot for me to grant. I promised myself I would never get involved in any sort of romantic relationship."

"I didn't say it had to be a romantic relationship. I know you, the beautiful girl with a heart of ice and stone who turns away every suitor. You only care about duties and bettering the lives of your planet, not feelings. I've learned of Aldura's history, and how, until fairly recently, arranged marriage was a common practice and many couples learned to be content with their lives. I have also learned that it still exists in some remote areas of your planet today. I think you would not be unwilling to marry someone you don't love for the right reasons. You're simply here for business, and my proposal is simply business and nothing else."

Ariella was taken aback and didn't know what to say. Casimir's words came as a great surprise to her and his brazen tone was a bit intimidating. Right now, she just wanted to exit the scene, but would not let herself appear weak or taken off guard. She maintained a cool composure. "Give me some time and I will consider it. I'm going back to visit Aldura next week, so perhaps I will be able to make a better decision after I've had some rest there."

"Take all the time you need, but I will keep in touch."

"Then if you'll excuse me, I need to get going," said Ariella and she got up and left. Ariella exited Casimir's chambers and found Amara and Vala who had waited for her nearby. "Let's go," she said.

"How did it go?" asked Vala.

"I'll tell you later," Ariella replied.

When they returned to Ariella's penthouse and Vala helped her undo her hair, Ariella answered Vala's question as promised.

"Casimir asked me to marry him, or at least get engaged. It's part of some plan he has to bring order to the corruption in the senate. He seems to know something that I don't, and warned me that if I refuse him, things may not go so well. I wonder what his plans are, and whether I should be concerned."

"What did you tell him?" asked Vala.

As Ariella pondered the situation, she remembered the promise she had made to herself. A promise that she would never allow herself to be romantically involved with anyone, or to be joined with any man. She had tried it once, but never again. She was better off on her own. Of course she wasn't going to marry Casimir, but if she was going to play his game, she wouldn't have to commit to him. Then she spoke up. "I wasn't sure how to respond. I told him I'll think about it. Maybe I should play along and at aleast get engaged. After all, I don't have to marry him. I can play the part of fiancé for as long as I need and then I can break it off. If he want's to play those kinds of games, and everyone else wants to play games, why not use their own devices against them? And if it does grant me extra safety and favor, perhaps I could use it for Aldura's benefit." She sighed. "Our break is next week. Maybe spending a few days on Aldura will help me see things clearly."

Vala was silent. She strongly believed Ariella should say no to Casimir, but she believed the senator would make the right choice once she was back home with her people.

As many senators and inhabitants began to make their plans for the break from sessions, rumors of a hostile fleet of ships began surfacing, though there was no evidence to prove the truth and many people dismissed the rumors.

"Captain, what do you think of the rumors of the hostile fleet? Do you think it's okay to travel back to Aldura?" asked Vala, who was loading the ship while Captain Camara and Amara prepared for launch.

"I never want to get carried away by false rumors, but with that being said, it's always best to play it safe. I don't think it's a big enough concern to cancel the trip, but I do believe we should be extra diligent and cautious, and put a few extra safety protocols in place. We will keep to the safest routes for travel and check in with Verona more often than normal until we've arrived safely," Captain Camara replied.

Vala seemed satisfied with his answer as she continued to stow the rest of hers' and Ariella's things. After one more hour, they were ready to depart and Ariella, escorted by Vala and Amara, came to the platform and boarded the ship. They began their travel as Captain Camara used the protocols he had described to Vala, and all seemed to be going well. Their travel continued on smoothly.

"We're at the half way point," said Captain Camara quite a while later, "so far so good. I think we're going to be just fine."

As soon as the words left Captain Camara's mouth, Amara tensed up in the co-pilot's seat and positioned herself to switch over to a manual control of the ship. Captain Camara caught this sudden change in her posture and suddenly became alert. He was about to ask her what was going on when all of a sudden, a fleet of mysterious ships seemingly appeared out of nowhere. Immediately, they began attacking Ariella's small ship with an intent to disable it.

"Take evasive action now!" exclaimed Captain Camara as he began to call Aldura for help. He did not get his message out, however, as a blast from one of the opposing ships suddenly drained all their power.

"Captain, the ship's been badly hit," reported Amara.

"Quick, find where it's been damaged and fix it!" replied Captain Camara. "If we can't get help quickly, we're in trouble," he muttered. After running diagnostics and studying the damage, Amara reported through her personal communicator. "It's bad Captain. I'll do what I can, but we'll need to land somewhere to do a full repair."

"Do what you can," he replied. "It may take a while to find a place to land. In the meantime, I'll try to send out more distress signals, I haven't received any responses yet."

"How much trouble are we in?" asked Ariella, as she and Vala approached the cockpit.

"It doesn't look good, but let me worry about it. We'll do everything we can," said the captain.

They attempted to creep along on low power while Amara did her best to repair the damage. They waited in suspense when suddenly, an object hit them. The large ship that was pursuing them had grappled their ship and started drawing it closer so they could attach a tunnel to pass into the captured ship. Captain Camara thrust the ship forward making it go as fast and hard as it could, but the grapple cables were too strong and the small ship was losing all it's power and quickly stalled. Amara ran up, her repair job was not fully complete.

"I think we're in trouble."

"So it seems," replied Camara.

"Then we'll give them a good fight. I'm not afraid of them," said Vala, taking a weapon in her hand.

"I'm right here for you milady." She gave Ariella a quick glance.

Captain Camara made sure all the doors were locked and secured and he and Amara barred them. The senator and those with her all took weapons and took cover.

"That door is strong, but if they're determined, they can tear their way through. Amara, will we have the power to attempt another breakaway once the engines have recharged?" asked the Captain.

"We should," replied Amara.

"Then let's hope we can hold them off long enough."

They waited in silence; then the attackers began cutting through the door.

"Senator, you'd better hide," whispered the Captain.

Ariella took his advice and Vala followed her as she took cover nearby. "They're almost through," said Amara and she pointed her firearm at the door. She took cover and froze, hearing what the others could not see. She shot just as the first attacker broke through and he fell dead. Then the onslaught began, both sides fighting, with the senator and her companions severely outnumbered. The defenders were able to hold off the invaders for a while, but were pushed back and the invaders were soon able to move themselves between the guards and Vala, and Ariella who was still hiding. The attackers did not see the senator, but they did see Vala and overwhelmed her and took her. Ariella would not have it; she jumped out of hiding with a small weapon in her hand and began firing. Captain Camara silently signaled Ariella to get out of sight, but she refused. They had practiced scenarios like this many times before; Camara could not understand why the senator broke from the plan they recited so many times. The captain had trained Ariella in many battle skills and tactics since she had been an aid for the previous senator. Despite the plan and scenarios they had gone through, Ariella could not sit and hide while they had taken Vala. She would not let her go without fighting. Captain Camara wanted to shout at her or at least get her attention but if the attackers did not know who the real senator was, Ariella Callista was in slightly less danger.

The Captain and Amara fought hard. Amara was doing a wonderful job; she read the faces and the movements of the enemies and could tell who was the biggest threat at any moment and who was about to attack or shoot next. She was processing many senses and movements. She had taken two weapons, one in each hand so that she could make herself function more efficiently by taking down two attackers at a time. Captain Camara tried his best to urge the senator back to safety, but she insisted on staying where she was. She fought fiercely and saved Vala from her captors and Vala then went straight to the senator's side. "We should retreat to safety," Vala said. Ariella finally began to back down, but not soon enough. As she and Vala were escaping to another compartment, a stray band of enemy invaders seized Ariella. Vala turned and began firing at them with all her fury but was unable to stop them. When Captain Camara saw them, he knew they were in trouble. The three remaining companions fought harder than ever and pushed the attackers back until they had the ship back in their own hands, but the senator had been taken.

"I think they were satisfied with their catch," said Amara, "they moved out of here too easily."

"Nevertheless, we need to make sure we maintain control of this ship," said Camara. "How much longer until we have enough power?"

"Not much at all, it should be ready any minute," replied Amara.

"Then here's our plan," said the Captain. "I'll go rescue the senator and you two stay here and prepare to break free as soon as we return."

"Captain, what if the plan fails? I mean, what if you don't make it? You know you're outnumbered," said Amara.

"You're smart Amara, and very capable of making choices. You know what happens if I don't make it back. You'll become the captain of this ship and the head of security in my absence. But right now I need you to stay here no matter how much you want to come with me. It's very important that you stay here."

"Yes Captain," said Amara, feeling very uncomfortable and nervous about his decision.

"Amara, remember everything I taught you. You've been my best student and I'm proud to have taught you."

Camara began to leave and Amara skulked to the cockpit.

"Captain! With all due respect, shouldn't I go too?" said Vala.

"Your place is here, Vala. I'm in charge of your security just as I am in charge of the senator's. I don't want to risk losing two of you."

"But I should be with her; at her side. I was trained to protect her and never leave her side! And now that's just what's happening. I can't leave her. I won't."

"Vala, I'll bring her back. I know things don't always work out how they were planned, but you must stay here and that is an order."

Vala stood where she was, battling between the desire to save her only friend, and following orders, when Amara came back out of the cockpit.

"Captain!"

Camara turned and halted. Kaiya Amara ran to Captain Camara and wrapped her arms tightly around him and he put his arms around her.

"In case you don't return," she said. It looked as if she was almost ready to break out in tears.

"Remember what I told you. You're strong and capable."

Once again, he turned and walked through the tunnel that had not yet been removed, and into the large spacecraft that had captured their ship. Ariella was still in sight, just barely. It seemed the invaders were not going to give up the little starship and were now preparing to bring it aboard. Camara kept out of sight as much as possible as he made his way to the captive senator. Amara didn't like the situation and she quickly sealed an emergency panel over the broken door. The panel had a window on it and she watched through it. The captain finally reached the senator, but was unable to keep undetected any longer. There was no way to rescue her except by open combat. Camara took a breath and charged the enemies. He seemed to be doing a good job at rescuing the captive but then Ariella gave a shout as Camara was hit on the head and fell to the ground. The guards quickly took Ariella away and began dragging Camara towards the captured ship. Amara cried out when she saw Camara fall. They had already begun dragging him towards the silver ship when Amara slipped through the emergency panel and burst through to the attacking ship. In her wrath, she slew everyone in her path and did not stop until she reached the captain. She kneeled down, he was barely alive.

"Kaiya Kaida Amara. You have made me proud," he said faintly and was with Amara no more. He had given his life to save them all. Amara shed a few tears, closed his eyes and with all her strength, managed to lift his body over her shoulders and staggered back. She laid the body down when she got to the ship and then closed the panel.

"We need to break free," she said.

"But we have to rescue the senator!" exclaimed Vala, getting herself together after the shock of the last several moments.

"You saw what happened!" replied Amara. "If we try that again we'll both die. Then there will be no one to save her."

The onslaught began again and the ship was attacked a second time. It seemed the mysterious attackers had changed their minds once again. "Vala, hold them off while I prepare to break loose!" said Amara as she ran to the cockpit. She began starting the ship up. Vala opened a small hatch in the panel and began firing a hand cannon through it.

"We have to get out of here. If the senator still has her tracking device we can trace her. We may have to contact Aldura to ask for the aid of battle cruisers. I was having trouble sending a message earlier. Once I get this ship free I'll try to keep this battle ship in sight, though with the damage the power will drain quickly. The ship will be giving almost all its power just to break free," said Amara.

"Ma'm, I was able to send a distress signal when you began fighting. It appears there were some

Alduran battleships in our area of space and they will be here any minute!" Seren came out of the hull where she had taken cover.

"You sent a signal? How?! I tried but we were blocked," exclaimed Amara.

"I hacked into the attack ship's network and used it," said Seren, calm as ever.

"There is hope," said Vala in a low voice.

"Might I ask where the senator and the captain are?" asked Seren.

Amara turned and left without speaking a word. She headed back to the cockpit and Vala briefly explained to Seren what she had missed. Suddenly, the engines roared to life. The little ship reached its maximum acceleration and shot free of the grapples. Then the engines died once more as they moved a safe distance from the enemy ship. Vala walked quietly into the cockpit. Amara was sitting down, drenching herself with tears and letting out big sobs.

"You handled the situation beautifully and bravely Amara. I could never have kept my mind that straight after such a loss," said Vala. After finishing the sentence, she stood silently, staring out at the distant stars. There it was again. She could not forget it. And now, perhaps, she had lost another special friend. Why had she even allowed herself to form that wonderful friendship? She should have heeded his voice.

"Maybe you will think twice next time you have the chance to start a strong relationship, hated child!"

"I know what you must be going through," said Vala quietly.

"Do you? Do you really?" replied Amara, thinking Vala could not possibly have experienced worse than she had.

"It's one thing to lose the one closest to you, but to lose everyone who is precious to you, that's something else," responded Vala who was gazing out into the stars. It was as if she was looking far out; to another place, in a time long ago. Her memories took her back to a time in her past. She was twelve years old, and she was in a field of wild flowers with her two younger sisters on Aldura, outside of Verona. They were gathering the flowers to decorate the entire house for the flower festival that happened every spring on Aldura. Once they were done, they rode their horses back to the house where their mother was preparing fruits and vegetables to bake some floral treats. Their father would just be completing his last tailor's project for the day and would help them get out the supplies and tools they would need to create garlands, crowns, and bouquets. Then they might go into the back garden together to cut a few more flowers to add to the decorations. Their friends would come over to join them in the celebration, and perhaps help with the decorating, and they in turn would be invited over to visit their friends and celebrate as well. They might also stop by their grandparents' house at some time during the week of festivities and perhaps bake a few extra treats or help with the flower gardens. They had all been robbed of their life too early, and Vala felt she had been robbed of her life as well. To Amara it looked as if Vala was bearing the weight of ages and she seemed very far off as the memory filled her mind and soul.

"You lost everyone?" asked Amara, still stained heavily with tears.

"Yes," replied Vala.

Amara suddenly began to open up. "I have no one left here. I don't know what I'm going to do now." A few more tears ran out of her eyes.

"I'll still be here for you– we all will. Why don't you tell me about yourself and how you came to Aldura?"

Amara looked at Vala. "Well..."

"Let's make a deal. I'll tell you my story and you can tell me yours," said Vala.

"Alright…" replied Amara, a bit hesitantly, but willing to meet Vala's request.

Vala began by telling Amara her story: about her life growing up on Aldura and the sudden slaughter of all those who were dear to her, with no apparent reason, and by a mysterious enemy. Amara sympathized with her, realizing that they both had something in common. She felt Vala could truly understand her and this gave her strength as she began to prepare to share her story.

"I should never have made such a close friendship with the senator," said Vala, "I feel cursed, or something like that. Every close person I've had has been lost."

"Don't say that," said Amara. "You don't know what happened to her; there is still hope. And it's our job to find her and keep her extra safe when we have her back."

"If we get her back."

"Don't talk like that. We need to keep going. I won't rest until I have found Senator Callista. Except... I'll have to bring Captain Adwin back to be buried." She was silent, then she began her story.

"On my home planet, our parents choose which occupations we will pursue. Sometimes they will choose with the help of counselors or those who are considered the wise men and women of the community. At a very young age, we are sent to a school where we live and train for the trade or position we will hold in the future, the one our parents choose and are able to afford. I was training to be a warrior, to defend our people and keep the peace. It was a respectable position and my status in society would secure me in a more superior class. We were taught to master our minds, senses, and emotions. Never were we allowed to let our emotions control us or influence us. In fact, even feeling them was discouraged. We had to be firm and unwavering. Sterile even, and controlled from the inside out. We studied the use of many different weapons, fighting techniques and tactics. We also learned to relax our minds and to be acutely aware of our own bodies. I won't say I didn't enjoy it, but as I grew older there was a boy in my class who I became fond of. It was difficult for me to focus sometimes. As I aged, I began to love him, but I knew it was forbidden. Not only were we not allowed to feel emotion or let it influence us, but like our occupations, our husbands and wives are also chosen for us. I knew he felt the same towards me. I tried to control my feelings. I tried to suppress them, but I couldn't. I couldn't stand the tension between trying to succeed in my learning and the constant feelings I was experiencing from a forbidden desire. I didn't know how to deal with it. We tried to see each other in secret but it was not easy. Eventually, the school found us out and imposed stricter rules on us to keep us apart and 'controlled.' I had an outburst and no longer had a desire to continue with my life where it was at. I escaped at night and ran away at fourteen years of age. I traveled through space and quickly found my way to Aldura where I was given citizenship and permission to train for a job. That was when I met Captain Adwin. And now I'm here, alone again."

"And I'm here too, alone again," said Vala. "We'll have to stay together." As they finished recounting their stories, the large battle cruiser that had been attacking them abruptly started up and left at full speed.

"They're getting away!" exclaimed Vala.

The Senator from Aldura

"We don't have the power to follow them for long, but we should have the senator's tracking signal," said Amara. She tried to bring up the tracking signal on the ship's computer but could find no trace of it.

"I can't find it, it's gone. Seren, you were able to send a signal. Can you locate the senator's tracking signal?"

"I will try ma'am, but under the circumstances I don't think it can be found. It may be deactivated."

"Well, try what you can," said Amara.

Seren did what she could. "There is nothing I can do ma'am, there is no signal. I believe the device has been turned off or destroyed."

"Well, thanks anyway..." replied Amara, who didn't look very happy about the report.

Then Seren suddenly seemed to brighten up. "Oh, the cruisers are here," she said as a few Alduran battle cruisers suddenly approached the small ship. Amara contacted them over the ship's communicator and the silver starship was taken aboard one of the larger ships. Seren gave them the information needed to search for the warship that had attacked them and they sent mechanics to repair the senator's ship. It was agreed that Captain Camara should be taken back to Aldura for an honorable burial service. Amara insisted on attending and Vala, not having much else to do, decided she would accompany Amara.

Ariella's Choice

Ariella had been hastened back deeper into the ship. There she was left with just a few soldiers to escort her and was led to the lower levels where the cells were. She was still shocked by the events that had happened so quickly, and by Captain Camara's death. He had been a good friend. As the guards continued to force her to their destination, they came into a passage and more armed men ran by. Suddenly, the passage was assaulted by a cloud of some unknown substance that looked like exhaust, and she was grabbed by the arm and pulled to the side into a tight storage chamber. She looked at the young man who had taken her and struggled, trying to get free. He held her tighter and pressed his hand against her mouth.

"Shh!" he said in a low whisper.

Ariella paused until the passage was clear. Then she broke loose, but he grabbed her again. "What do you want?" she asked in a loud voice.

"Shh, be quiet!" he replied in a whisper.

"Why should I be quiet?" asked Ariella in a conversational tone, still struggling.

"I'm trying to get out of here and it doesn't help if I draw attention to myself. I'll get noticed for sure," he continued to whisper.

"Then why don't you just let me go?" protested Ariella.

"Because you just may be able to save me. If I make a deal with the Steelar-Romlinians, or Roecatans, perhaps they will forget me."

"What?!" exclaimed Ariella, who was being pulled along through the corridors by the man.

"The Roecatans, the people who own this ship. I sort of got in trouble with them and they took me and my ship captive. Seeing as they want you, I may be able to make a bargain."

"Roecatans? Bargain? I don't even know your name! You must be mistaken; this is not a Roecatan or Steelar-Romlinian ship and they don't want me. They wouldn't dare capture me – that would not be tolerated by the Galactic Union or Senator Blade."

"Corin Rogue Rebel. And you're the one who's mistaken. These ships are made on a remote part of Steelar-Romlin, on Roecata. I've seen them– and you must be someone of importance if the Galactic Union won't tolerate your captivity. Perhaps my fortunes have increased."

"But the ships aren't marked, and the crew don't even look like typical Roecatan or Steelar-Romlinian soldiers or pilots."

"Yes, it is odd; but I saw them, and they didn't like my sneaking around." Corin Rebel dragged Ariella to a ship just a bit larger than hers. It had been taken to a small hangar and secured. "Oh good, she's still there. I think we can get past the guards, there aren't very many of them around here since that onslaught."

He began to take Ariella to the ship, and she began to struggle once more as he quickly tried to force her on board.

"I will not go with you. I don't trust you and I certainly don't like the idea of being baggage to be traded!" she said again in a raised voice.

Corin winced a little and covered her mouth. The guards nearby heard her voice and ran over. Corin, with one arm around the senator, took out his weapon and fired at the guards as he backed into the open ship. He rushed to the cockpit, dragging Ariella behind him. He quickly closed the ship's door and started it up. "They will have alerted most of the cruiser's personnel by now, we'll have to get out of here fast!" He took off and blasted out of the hangar. Turrets began firing but he skillfully dodged them. Ariella gained her composure and noticed a monkey sitting in the co-pilot's seat. It had a headset on and was holding a small tablet.

"Well, now that you've got us free you can take me home; back to Aldura. If those really were Roecatans back there, the Galactic Union must know. We have to send someone to investigate."

"So you're an Alduran? You seem to be very concerned over this matter. What's your name?"

"I am very concerned; this is important! Many planets could be in trouble if someone is building warships in secret, and you don't seem to care! And why should I give you my name if all I am to you is a ransom for your safety? You should stop meddling in other peoples' business. Then you, and I for that matter, wouldn't be in this mess!" responded Ariella.

"Would you rather be back on that cruiser down there? I'm be happy to accept a bribe from them and return you…and I was just trying to be polite by asking your name."

"Well you're certainly doing a good job at it! I'm Senator Ariella Callista and once my people pick up the signal from my tracking device, they'll pursue you, rescue me, and you will be in even more trouble!"

"You mean this?" asked Corin, holding up a small tracking device.

Ariella stared at him in fury and disbelief. It was a secret that she kept one on her. How did he even know about it? She fiercely grabbed at the device but Corin grabbed her wrist, dropped the device on the ground and crushed it with his foot.

"I took it when I stole you from that guard. I'm not taking any chances. You're a senator? In that case it looks like I could get a good reward for returning you safely." He released her. Ariella stood flabbergasted, then she recovered herself and rushed to the ship's controls and began changing its course.

"No! No! No!" cried the captain. He rushed over, pulled Ariella away, and set the ship back on its course. "I'm the captain, this is my ship!"

"Well, if you're not going to take me home then I'll just have to take the action into my own hands," said Ariella, showing her fury.

"I never thought I'd meet my match in a woman," muttered Corin with a hint of wonder in his voice.

"Well, maybe it's about time you did!" Ariella stormed off. No one had ever outwitted her and no one had ever handled her the way Corin did. He was not soft and flattering like the men she was accustomed to dealing with. Ariella didn't know what to think; she had met her match.

After sitting alone for a while, Ariella returned to the cockpit. The ship was on autopilot, and Captain Rebel was sitting silently with his monkey companion, thinking to himself.

"So, where are we going, Hot Shot?" asked Ariella.

"Just call me Corin. We're going to a neutral zone."

"Well, you're getting a bit friendlier," she said.

"So are you," he replied.

"You're taking me to a neutral zone?" she asked, "What exactly do you do?"

He was silent, then replied. "I do things for people. I take them places, ship things, gather information...I do all sorts of things, anything to get money. Sort of like a bounty hunter or free-lancer. I've been on many adventures all throughout the universe. I've seen many things, been to many places..." he said thoughtfully.

"And meddling in other people's business, apparently," said Ariella.

"Well, some fishy things started happening so naturally, I got curious," replied Corin.

Ariella suddenly became intrigued. "What kind of things?" she asked.

"Well, we started seeing an increased demand for certain supplies. They were being bought in what seemed to be random quantities by random people, or entities, across the galaxy. Many supplies were being transported in unconventional ways. It was subtle enough so that it wouldn't be suspicious to government agencies or even the suppliers, but in the underground - the places where the law doesn't extend - we started noticing things. Many of the transactions and the transportation were taking place through us and we began to notice something was up. It was clear these buyers didn't want anyone to know what was going on, including us."

"But it seems you couldn't stay out of trouble," said Ariella.

"No," replied Corin. "I managed to get a job transporting supplies to Roecata. Maybe I got a little too curious for them and outstayed my welcome."

"And then we ended up here..." said Ariella, thoughtfully. They were both quiet, then Ariella began again. "So, you'll take me to this neutral place of yours and then you'll just dispose of me for a reward. And we'll have to stay there and wait until someone, maybe a complete stranger, comes along to take me somewhere else?"

Corin remained silent. "I suppose..." he began slowly, "...unless you'll give me something."

"Purchase my own self? How dare you! I hope no one else makes an offer either!" She was silent once more, then gathered her thoughts and began again. "If you're going to keep me here, there'd better be a place where I can have privacy." Corin got up slowly and beckoned her to follow him. He led her to a room with a few furnishings and a door, it was not a large ship.

"Here," he said. Ariella walked in.

"And thank you very much!" she exclaimed. She slammed the door in his face and Corin walked away in silence.

A few hours later, Corin returned to see how the senator was. He knocked on the door. Ariella was glad Vala had done her work. In a large seam in an underskirt Ariella happened to be wearing, Vala had sewn in a small Alduran firearm. These weapons were unknown to everyone but their inventors and certain government workers and officials. She hid the weapon in her hand and walked up to the door. She unlocked it, opened it, and stepped out, pointing the weapon at Corin. He stepped back.

"You will take me home or I will do it myself," demanded Ariella. Corin looked her up and down and then a small grin appeared on his face.

"You wouldn't dare," he said with a smile. Ariella fired a shot at his toe. "Do you still think so?" Corin didn't move and he still had a smile on his face. "You couldn't really bring yourself to kill me."

"Well, there's only one way to find out. And even if I didn't kill you, I could still injure you so that you'd become helpless and then I would have control over this ship and you." Ariella smiled smartly at the thought. Corin quickly moved forward towards Ariella's wrist. With some elegant and artful tactics, he overpowered her, took the weapon from her hand, and looked it over. "You are a fascinating young woman, Senator Callista. You're very different from the others. I think I'm beginning to like you."

"Well, if you like me, maybe you will be kind and let me go," said Ariella in a mock-charming manner.

"Oh really, I thought you were beginning to like it here," said Corin.

"Like it?"

"You said yourself you hoped nobody would offer a reward for you."

"You know what I meant." They stopped there as Ariella was defeated once again and once again, they said no more and went their own ways.

Another hour passed and the monkey decided it was time to turn on some music; he loved to listen to it. Ariella recognized the song. She knew it well and began to discreetly dance to it. How wonderful would it be, she thought, to be able to dance with a partner again. But there was no one here who could do it with her, so she just subtly moved her feet to the music while her mind drifted off to the pleasant memories of balls back home. Corin stepped in from another part of the ship and saw the monkey with the controls to the ship and Senator Callista moving her feet to a dance typically done in pairs, seemingly caught up in the music. He walked up to her.

"May I?" he asked, holding out his hand to her.

Ariella was startled and froze. She was rather embarrassed to be found dancing, especially by this man. She didn't know how to respond to this gesture. She could hardly believe that he would know anything about dancing. Besides, this was her captor. Why would she want to dance with him? If this were any other situation, she would have immediately refused him... but this was dancing, and she loved it so much, the offer was hard to resist. The slightly repulsed look on her face began to vanish. She cautiously took his hand and then they began.

"I guess Cosmo there decided he wanted some music," said Corin. "He's unique, his species are very rare. They're very intelligent and can learn things quickly. They can understand us as well, though they can't speak. Cosmo happens to be an expert in technology. He was used for an experiment; that's how he learned most of what he knows and then he ended up with me; he won't leave. It's nice to have him around though, he's quite docile, and helpful when he wants to be."

As they progressed farther into the dance, they began to impress each other with how well they each led and followed. They both tried more difficult moves, calls, and responses, gauging to see how good the other really was at dancing. It soon turned into a competition of who was the better dancer and Cosmo, enjoying it, began selecting songs that were quicker and more intense so that they were flying across the floor and suddenly began throwing air steps into the dance, dancing to their maximum potential. When they could dance no more, they both sat down to catch their breath. Ariella could barely hide her smile. She had not had that much fun in quite a while and was excited to have found a partner who matched her talent. It had been a wonderful experience. Corin had enjoyed it as well and was almost equally surprised by Ariella's talent as she was by his. They both stared at each other with looks of wonder. How did the other one know how to dance so well?

"Maybe you're not quite as bad as I thought," said Ariella.

"You're not bad yourself. I think I'll delay our original course, there's no rush to lose you so soon," said Corin.

"Where do you intend to go then?" asked Ariella.

"Well, there are lots of planets. Any place in particular you would like to see?"

Ariella pondered the question for a moment. She could use this opportunity to ask to go back home, but would Corin oblige her? Besides, somehow she wasn't sure if it was really what she wanted to do right now. There were so many other planets and places to see.

"Well, seeing as I have nothing else to wear, how about shopping?"

Corin stared at her. His face clearly showed his bewilderment and disappointment. "Is that all you can think of?" he asked.

"No, but it's a good start."

"Alright then...shopping it is. I'll take you to the biggest shopping center in the universe, you can find just about everything there." Corin reset the course and they began heading to a new destination.

When they finally arrived, they came to a planet that was like most heavily populated planets, but it had a massive trading center the size of a city and Corin landed the ship. He gave Ariella back the weapon he had taken from her.

"Are you sure you want to give it back?" she asked.

"You didn't stop me with it last time. Besides, there are places here where you really have to watch your step. Even though there are security guards, the center isn't always safe. You may need it. Just stay close to me," said Corin, strapping extra weapons to his waist.

"Oh," said Ariella, with some hesitation in her voice. "So, you couldn't take me somewhere else? Somewhere a little safer?"

"Well, I thought I'd take you to the best place I know of. Besides, like I said, it's only certain places... are you having second thoughts?"

Ariella stared out the hatch to the city, contemplating what the results of her decision would be. "No, no...let's go," she said. They left the ship and went in search of the clothing center.

Ariella had a wonderful time looking through all sorts of exotic styles of clothes, as well as familiar ones. She chose a few dresses and outfits that she liked as well as a few exotic ones that appealed to her. She didn't stop there though, next she purchased a few hair accessories, a bit of exotic jewelry, and some beautiful fabrics from places she had never been. She didn't stop there either; she also found a few foreign cosmetics and bath supplies. As they walked through the many different sections, Ariella proudly pointed out the fine merchandise from her own planet. When dinner time came around, they stopped at one of the higher-class cafeterias. There were many different restaurants serving food from all over the universe and there was also a buffet style restaurant that served dishes and samples from all over. Ariella insisted on the buffet so she could try as many of the different foods and drinks as she could. She saved her favorites from home for last. Meanwhile, Corin found himself carrying many of Ariella's packages and bags and wondered why in the universe he had agreed to this. Cosmo helped carry some things as well, but only the items he found fascinating. Most of the time, Corin just followed Ariella around, not saying or doing much. Finally, being an Alduran, Ariella had to look at the equestrian and archery sections, though there wasn't anything she purchased from them. She already had the finest equipment and supplies which were made on her home planet. As they began to return to the ship, Corin drew closer to Ariella and spoke in a low voice.

"Don't look now, but there are two bounty hunters following us. Just follow my lead and I'll get us back to the ship safely."

Before Ariella could argue, Corin began making his move.

"Alright woman, I've had enough of this!" he said out loud. "I'm not going to be your pack animal; you're going to carry your own stuff."

He began tossing Ariella's merchandise, and his own as well, at the senator who struggled to pick up on his sudden move. She began fumbling around to gather up all the packages.

"Be careful," he demanded and bent down with Ariella to help pick up the packages. They were now under the cover of the crowd, on the edge of the walkway.

"Don't worry about this next move, they won't hurt you. Be prepared to fight as soon as you're free," he said to Ariella in a low voice. "And don't try anything cute."

The bounty hunters quickly approached them. As soon as Ariella had all the packages in her arms, Corin stood up and took her with him. He turned to face his pursuers and held Ariella in front of him. Ariella gave him a look of distaste but didn't struggle too hard. Corin smiled at the two hunters.

"You wouldn't want to harm the precious bounty now, would you? I know her life is worth more than mine."

He continued to back away slowly, still holding the senator in front of him. The bounty hunters continued to walk slowly towards him, and one began an attempt to circle around behind him. Corin caught this subtle move and shoved Ariellla into the hunter who was closing in from the front while he jumped sideways to tackle the other. As Ariella stumbled into the first attacker, she let the packages fall and used the moment to take some small concealed weapons out of her hair and sleeve. She shot the hunter's hand and destroyed his weapon. He fell back. As Ariella dealt with her opponent, Corin found himself locked in a battle of bare hands against his opponent with Cosmo chittering and cheering him on, dealing blows and bites when he deemed it necessary. Ariella turned towards Corin, but her opponent was hardly phased by her attack and quickly snapped back into action. Ariella reacted again, getting more aggressive this time. If he died, there wasn't much she could do about it. Both brawls didn't last much longer and as soon as they were over, Corin and Ariella gathered up their belongings and ran through the walkway back to the ship. As they ran, Ariella pointed out a sign with her's and Corin's pictures on it and words in several different languages scrolling through.

"It looks like they've finally realized you're gone," said Corin.

"And obviously, they know who did it!" responded Ariella. "I told you!"

"And I told you! You haven't escaped me yet!"

When they reached the ship, Corin immediately began the take-off as Ariella placed all the remaining merchandise out of the way.

"We're getting out of here and then we're going to lay low for a while. This time, I'm choosing the place," said Corin.

Ariella didn't argue. Although she wanted to be back at home and safe, she was somewhat intrigued by this misadventure.

Once they were safe again, Corin spent several days dodging adversaries and taking Ariella to other planets, sticking to the ones with a g-force at or near 9.81 so that they wouldn't have to wear protective suits. They visited a desert and another place with snow; they ice-danced there and discovered that they each had a talent for this kind of dance too. As they ran from planet to planet, they climbed large mountains and trees and enjoyed beautiful caves full of crystals and other fascinating places. Then the day finally came when Corin decided to address the issue that was growing on his mind.

"I've been thinking…for a while actually," said Corin. "I should take you home…"

"What?" asked Ariella, forming a small smile.

"I was wrong, I should have just taken you home when I first found you. I should not have treated you like a hostage. I'm sorry."

Ariella smiled. "I forgive you. And actually, I'm glad I got stuck with you. I've had a wonderful time." She wrapped her arms around him, with a bright smile on her face. Then she suddenly backed off, realizing what she had just done, and retreated to be alone.

Ariella's Choice

On their way back to Aldura, they stopped at a large, beautiful city to refuel and restock. As they made their way back to the ship, they were followed by soldiers who appeared to be of the same faction Corin had seen building ships on Roecata - the same ones they had escaped from - and an ambush began. The soldiers tried to take them but did not succeed and began firing at them. Ariella, Corin and Cosmo ran towards the ship, firing back at the attackers. After a brief skirmish, Corin and Ariella decided the best move would be to outrun the soldiers. They seemed to be succeeding with their plan as Corin expertly guided Ariella through the maze of the city, until they ran into a blockade. They stopped and fired at the soldiers and when there was a quick break in between shooting, Corin, seeing a chance of escape, lightly picked up Ariella and swung her over the blockade. He made a few more shots and jumped over after her. They began running again but as they neared the ship, they discovered that the area was heavily guarded. Ariella and Corin took cover and slowly fought their way to the ship. As the fighting continued, they were separated. Ariella was firing and stabbing her hair accessory that doubled as a weapon at some soldiers who were about to take her. Corin managed to break through and rescue Ariella; then they ran together, hand-in-hand so as not to be separated, to the ship. As soon as they were inside, Corin closed the door and before Ariella could go her own way, he pinned her against the ship's wall with one hand on either side of her. He had a cheeky smile on his face, but it suddenly faded into a more soft and serious expression, and he seemed to be about to say something. Before he could get a word out, however, Ariella picked up one of the ship's larger tools that happened to be behind her, raised it above her head, and began to swing it down towards him. It swung down past his face and over his shoulder. Just as he moved out of the way in surprise, the tool went past him and right down onto another person who was on the ship with them. It was then that Corin realized their fight wasn't over yet, there were more soldiers on board waiting.

"I'm not a woman to be messed with," she said in an austere tone, her cold blue eyes burning as if there was a fire within.

Ariella and Corin fought, often side-by-side or back-to-back, until they finally regained the ship. When they were free, Corin quickly took off and landed nearby in a safer area where they could clear and clean the ship after the battle. It was not pleasant work, but Ariella took it well. After the work was done, she noticed that Corin's forearm had been injured.

"Corin, you got hit."

"It's not bad."

"Still, I think we should do something about it." She examined it closer and found that it was worse than Corin made it out to be. "Not bad? I think it needs stitching." Ariella took out some medical supplies for the ship's first aid storage. "I know just what to do," she said. "My father is a doctor, he taught me a lot."

"I really don't think it's necessary," protested Corin who didn't like needles.

"I disagree. Don't worry, it won't hurt. I'll block it before I stitch it." Corin was hesitant, but this time, Ariella got her way.

She cleaned the wound and gave a subcutaneous injection in the surrounding tissue to numb the nerve signals in that area before stitching it. As she cleaned and stitched up Corin's wound, she began thinking about home. She now longed to be home. Everyone must be worried about her and searching for her while she had been off having fun.

"I think it's time I went home. I have work to do and nobody else knows where I am and that I'm safe," she said.

Corin agreed to take Ariella home but requested a stop at one more place first. He took Ariella to a remote planet with many oceans and beaches. They spent the day enjoying the sun, the sand and the waves and stayed until sundown. As the sun disappeared, they sat on the beach watching it set. Deejay Cosmo suddenly decided the situation called for dancing, and began playing a selection of mostly slower dance songs. Corin and Ariella glanced over at him, then Corin looked at Ariella with a smile on his face.

"Shall we give him what he's asking for?" he asked.

Ariella responded with a soft smile. She said no words but gave Corin her hands and they got up and danced to the music until the sun had completely set, then they sat down once more without speaking a word. Both were silent, but their heads were full of thoughts. Then Ariella broke the silence. "I've enjoyed this so much…seeing all those places was wonderful. And the dancing…I'll never forget it. I'll never forget you. What are you going to do now? Once I'm home and back to normal life?"

"Well…I guess I'll go back to what I've always been doing. I'll be flying across the universe – just Cosmo and me. I may have to hide out for a while though. Apparently, I'm now a wanted man."

Ariella began turning thoughts over in her head. Corin could see there was something on her mind but whatever it was she was thinking, she chose not to say it and kept silent. Suddenly, she had another thought. "It's spring-time on Aldura, one of my favorite times of the year. When you take me back, stay for a day or two, I'll show you how wonderful and beautiful my planet is and some of our favorite activities. My family owns a home far out from the cities. We could go there."

"I wouldn't want to intrude"

"Oh, you wouldn't be at all. You'd be my guest and besides, I don't think anyone will be there – at the house."

Corin brightened up a little. "Well…I suppose I will. The place you come from has to be nothing less than the most beautiful place in the galaxy."

Ariella smiled. "Don't try to flatter me."

"But I mean it," said Corin, looking her in the face.

Ariella held her smile, but then turned away as the smile faded. She knew she had to get back to reality. She stood up and walked along the shore, with the waves lapping at her feet and the moon and stars shining down, thinking to herself. Was her heart getting soft? She had told herself no more. No more opening up her heart. She couldn't trust the young men. They had proven that at the capitol. She was done with broken hearts, with games and false motives, and the one she trusted most not showing up for her to support and defend her when she needed it most. How could she let this vagabond steal her heart? He was different than the others. He was exciting, had conviction, and was always dependable. But would he stay that way? Was this his true self? Could she really trust him with her heart? And would she really go back on a vow she had made to herself?

The next day, they began the trip back to Aldura. When they arrived, it was a beautiful late spring day. The house was located in the subtropical region of Aldura. It was warm and humid, but also windy on this particular day. There were flowers everywhere and the grass was green and tall.

"We call this region Florina, it has a subtropical environment. Aldura has a variety of climates, but the majority of our planet is either tropical, subtropical, cold semi-arid or dry-summer subtropical in climate. It's a particularly good place to grow our fruits and flowers, and vineyards. I love walking through the vineyards," said Ariella, smiling and excited to be home again. The weather brought back memories of the carefree days of her childhood and made her feel free again. After they landed, she ran out across an empty field as the wind blew through the tall grass and her golden hair. Her light spring dress billowed behind her. Cosmo was in a frisky mood and decided to run after her. Finally, being left by himself, Corin ran after both of them. When Ariella was out of breath she sat down in a sea of grass and wildflowers, still smiling.

"It's so good to be home! Especially at one of the best times of the year!" she exclaimed, smiling up at Corin who was approaching her after the run. "I feel so free here," she said as he sat down next to her. He was silent, it was a wonderful place.

"I can see why you like it here," he said. They sat in the grass and the flowers for a while, while Ariella told Corin about life on Aldura. As they talked, Ariella suddenly noticed a few horses nearby.

"Those are some of our horses," she said. "We usually keep horses at both of our houses, but we like to take our favorites with us to wherever we're staying; and look, my favorite is here! My parents must have sent her here for the spring season." She walked towards the horses with Corin and Cosmo following. When they reached the horses, Ariella began stroking them. Corin was not unfamiliar with them and after a short while, stroked a few of them as well. "Do you have much experience with horses?" asked Ariella.

"A little," said Corin.

"Can you ride?" asked Ariella.

"Good enough."

"I'll have to see how much you know."

Ariella walked up to her favorite, a mare of desert origin. She grabbed her withers with her left hand, placed her right hand on her back and lightly sprung up. She swung her right leg over to the other side of the horse, grabbed the mane with both hands, squeezed the horse gently while leaning forward very slightly, and coaxed her easily into a gallop. She began galloping all around the field, laughing and smiling. It was clear she was really enjoying herself. When she was ready to slow down, she sat back and slowed the horse to a trot and finally, a walk as she approached Corin.

"Well?" she asked, "Can you do that?"

"Maybe I'd better start with a saddle and bridle," said Corin, looking a bit intimidated.

"You don't need a saddle and bridle, at least not for what I did. Besides, we would have to go all the way to the barn to get them. Just do what I say and you'll be fine. You'd better have good balance though, and be soft and gentle with the horse. There are times when you need to be tough, but only when it's necessary. Go on, find one you like. Mount just like you saw me do it."

Corin tried and managed to get on the back of one of the horses with ease.

"Good! Now squeeze gently to bring him to a walk. Give some pressure with your right leg to go left, and press with your left leg to go right; you may need to move your leg slightly in front or behind the girth area when you do this. Sit back and deep to slow down and squeeze to transition to the next gait up, these horses are well trained."

Corin followed Ariella's instructions and it wasn't long before he was able to ride without the help of a saddle or bridle. His skills were good, though not as good as Ariella who had begun riding at a very young age.

Over the next few days, Ariella showed Corin some techniques for shooting a bow, starting with a light bow and making sure he understood important parts such as anchoring, posture, bow arm position and alignment. She found, however, that he also had picked up the skill of archery from his many adventures and was quite good at it. They went on trips to nearby springs, rode some cross country, and went for walks through fields and the country roads. It had been a wonderful time, but as Ariella kept telling herself, she knew she had to go back where she belonged and let the rest of the planet know she was safe. She finally contacted Amara and Vala and after telling them all they insisted on knowing, arranged to meet them in Verona, Aldura's capital. Ariella's and Corin's last day together before the departure to Verona ended with a dinner in the dining room which had a corner open to the outdoors. The table was glass and the candlelight, chandelier, and glasses sparkled and reflected in the table. It was the finest house and finest dinner Corin had ever experienced in his entire life. As they ate, they discussed their backgrounds. Ariella began first by describing her life growing up.

"I was raised in Verona in an upper-middle class home, but I spent many summers here at my grandparents' ranch. I was an only child and my family was well off. My father is a doctor and mother was a horse doctor before she retired early to focus on caring for the house and our family. Her parents were ranchers. My family worked hard to build the life they're living now, and my parents worked to make sure we had a good life. I've always had an interest in the Alduran court and law-making, so my parents focused my education on preparing me for politics and life in the Alduran court. In our past, Aldura was a monarchy for many years and as a result, the court today is still particular about many things and can be a bit exclusive or cliquish. It's not always easy for someone who's not already part of the court society, either through birth or recommendation by someone in good standing, to navigate the system or find favor. In many regions, it's still easier to get elected as an official if your family is already a part of the court society. Fortunately, that is changing with the new administration under Queen Selina. But with all of that, it was not easy for me to get involved in the legislature as a youth. I had to learn their ways, how to develop a personality that caused them to favor me, and how to make friends who would support me and help me get court positions that would allow me to grow through volunteering, networking, and mentorship. I enjoyed being at the capitol, but sometimes I would miss the freedom I had here on my visits to the ranch where I could fully be myself. I also learned ranch work here - how to take care of the animals and equipment, and how to care for the land. Tending to the living things… being among them when you're alone in the middle of wide, empty spaces really brings you back to a life that's much simpler and more free. I just want my people to experience that kind of peace and freedom." She finished her story and looked at Corin. "Where did you grow up?" she asked.

Corin looked a bit intimidated at first. His story was not like Ariella's and neither was his upbringing. "Well… my childhood was very different from yours. There's not much to tell really. My father was a pirate flying all across the galaxy so we never stayed in one place for a long time. Our ship was our home. I lived with my mother in my early years, but in a raid by a task force from the Galactic Union, she became the victim of gun fire and died. It was unjust, and I have a hard time respecting their authority. After that, I was raised traveling all across the galaxy with my father, so most of my time was spent around thieves, bounty hunters, black market dealers, and the like. You'd be amazed at some of the skills I learned from them though. When I grew older, I decided I wanted to do my own thing. Though I don't always agree with the law, I was tired of running from it and living life as an outlaw. Fortunately, I had no bad records to my name since I was under my father's care as a minor. I decided to leave that life and do something that would draw less attention from the authorities, and I was tired of being subject to someone else's orders. I wanted to live my own life and have the freedom to choose my own path. So I left the crew and I've been flying solo ever since, though I still have friends and connections in many different places."

"Yet now you've found yourself on the run again…" said Ariella.

"Yes, not my preferred way to live, but it'll work out. I'm an outlaw's son… I guess it was bound to happen sooner or later." He paused and a question began to form in his mind. "How did you manage to climb all the way up to your position as a senator in such a short time?"

Ariella was pulled out of her deep thoughts and responded. "Well, I mentioned my training, mentoring and conditioning, and how I participated in activities and programs to help me get experience and connections. I began traveling to the palace every day and paged for Aldura's legislature where I got to know people and gain a good reputation with the legislators in higher circles. There were a lot of politicians who showed me favor, liked to have me in their company, and some even offered to give me help and advice. Then I met Senator Valencia, Aldura's last senator, and he enjoyed my company so much that he asked me to come with him to the galactic capital as his aid. When his term ended, some legislators I had previously worked with encouraged me to run, so I did. I won by a close margin."

"It sounds like you've had lots of favor on your life," said Corin.

"Yes…it was great, it's what I worked for…but it became too much favor, in fact…"

"Too much favor?"

"When you're young, and you're around other young adults who are trying to secure a good future and earn significance and prestige, there can be drama. Being the darling of the capitol, there were many young men who were after my affections. Not all them were genuine, unfortunately, and those who seemed to be, or perhaps were, still proved they could be moved by outside circumstances. Those young politicians and politician want-to-bes did not prove to be trustworthy or stay true to their convictions. It turns out I couldn't trust any of them."

"Well...maybe politician is not your type."

Ariella kept silent. She had a lot running through her mind: what her return to the senate would be like, her past experiences with the young men of the capitol, Casimir's proposal, her vow to herself, and now, Corin who had turned her world upside down. She couldn't express it all in words, nor did she want to disclose everything right now.

After the dinner, they danced a few songs for the last time, and then both sat in silence, contemplating what was to come with the morning. It had been such a wonderful adventure. They didn't want it to end, and both knew that tomorrow would probably be the last they ever saw of each other. How could Ariella let Corin go? She had grown very fond of him. He wasn't like the other men she had spent so much time with. He was strong and though he had his flaws, he was unwavering. He wasn't trying to get anything out of her. He wasn't trying to use her - at least not anymore. He had no political ambitions. He just lived a simple life and was content to keep it that way and yet, with him there was always some new adventure to be had. She had grown to enjoy the spontaneous adventures that had disrupted the normal flow of her steady life. She had been stalling, using every adventure as an excuse to delay her return to the senate and the life it promised to give her. But she couldn't keep it up forever. She couldn't believe it - she even hated the idea, that this man could rock her world - but she finally admitted to herself that her feelings for him were growing.

"Are you feeling how I'm feeling about our parting? About this evening?" she asked.

"Maybe. It depends on how you're feeling," answered Corin, "Are you glad or sad to see me go?" he asked.

"I think you know," replied Ariella. She continued, "Have you ever met someone, a woman, who you felt was the right one for you? The one you could spend the rest of your life with?"

"Yes…one," he said.

"Did you regret leaving her?"

"I suppose I will, once you're gone."

Ariella didn't seem to take Corin's hint, so she continued. "Did you ever tell her that?"

"No, I didn't think it would work out between us. She lives in a very different world from me, and I'm not sure if she truly returns my feelings."

"Well, I think next time you see her, you should tell her. You may be surprised. She could be very happy to hear it from you. You never know what could be without saying something and at least trying it."

"Well then," he began slowly, "seeing as this is the last time I may ever see her again, other than tomorrow, I'll say it now. I'm saying it now."

Ariella's Choice

Ariella felt her heart beat a little faster. What did he just say? She looked him in the eyes with many emotions flooding in. The joy she felt that he felt for her just as she felt for him, but there was also fear and uncertainty. Could she really let this happen? Her feelings seemed to show as she looked at Corin.

"Ariella Callista, you're the only one I could ever love, and I will remember you all the rest of the days of my life. You have a fire and spirit in you that will change the world as you've changed mine. It turns out not every politician is greedy for gain and willing to compromise and allow injustice, and you are a strong woman. You must be feeling something too, I can see it."

Ariella didn't say anything, she was struggling within. She had grown to take pride in her singleness and independence, she had promised not to let passions, emotions and desires sway her any more, and here she was falling in love again. Could she risk this? She began to look for reasons why she shouldn't give in, then she broke the silence. "If what you told me about the Roecatans is true, I don't think it would work between the two of us. Besides, like you mentioned, we are living two very different lives. You're the son of a pirate, now wanted by the Galactic Union who killed your mother. I'm a leader in the Galactic Union and part of the senate. And to add to that, if those were Roecatans who were after us, then we'd both be in greater danger if we were seen together; maybe a lot of people will be in greater danger."

Corin pondered her answer. "But as you said, it's at least worth a try. If you want this enough, I'm sure we can work it out. I know you'll make something work if you really want it. Even if it meant turning myself in, I'd still be willing to do whatever it takes."

Ariella knew he was right, but she was still afraid. More thoughts flooded her head. If it meant abandoning her role as a senator, what would her life look like? How would Aldura take this? What would those in the Galactic Union say? What kind of representation would her people have without her? Then she remembered Casimir's proposal again. What would this mean for her and Aldura? What would she tell him? She hadn't even considered her answer since her captivity. "I don't know... I don't think it will be that easy. At least, not right away. It has something to do with me, it's a diplomatic agreement of some sort. I would have to take some time to figure out how to resolve it. Right now, if we were seen together, you would be in greater danger because of what you saw, and if it was suspected that... that I might have feelings for you, I would lose an advantage I currently have. I don't think it could work between us."

"But you do admit it; you do love me," said Corin.

Ariella was silent and deep down, very sad. Some of it showed on her usually proud face. Then, she went for a cutting tool, cut a lock of her golden hair off and handed it to Corin. "If you wish to remember me, you may have this," she said.

Corin took it. "I will always remember you, and I will keep this with me at all times." He fished around in his pocket and took out a necklace of rare gems and materials. "You keep this. I found it at an archeological site, it's very rare. I could make some good money out of it, it's a lot to give up; but you are worth far more that this relic to me. I want you to have it."

Ariella took it carefully. She looked at him with a faint smile and was about to cry. "If you'll excuse me…" she said as she got up. She went to her room and stayed there the rest of the night. She could no longer keep herself composed and she dare not fall apart in front of anyone. She was supposed to be strong.

The next day, they loaded the ship and reached Aldura's capital where Vala and Amara were waiting. Ariella and Corin spoke very few words that day. After they landed in the capital, Cosmo and Seren were sent to load Ariella's things on board her ship which had been cleaned and repaired like new. Everything was ready, and here they would depart. Ariella and Corin turned to say their goodbyes and Ariella held back a few tears as she hugged Corin for the last time.

"It was wonderful," she said, "goodbye."

"Goodbye," said Corin. He watched her turn around and leave with an empty feeling inside, with Cosmo at his side.

When Ariella saw Vala and Amara standing by the ship, she remembered that Captain Camara had been killed rescuing her. She would have to pay her respects to him and his family when she had an opportunity. She approached Vala and Amara who were relieved to see her, while she came to them with a heavy heart, her thoughts running rapidly. This was it. The last time she would ever see Corin. She was leaving him behind, forever. Could she do that? But it seemed like the best thing for both of them, though her heart was not with her in this decision. It was pulling her back to Corin who was standing at a distance, growing father apart from her with ever step she took. Then another thought overtook her. She stopped, turned, and looked back. She could take it no more, despite all her reasoning. Her heart won her over and she ran back to Corin and took hold of his hands.

"Come with me. We could use you. My guard and captain of my ship died defending me, I need someone to replace him. Seeing the way you were able to keep me safe, I think you would do a wonderful job at it."

Corin looked stunned. "Do you really mean it? What about the danger you spoke of?"

"Like you said, we'll work it out. Perhaps having you as my captain of security could help solve some of the problems I spoke of, and we can keep things secret if we have to. Please come with me."

Corin's bewilderment morphed into a smile. "Of course I'll come," he said. Then the two, in high spirits, walked together towards the others.

"Vala, Amara, this is Captain Corin Rebel; the one who rescued me. He's going to be my new head of security."

A look of shock flashed across Vala and Amara's faces at Ariella's unexpected words. Who was this strange man that Ariella was putting so much trust in?

"Corin, this is Vala, my handmaid, and Amara, my other bodyguard; you two will be working together a lot and Amara will help you learn what you will need to know. There may be a few requirements and tests you need to meet to take this position officially, but we'll help you get through it all. I'm sure I can have most of them waived, it shouldn't be too difficult."

Amara and Vala had so many questions they wanted to ask, but this moment didn't seem to be the time. They needed to make sure Ariella was settled and all was well first. Ariella and her companions were to stay at the palace that evening (Vala and Amara had already been there since they arrived on Aldura) before departing the next day. They only had a few hours to themselves before Ariella would have dinner with Queen Selina to catch up on her adventure and to discuss the current political issues on Aldura and in the Galactic Union. As they were shuttled from the landing base to the palace, there were some questions about whether Corin was allowed entrance, but at

Ariella's word, no objections were made towards him. As Amara and Vala assisted Ariella in preparing her room for a short stay in the palace to debrief before returning to the galactic capitol, the question of who Corin was was still on their minds. Ariella had not told them much since she made contact with them on Aldura. Vala gave Amara a look and finally, Amara spoke up.

"Pardon me, Milady, but I think it's important for me to know. Who is Captain Rebel? And did the capitol security or the military assign him to you? Because I didn't receive any orders from them."

"No, he was not assigned to me. I'm appointing him myself."

"I was not aware that he was approved by Aldura's Department of Security," Amara responded, confused.

"He's not. But I approve of him so I will inform the queen of my choice to appoint him as my new captain so that the formalities and approval can begin."

"Has he been trained in our methods?"

"He has not. But his experience will qualify him, and I'll trust you to help him learn the protocols and whatever else will be required of him."

Amara didn't look happy with Ariella's answer, but it wasn't her place to argue. Her responsibility was to follow orders, and she would have to trust whatever decision her superiors made in regards to Corin. She remained quiet and said no more on the matter. When she was no longer needed, she went off and skulked.

How could this foreign man with an unknown history, with none of Aldura's rigorous training which went on several years before one could become an officer or captain, suddenly be offered this position of high importance, and be placed in direct command over her? She had served in her position for several years. She had been faithful and knew all the protocols. She had worked hard to be able to take on this position, and yet, now that the opportunity was before her, it was being taken by a nobody who didn't even have to work for it. She should be given the position of captain of security over him. She had been specially trained for it. It didn't make sense and it frustrated her and even made her feel betrayed. However, she must follow the commands of her superior officers and do whatever they ordered. Maybe they would see he was unqualified and refuse the senator's request. On top of all that, she still missed Captain Camara. She kept her cool and kept her opinions to herself, though she did express them to Vala when they had a moment together. Vala understood Amara and was on her side, though she trusted that Ariella had a good reason for appointing Corin as her new security captain and was curious to learn what that reason might be.

    That afternoon, Corin was given his own room and left to himself. The decision on what to do with him would be made during Ariella's dinner meeting with Queen Selina, which would start in a few hours. Reporters from all over had been seeking Ariella for an interview and Aldura's legislature was desperate to hear from her what had happened. Had Vala, with Amara's help, not insisted that she needed some rest before having any conversations, Ariella might have had no down time to herself and been completely overwhelmed the rest of the day. Meanwhile, the media was confined to the public places of the palace, waiting earnestly for an interview, press conference, or anything they could get from anyone who might have information on Ariella's capture and return. Ariella, her companions, and the queen all refused to give any comments until things were settled and it was safe for Ariella to return to the galactic capitol. Some of the press had already identified Corin as the man who was wanted and had been associated with Ariella's capture. Many questions and speculations about him were being passed around and discussed live on broadcast.

When the time came, Ariella was escorted to the queen's private dining room where thankfully, only a small number of people were there to join them. Queen Selina welcomed Ariella and was delighted to see her unharmed. Her first order of business was to ask after Ariella's well-being. Next, Ariella was updated with the latest events happening on Aldura and in the Galactic Union, and the senate in particular - one of Ariella's trusted advisors had been able to stand in her place during her absence and keep Verona updated. One thing that was of particular concern in the galactic senate was the safety of the galactic senators. Since Ariella's capture, volatility in the union and attempted assassinations, captures, and even small, local uprisings had increased. The queen wanted to ensure new measures of higher security were taken for Ariella. This finally landed them on the topic of Corin. Aldura's Head of Security was present at this meeting and there were many questions about Corin – about who he was, his past records, whether he could be trusted, whether he was truly fit for the job, if he could follow orders and protocols, and if he could learn and follow all Aldura's methods for both millitary and security officers. Ariella affirmed that he was capable and trustworthy. She argued that his unconventional methods might be better for her, as they would be unpradictable to anyone who might be more familiar with Aldura's ways. And she was fully confident that with some help, he would easily learn the protocols that were important to know. With her reasoning, she was able to convince the queen and head of security to come into agreement with her. Even though she had a right to choose her own security officer regardless of their opinions, having their support would help speed up his processing. It was agreed that Corin's appointment and the processing of his credentials would be expedited. Ariella would stay on Aldura one day longer so that Coring could be processed and fully ready to serve in his new position by the end of the next day. The day after that, Ariella would return to the capitol. There was however, one condition. Corin was approved by Aldura, but he would still have to be set free of any charges the Galactic Union held against him for the supposed capture of Senator Callista. It would be Ariella's responsibility to set him straight with the courts as soon as she arrived at the captiol. If he was convicted, he would loose his position, though the leadership present at the dinner were confident he would be aquitted after hearing Ariella's story. At the end of their conversation, Ariella also requested that no public comments be made on Corin for security purposes. To that, the head of security wholheartedly agreed.

When they finished their dinner, many reporters were still eagerly waiting to hear from them. They made their way from the dining room to the public space and began answering questions. The reporters, though they pushed and tried their best through the use of different questions, could get no information on Corin, and Ariella refused to disclose what had happened on their misadventure. She made sure that one truth was known, however, and that was that Corin had rescued her.

The next day was a busy day. Thankfully, Vala and Amara had already loaded most of their's and Ariella's belongings on the ship, so they only had a few more things left to pack. Corin, however, had his own belongings, supplies, and extra weapons that needed to be loaded. On top of that, he had to go first thing in the morning to get measurements for his new Alduran uniforms. He would be given two to start with that would be tailored to fit him, and more sets of uniforms that would be constructed or tailored and shipped to him at the capitol at a later time. Next, he would have to go give all his required information and sign documents to not only receive his credentials and be officially recognized and authorized as Ariella's Captain of Security, but also to be given citizenship, which was another requirement for his position. Then he would be sworn into his new office, meet his superior officers to receive some instruction and training, and finally, attend to any personal matters that still had to be dealt with. The following morning, they would depart for the capitol. Amara also received instruction that Corin would be Ariella's new Captain of Security and she was expected to submit to his orders and help him learn all the standard protocols a captain of security should know. Amara felt rather uncomfortable with this decision, but there was nothing she could do so she submitted to the orders she was given.

    Corin was also feeling rather overwhelmed with all the new information he was supposed to retain, and with the sudden change of going from a free, independent traveler, coming and going as he pleased with no one to give him orders and no one under him to have to lead. Now, all of a sudden, he had both. He had allowed himself to be plunged into a new reality without thinking it through. He wondered if he would regret this choice. But then he remembered why he had done it without a second thought. It was for Ariella. To be with her and keep her safe, though they would keep his true motive a secret.

    The next morning, Ariella and her three companions, as well as Seren, prepared to board her ship to return to the galactic capitol. Corin had arrived at the ship hours before the rest to acquaint himself with it and to prepare it for the flight ahead. He had carefully examined the exterior and interior, the structure behind it all, the materials it was composed of, and the engines to the best of his ability. He was impressed by it, but had some ideas for modifications that could be addressed at a future time. When the time came for their departure, Ariella arrived, escorted by Vala and Amara. Seren had come shortly before they did and Cosmo, of course was going to join them and had been hanging out with Corin since the early morning.

    "Captain Rebel, I haven't seen you at all this morning. I was hoping I would catch a moment to check in with you," said Ariella, brightening up as she approached him.

    Amara immediately noticed a change in Ariella and Corin's demeanors as their attention was drawn to one another.

"I needed to make sure I understood how this thing worked before flying it, and to make sure it was safe enough to carry you to the capitol," Corin replied.

Vala also began to pick up on Ariella's brightness. Ariella smiled at Corin as she passed him and entered the ship, with the others following. Corin boarded last and sat down in the pilot's seat. He would start the flight and as they neared the capitol, Amara would take over and fly them in. Corin was still on trial so they thought it would be best for Amara to take the ship past security and escort them to the government complex.

When they had been flying through space for a while, Vala decided to take a moment to get to know Corin better while Amara was taking a break from co-piloting. There was clearly a reason Ariella had chosen Corin as her head of security, and she wanted to know who he was.

"I thought I should get to know you a little better," she said in a friendly tone. "What's your story? And how did you find the senator? She told me a bit about your adventure together."

Corin began by telling her about his past, but only disclosing a few details. Then he told her his side of the story of their adventure but again, without giving too many details or disclosing anything about their relationship.

"And then she asked you to take the position of her head of security?" asked Vala.

"She did."

"And you accepted? You both surprise me."

At this point, Amara was just outside the cockpit, returning from her break which she decided to shorten. As she heard Corin's and Vala's conversation however, she paused and waited outside, listening in.

"Why is that?"

"Well, for Senator Callista to trust a younger man who she hasn't known a long time - that's not like her. Something really big must have happened to cause her to ask you. And for you, I imagine this is such a big life change and you seemed to take it on without a second thought. Some might suggest you took it just for the chance to be pardoned by the galactic union, or even that the Senator may have been threatened to appoint you. But maybe there's another reason."

Corin was silent, carefully evaluating his answer. "Well…I suppose you'll suspect it eventually, so I might as well tell you straight, though we believe it needs to be keep it a secret so you need to promise not to say anything."

"I promise," said Vala, perking up a bit.

"We wanted to stay together… because I love her and she loves me."

A look of shock passed over Vala's face but then it was replaced with an expression of delight. "Well, I'm surprised to hear she allowed herself to fall for you, but I'm happy for her. Perhaps you are the best choice for her captain of security then. They say there's no force stronger than love." She trailed off, and her thoughts did the same. The thought of love...she was still afraid to love or be too close to anyone again, outside of the necessary bonds she had built with Amara and Ariella. And even those relationships still made her nervous at times.

"Is something wrong?" asked Corin.

Vala suddenly broke out of her thoughts. "No, nothing's wrong. I was just thinking about something but it's not worth discussing. I didn't know why the senator chose you, and I didn't know much about your relationship with each other, but then we haven't had much time for a conversation." She considered it some more, still surprised at this unexpected change, but maybe it would help the senator make a sensible decision in regards to Senator Blade's proposal. "Well, I should get going," she said, getting out of her seat to leave the cockpit. As she did, Amara slipped away from sight before anyone saw her. Amara decided she would come back a little later. It all made sense now as to why Captain Rebel was given his position. She felt far better about the situation than she had before. When she finished processing her feelings, she returned to the cockpit and joined Corin.

"You know, you may not have known this, but I was bitter towards your appointment for certain reasons, but I can see now that I was in the wrong. I think you are a great choice. Will you forgive me?" she said.

Corin, who had no idea Amara had felt that way towards him, was a bit surprised and touched. "Well… certainely. And thank you for forgiving me," he said.

"We're all good then," replied Amara. She perked up a bit and began telling him about the protocols of Aldura's security and military forces, and answered his questions and in the process, their bond as a team began to grow.

When they finally arrived at the capitol, Amara flew them in, landed, and escorted them to Ariella's senate chambers. They would unload everything at her penthouse later. Many questions had been asked by security as they arrived because of Corin, but they didn't have too much trouble since the capitol had already been made aware of Corin's situation by Councilor Betulace-cay, who acted as one of Ariella's advisors and helped both her and Aldura in matters regarding the Galactic Union. These advisors were not normal office holders, but were knowledgeable people chosen by certain parties on Aldura to advise her. They represented the people of Aldura, the government of Aldura, and sometimes minority groups. Councilor Betulace-cay was a representative of the Feirae people – Aldura's ancient natives that generally preferred to keep to themselves and stay secluded from the outside world. He frequented the capitol to keep in touch with what was going on in the senate and to act as a lobbyist towards his people's best interests. He had been standing in for Ariella in her absence and had already been at work helping her with Corin's situation. After Ariella's conversation with Queen Selina, they had thought it very important to set up a meeting between the president of the union and Ariella and Corin so that he could hear what Corin observed about the strange happenings on Roecata. Councilor Betulace-cay had helped arrange this meeting for Ariella upon her return.

When they stepped out of the ship onto the capitol building's landing pad, Casimir Blade was already making his way towards them. When they intersected, Casimir pulled Ariella off into a private conversation as they headed back to the offices, Amara, Corin and Vala keeping within sight of the two senators but outside of hearing distance.

"I'm so glad to see you back safe, we were very worried about you. I even sent out some soldiers and hunters to find you and get you back to safety. Fortunately, I heard you somehow made your way back to Aldura unscathed," said Casimir.

"Thank you for the sentiment. It was an adventure," Ariella replied.

Casimir barely seemed to hear her response however, and continued on as if he had something more pressing to discuss. "I heard of your attempt to persuade the president to start an investigation of Roecata."

Ariella's tone changed a little. "News sure travels fast around hear. I suppose everyone has open ears and loose mouths, especially when bought with the right price. Yes, I have. I imagine you'll take a strong interest in this issue since it's happening on your own home planet."

"I certainly do. I know nothing of this matter. Strange ships and armies coming from my home world? And who is the one who discovered this? Just a low life from nowhere with a rather offensive reputation. It's his word against mine, and all the other Steelar-Romlinians out there. And what proof does he have? I would caution you not to trust him. His kind can't be trusted, they don't have it in themselves to be trustworthy. There is no evidence to even build up an investigation...I wonder if someone might be after me?" he raised his eyebrow ever so slightly.

Ariella was silent and Casimir continued. "I will make sure this issue is put to rest quickly. And as for your chosen captain, I would advise you to replace him, or at the very least give him none of your trust. You know he is suspected of illegal activity. What if it doesn't end well for him?"

Ariella could not keep silent at this last comment. "I've seen the charges and the only thing he was suspected of was my kidnap, which as you can clearly see, is not true. He was able to save me and keep me safe when no one else could. He rescued me from my captors when no one else was around to give us aid. I would say he's more capable of keeping me safe than the entire government! And I won't let the issue of

Roecata rest. I trust my captain's word and regardless of where they came from, a brand-new, unheard-of faction should not be ignored."

"On that last point I do agree, but we need to be in possession of all the facts first. I would advise you to stay out of this business and let the president deal with it on his own. We want to be very careful about issues that could lead us to war." They both gave each other a hard look. "And may I remind you that you still have yet to give me an answer to my proposal. You may want to make a decision quickly before the tide changes."

Ariella said nothing but stared at him again with her icy blue eyes, then departed. Her companions caught up to her and Vala noticed the irritation on Ariella's face. "What is it?" she asked.

"I don't want to talk about it right now," said Ariella looking very determined and ready to fight.

They walked in silence straight to Ariella's senate chambers where Councilor Betulace-cay was waiting for them.

"I'm glad to see you back," said the councilor.

"Thank you for holding everything down," said Ariella, looking flustered.

"I've already relayed your request about Captain Rebel and the important information he possesses to the president's office. I believe they have also contacted you to arrange a meeting this evening."

"Yes, I just received word. We will both be there."

"Well then, I hope everything is in order and it goes well for you."

"Thank you. I'm truly grateful for all your help in this," said Ariella.

Their next task was for Councilor Betulace-cay to help Ariella get updated on everything that was happening so that she would be ready to continue with business the following morning. After that, she and Corin would have just enough time to get prepared and meet with the president.

When the time arrived, Ariella and Corin were escorted to the president's office. There, they discussed the details of Ariella's capture and what Corin witnessed on Roecata and what had led him to go there in the first place. The president seemed very concerned over this news and expressed his wish to send investigators right away. He would also assign someone to interview Amara and Vala who had witnessed the attack, and someone to withdraw memories from Seren's memory bank of the entire incident. As for Corin still being held suspect for Ariella's capture, the president explained that he would still have to go through the normal court procedures, but it was clear that he was innocent and would be acquitted easily. His case would be escalated and decided quickly. The meeting seemed fruitful, and Ariella was looking confident when they returned to her office chambers. When all their business was finally completed for the night, Ariella sent Amara and Vala to go prepare the ship for them to return to her penthouse. She and Corin would join them in just a moment.

"Busy life," said Corin as soon as the other two had left.

"It is," said Ariella, "though today was a little more than normal... but that's my life. Meeting in the senate chambers every normal work day, and after hours there's other business to attend to, and often there are meetings or parties with politicians and other kinds of people."

"Who was that man who came to greet you on the platform earlier today? Was he a senator?"

Ariella stiffened up a bit. "That was Senator Casimir Blade from Steelar-Romlin."

"What's his deal?" asked Corin, who had noticed there was something between him and Ariella.

"I don't know... I'm still trying to figure that out."

"Is he someone we should be wary of?"

"I don't know... but I will be watching him closer. I suspect he's up to something."

Corin was silent, considering what Ariella had just said.

"We haven't had much time together since arriving at Verona," said Ariella, "how are things going for you?"

Corin pondered her question as they both gazed out the large window at the night time cityscape. "...it's a lot... I made a big change. It's been very overwhelming at times. But, I'm looking forward to the days ahead. I think it will be a good adventure. And working in palaces and senate chambers: that's something I never thought I'd get to experience. I never wanted anything to do with these kinds of people, but why not at least enjoy the beauty this place has to offer?" He held Ariella's hand as they continued to stare out the window. In this moment, she seemed to find peace.

"I hope this place becomes enjoyable for you," she said. They stood a moment longer in silence and then Ariella gently pulled her hand away, with the trace of a restless expression over her face." We need to be careful around here. I still think it's best to keep this secret. Especially from Senator Blade. And we should go join the others before anyone begins to suspect something." Ariella stepped out of her office with Corin following, then she locked it behind them and they went outside to the landing pad to catch up with the others.

After Corin was presented before the court a few days later, he was released of all charges, as there was no evidence that he was guilty. Ariella's words and the support of the president's office also aided in his acquittal. There were, however, rumors circulating that Ariella was being held hostage to Corin's will, and that he had forced her to swear on his innocence. As time passed, however, those rumors began to fade and Corin settled into his new position. Though Corin did

Ariella's Choice

some things unconventionally due to his background, he proved to be good at his job and over time, earned more of Amara's respect. Corin learned all his duties easily and quickly and continued to practice his equestrian and archery skills to meet the expectations of his role. Ariella told no one but those closest to her of hers and Corin's story, so he was known only as Ariella's head of security. When they danced, however, the passion they both had for dance and each other could not be masked, and eventually, on Aldura, they became well-known as a dance pair.

Vala's Choice

As Ariella continued in her career for several weeks, she was sent a second handmaid from Aldura who would help with the tasks done by Vala and Seren. Like Vala, she would also serve as another secret defender of the senator. Her name was April Rain. She had blue eyes and curly blonde hair and was about the same size as Ariella. She was only eighteen years old. When she arrived, Vala instructed her in the tasks she would perform and the two of them became good friends over time. April came from a family who lived in a townhouse back on Aldura, in Verona. She was bright, cheerful, and loved to talk - she complemented Vala's subdued personality well. Her mother was an artist, and her father served on Verona's police force. She had a younger sister at home as well. Ariella had still not given Casimir an answer to his proposal, and continued to make excuses for delaying, neither giving him a yes or no for fear of how he might react, especially with tensions arising. She and Corin continued to build their relationship, but it wasn't always easy for them when Ariella feared making it public.

As the middle of the year approached, a sickness spread through the galactic capital. It was a new one that had never been encountered and so many of the capital's inhabitants were taken by it that the hospitals began to fill up and the city had to be quarantined. No one and nothing could enter or leave without thorough testing. Ariella couldn't help but wonder if it had been caused intentionally by someone as a biological weapon. She still remembered the ships that had tried to capture her, and hearing the fate of the one that had taken her captive. When the Alduran ships had finally caught up with it and captured it, it was suddenly destroyed from the inside, as if it had self-destructed, killing its whole crew in the process. She wasn't the only one with suspicions about the sickness, there were a few others who held similar speculations, and she met with them regularly to discuss it. Soon enough, the virus made its way to the senator's penthouse and Vala got sick. April stayed with her to watch over her, hoping she and Ariella could keep her from getting worse. Vala did get worse, however, and there was no choice but for April to take her to the hospital. It was a dangerous virus. As they arrived at the hospital, with Vala seeming to lose consciousness and not entirely awake, April noticed a young doctor with an irritable expression exit a treatment room with someone who was probably a nurse. They seemed to be heading in her direction.

"...I expect everyone and everything to be ready and properly prepared, there is no room for incompetence. When I need things done, I need them done right away; the life of the patient depends on it. Being kept busy with more patients than normal should be no excuse, there are other less important things that can be dropped if necessary," the doctor was saying.

The nurse seemed to be about to reply when the doctor suddenly caught sight of Vala. "Oh, not another one," he said in a taxed expression, but April could detect some compassion in his voice. Accompanied by the nurse, he approached Vala, asked a few questions, and briefly examined her. When his findings brought him to a conclusion, Vala was taken to a treatment room by the nurse and a few attendants. The doctor stayed behind and introduced himself to April as Dr. Swann and asked her some more questions before starting a more thorough exam and prescribing a treatment. Dr. Swann was a young doctor, but already very knowledgeable and gaining a good reputation. He liked everything to be perfect and just so. Though mostly unintentionally, he was often hard on those who failed to meet or perform to his standards. On this day, he was a bit more stressed than usual, as was most of the hospital staff due to the overwhelming number of patients and lack of sleep.

After Vala was examined, she was kept at the hospital due to the severity of her illness and was well treated and cared for by nurses and by Dr. Swann. She had been asleep and not completely conscious for several hours. When she finally awoke, she first laid eyes on Dr. Swann who was checking up on her. He was always kind to his patients, even on rough days. The first things Vala noticed were his deep dark blue eyes. She thought they were beautiful and kind and were a captivating compliment to his dark hair.

"I'm Dr. Galen Swann. How are you feeling?" he asked.

"A little better I guess," said Vala, smiling faintly up at him, "I still feel very weak."

"Well, you should get stronger every day now that you're being treated. I don't think you'll have much to worry about now, but I do want you to stay for a few days until I'm confident your condition is stabilized. The virus took quite a toll on you," replied Dr. Swann as he began to leave the room.

"Will you stop by again soon?" asked Vala eagerly.

"Well… I might," said Dr. Swann with a friendly smile.

There was something about Dr. Swann that Vala liked, something that attracted her. Was it his kind attitude towards her? She thought about it for a while

while she lay alone on the hospital bed, enchanted. Dr. Swann too, began to ponder over Vala. He had only just met her when she woke up, but she seemed like a kind, innocent girl, though there seemed to be something sad hidden deep inside. There was something about her that attracted him as well. At first, he hadn't been sure about going to see her again that day, but there was something about Vala that he couldn't shake and for some reason, he wanted to go back and check in with her. He decided he would give her another visit if and when he had a chance. That chance did come later in the day and he decided to visit her again towards the end of his shift. When he arrived, they entered into a conversation of small talk.

"Your name is Vala, I'm told," said Dr. Swann.

"That's correct. I suppose you met April Rain, she's the one who took me here isn't she?" replied Vala.

"Yes, I met April. She seemed to have her hands full, but still very calm and pleasant," continued Dr. Swann.

"Yes, poor April. She's got a lot more work now that I'm here," said Vala.

"She said you both work for Senator Callista from Aldura."

"Yes, we're her handmaids."

"What is it like being a handmaid for the senator?"

"Well, our job really never ends. We need to be ready to serve the moment we're needed no matter what the hour is. We assist the senator in ways normal handmaids would, and tend to normal household duties, but we also perform some of the tasks an aide would normally do when extra help is needed. The living isn't bad though. We have our own room in the senator's apartment so we can always be wherever she is and attend to her needs."

"Do you ever get much free time to yourself?"

"Not much. By law, we are given the choice to take some time off for ourselves, but it isn't much and I usually choose not to use my spare time. I really have no reason to use it, and no other places to go. My life is with the senator and the other staff."

"It's good to have a job you're passionate about and devoted to, but I do hope you get to visit family on occasion and take some time to rest."

Vala paused and looked off into the distance. The dark figure came to her mind, and she suddenly appeared to be struggling within; struggling against sadness and bitterness, and the doctor noticed.

"What's wrong?" he asked.

"I-it's just...I lost my family. Not one of them is around anymore."

"I'm sorry. What happened?"

"I'd rather not talk about it. Just- please leave me. I'll be fine in a little while."

"Are you sure there's nothing I can do for you? If you're struggling with any kind of trauma I want to make sure you're not left to deal with it alone."

"Well then, do whatever you want, only don't talk to me about the subject. In fact, I'd rather not talk at all right now."

The doctor made up his mind and sat silently observing Vala until she seemed to get over her grief. When he got up to leave, he turned to speak to her. "You know, if there is anything you're struggling with emotionally, a counselor or therapist could really help you. We have a few here if you would like to talk to someone."

"I appreciate the offer, but I'm not sure I'm quite there yet," said Vala. The doctor gave her one more glance before exiting the room.

As Vala grew stronger, Dr. Swann would escort her on walks in a garden on the hospital grounds and she would lean on his arm when she was weary. When Dr. Swann returned from one of their walks, one of his colleagues, Dr. Faye cut off his path and drew him to the side.

"You know, you can always ask a nurse to do that. I'm sure you've got other more important tasks to spend your time on. Besides, you know you have to be careful about your relationships with your patients. We wouldn't want an emotional bond to start forming, after all." She gave Dr. Swann a serious look. "Of course, what you do at home and with your time outside of work, that's completely up to you."

Dr. Swann thought he saw a small wink flash on her face as she finished the sentence and walked off at a brisk pace. What was she implying?

Two days later, Dr. Swann returned to the hospital; he had been sent on a much-needed break the day before. When he returned to his office, Dr. Faye came in to meet him. "I hope you got some good rest yesterday." She handed him something that was wrapped up.

"What is this?" asked Dr. Swann.

"I took care of your patient yesterday while you were out. She likes orange roses."

Dr. Swann stared at her; a bit bewildered. "You know I have lots of patients here," he said.

"Yes, but you know which one I'm talking about," said Dr. Faye. She turned and began to leave. "You're welcome," she said as she made a swift exit.

Dr. Swann sat at his desk for a minute, trying to wrap his head around what had just happened. Finally, he got up and found an attendant to deliver the rose to Vala's room when she was asleep. He told them it was from someone else so no one would begin to make assumptions. Besides, it was technically from Dr. Faye anyway. When Vala awoke, she saw the orange rose on her bedside. She wondered who could have sent it. It couldn't have been Dr. Swann, could it?

Finally, the day came when it was time for Vala to be discharged. Dr. Faye, who had seen Vala when Dr. Swann was not available, issued a discharge for her and personally came to see Vala out. As they began to walk out, Vala spoke up.

"I was really hoping I could say goodbye to Dr. Swann before I leave, he has been really kind to me."

"Oh, well, I believe he's scheduled to leave at this time. We may be able to catch him before he leaves," replied Dr. Faye, as the trace of a smile formed on her face.

"Let's go this way," she said as she turned a corner after exiting the main entrance. She walked Vala a little closer to where the staff exited and lo and behold, there was Dr. Swann, taking his leave for the day.

"Dr. Faye! What are you doing with my patient?" he asked when he saw them.

"I decided to discharge her a day early. We need the space and I think she's okay to go."

Dr. Swann looked upset and a little angry. "And you didn't think to consult with me first? You know I was assigned as her primary physician."

"Well, I was responsible for her when you were out, and I needed more rooms. I checked her records, and they looked good to me. You know well that in times like these, we can't always afford to stick to all the normal protocols. Anyways, I've been out here long enough, I need to get back to work."

Dr. Swann began to protest but Dr. Faye was quick to leave. Dr. Swann looked frustrated. "I'm sorry about that," he said.

"It's okay. I'm sure everyone is doing their best right now. I think you all are doing well considering the amount of work you have to do. Besides, I do think I'm feeling well enough to be home now," said Vala.

There was an awkward pause. Neither of them seemed to know what to say. Then Vala spoke up. "I guess this is the last I'll see of you unless I happen to get sick again."

Dr. Swann replied, "I will certainly miss you, and I don't think you will have to worry too much about getting sick. You've survived it and the labs have begun producing vaccines and treatments for the virus. We should soon be back to normal."

"Maybe I will keep in touch with you, whether I see you soon or not," said Vala, feeling a bit sorry to leave.

"I hope you do," said Dr. Swann, not fully realizing what he had just said. Vala turned and left and returned to the senator's flat. Fortunately, the others had all escaped the attack of the virus. As soon as they learned that Vala had been taken sick by it, the capitol assigned Ariella a health care official to monitor her and make sure precautions were taken to prevent her from catching the disease.

When Vala returned to her work, she was quite rested and ready to get going. The others, however, seemed quite tense.

"What's going on? What have I missed?" asked Vala upon her return.

"You must have really been insulated from normal life during your recovery," said April.

Then Ariella spoke. "Yes, the union's president died just died yesterday. They say the virus killed him, but I have doubts about it. Everyone is restless, we don't know what will happen now. He started secret investigations into what Corin witnessed on Roecata and now he's gone. There's something very suspicious about what is going on. How could you not know he was dead? It was broadcast everywhere!"

"I suppose I was too caught up in other things," said Vala.

"What is there at a hospital that can attract that much of your attention?" asked April.

"Well…I just wanted to do something different staying there. I wanted to disconnect from the outside worlds for a change," said Vala, not wanting to mention what had really drawn all her attention. "Oh!" she suddenly exclaimed, "If you think he died because of what you told him, then that means you and Corin are potentially in more danger!"

"Exactly," said Corin, stressed himself. "We're glad to have you back, we need you."

Vala got back to her normal work that week and was glad to be performing her regular duties again after feeling so bad the week before. She continued to correspond with Dr. Swann and when she went out on errands, would often use the time as an excuse to briefly meet up with him, though no one else knew.

The Senator From Aldura

As the weeks progressed, the immunity of the galactic union's population began to build up and strengthen. Though caution was still to be exercised, most were confident that things would open up and be fully operational again by the end of the year. This was the hope of Ariella, her handmaids, and her protectors, who were anticipating their end of the year return to Aldura for a much-needed break. They were all restless after the events of the pandemic.

On one day in particular, once business in the capitol was mostly back to normal, Vala and the senator were preparing themselves for a reception they would be attending that evening, one that several senators and government officials had been invited to. Ariella was not enthusiastic about going, but because Casimir Blade insisted she be there, she agreed to attend. April had gone out to run an errand and Amara was asleep after her watch, though she would wake up shortly to accompany them. "We should be leaving soon, but I think I'll go late. It's not important that we be there on time anyway," said Ariella. She thought she heard Corin stifle something that sounded like a grunt or scoff in response to her statement. "Is there something wrong?" she asked him.

"No, I'm just surprised you don't want to get there sooner considering the reason you're going."

"I would really prefer not to go at all, but good relations are important and to not go-"

"Yes, you need to stay on Casimir's good side, I understand," interrupted Corin.

It seemed to Vala that this obscure conversation was starting to get a bit heated, and Ariella looked provoked. "Is anyone hungry?" Vala asked. The other two suddenly turned their attention to her. "It's dinner time now and the reception is not exactly going to be a dinner, just light refreshments." Corin and Ariella seemed to cool down.

"I'm fine," said Ariella.

"I'll have something later," said Corin.

"Well, I am," said Vala as she went to get a quick bite to eat, then she returned to assist Ariella with a new dress Casimir had sent her. It was a new fashion; Casimir had sent it to Ariella and insisted she wear it, as ambassadors would be present at the dinner and he wanted her to represent the latest fashion. Ariella felt the real reason was deeper than that, however. Perhaps a means to attempt to assert some control. When Vala entered the dressing room, Ariella was already in an opaque slip-like garment that would go under the dress for extra comfort and modesty. Her hair was already done up on top of the back of her head. Corin was lounging on one of the couches and Vala shot him a brief look of annoyance as she passed him. Didn't he have somewhere better to be than hanging out with them in the dressing room right now? Besides, she didn't feel a ladies' dressing room was the most appropriate place for him to be, even though

Ariella was decently dressed in the undergarment. She picked up the dress and began examining it. It wasn't like normal dresses with lots of seams stitched together, its construction was rather different. It was more like one long cut of fabric with all four ends finished off very neatly and almost invisibly. It was designed to wrap around the wearer, somewhat like a bandage, over the entire body and fastened at the back and a few other places, except that it was shaped in a way that allowed ample movement of the wearer. There were no sleeves. The dress was fastened at the top around the bust, wrapped around and attached at certain points provided by the design, and finally, ended by trailing on the floor behind and slightly to the side of the wearer. This design was the reason for the other garment being worn underneath; Ariella was not comfortable in just the dress alone. She stared skeptically at it, but Vala began to help her into it after she gave it a good exploration.

"I'm not sure how I feel about this dress," said Ariella, not showing any enthusiasm towards the garment.

"Then why not wear something else?" said Corin with unappreciation.

"Because Casimir insisted," she replied.

"So what? You're a strong woman, you show him that you're the mistress of your own life. You never do something that you don't want to do so why should you do it now all of a sudden?"

"In this job, some sacrifices need to be made. And no, I don't always choose to not do something just because I don't want to; I make plenty of sacrifices as Aldura's senator!"

Vala felt some pain and weakness build up in her abdomen and muscles and she began to falter a little. Then Corin looked as if he was about to respond again so she composed herself and interjected. "Well, I think it actually looks flattering on you Ariella," which was a true statement. "It compliments you well, and I've never seen anything quite like it. The craftsmanship is very unique and original, it's truly a work of art."

"Ah, so it's a work of art. I can see it now; that's why this dress is so important. You high-class people are so into critiquing and interpreting art." He assumed a mocking expression "'Ah, this line over here means solidarity...oh! And this circle represents great sadness! I don't understand how something so dull can be so fascinating and so essential to high society."

"Well, I do agree that some people take it too far, but it's obvious to me that you've never been taught to appreciate art; and it's more than just the high society that appreciates art. Anyway, you have to admit that she does look good in the dress," said Vala as she finished fastening it.

Corin looked un-amused and sported a bit of a saucy demeanor. "Well, I can't say she doesn't."

"Well it's settled then," said Vala. She began to feel strange again.

As Ariella and Vala made their final preparations, Vala began to feel worse. Finally, she asked if April could go in her place if she came back on time.

"Why do you want to stay? Is something wrong? You don't look so good," said Ariella.

"I don't feel well," replied Vala, "I think I just need some rest." She got up to go to her bed but had difficulty and stumbled.

Ariella rushed over to help her and Vala dropped down to the floor.

"Oh, I feel terrible," moaned Vala.

"Vala, what's wrong?" asked Ariella.

"I..."

Vala said nothing more, but she was respirating rapidly and looked ready to pass out. Ariella looked at Corin with concern. "It could be poison," she said, "I'll have to get her to the hospital quickly."

"I'd better leave a note for Amara telling her what happened," said Corin.

"Why don't you just tell her yourself when she's awake?" asked Ariella.

"Because I'm not going to wake her now and you and Vala are going nowhere by yourselves. I'll take you both to the hospital and then we're going someplace safe to find dinner. I'm not taking any chances, and you can forget your plans for the evening."

They quickly brought Vala to the hospital and Ariella waited in anticipation to find out what happened. Dr. Swann treated Vala and gravely informed Ariella and Corin it had been poison. Vala was saved, but she would have to stay a few days.

"Well, I guess we'll have to do without her again for a while. Poor Vala," said Ariella.

"At least she's in good hands and you're safe for now," said Corin, giving her his arm. He seemed very ready to leave.

Ariella was hesitant.

"Don't worry. Like he said, she's in good hands," said Dr. Swann.

Ariella seemed satisfied enough and went with Corin, though she was silent most of the evening. When they returned to Ariella's personal transporter they had arrived in, Corin was silent and began to ponder the incident. He had almost failed at protecting the senator. Now it was his responsibility to solve this problem. How could someone have managed to slip poison into their penthouse? Ariella saw his concern. She was sitting in the back of the transporter as was customary, but she moved off her seat to get closer to Corin when she saw the concern on his face. She put her hand on his arm, not wanting to look too conspicuous, but also communicate her concern and understanding. They had both come to the realization that they had almost lost Vala, and this could mean that someone wanted Ariella's life.

"I'll have to review our safety protocols and figure out how this could have happened. This is serious. We almost lost Vala... we could have lost you. I failed to do my job." He stared into Ariella's beautiful face with a grave look. "I'm not going to rest until I figure out how to keep you safe. For a start, we're not going to have anything delivered anymore. Vala and April can pick up the things we need themselves. I'm going to keep you safe," he said, taking Ariella's hand.

Ariella was aware that though they were likely alone, they were still in a public space and someone could catch sight of them, so she removed her hand from Corin's but gave him and expression that said she understood him and was grateful for him. This was all still a shock to her, as it was to Corin. They remained in silence a brief moment longer before Corin finally decide it was time to leave.

Meanwhile, Vala was delighted to see Dr. Swann again; they had continued to correspond with each other though most people did not know it.

"I've missed you," said Dr. Swann.

"So have I, though I really didn't want our next meeting to begin like this. Still, it is nice to have you caring for me."

"That's what I'm here for. Maybe you should get sick more often," said Dr. Swann lightheartedly.

"If everything was different, I probably would," said Vala sarcastically with a smile. "I am worried though, about the others."

A few days passed and when Vala was discharged, Dr. Swann came out to meet her in the same place they had departed from after Vala's first hospitalization.

"I'm leaving for the day and since you're also leaving, I was wondering if you would like to go to dinner," he asked.

"Well..." began Vala, hesitantly. "I don't have anything nice to wear here with me, I'd have to go back to the penthouse to get something or go as I am."

"That won't be necessary, I have clothes for the occasion and I'll buy a dress for you. We'll go to one of the shops with the latest fashions."

"You're offering way too much, I can't accept any of this."

"But I want to do it. I only have myself to spend on and I don't need much. Please do it, it's not often I have chances like this."

"...Alright, If you really want to do it," said Vala with a shy smile.

"Then I'll get ready and wait for you," said Dr. Swann, looking delighted.

Inside, Vala was very excited. She had never been treated so special before. When they were ready, Dr. Swann escorted Vala to one of the finest boutiques in the city. Vala looked at price tags on the dresses and chose a cheaper one from the back rack.

"Are you sure that's the one you want? Why not try one of the latest ones? I'm sure you'd like one," said Dr. Swann.

Vala smiled shyly again. She was reluctant to go for the more expensive items, especially when someone else was paying for it, but there was one new and more expensive dress that had caught her eye and Dr. Swann had noticed it. She brought herself to try it on and liked it.

"Would you like to keep it?" asked the doctor.

Vala was hesitant again. "Well, yes, but I've just never had anyone purchase nice things for me…at least, not in a very long time…I feel like I'm doing something wrong…"

"You're doing nothing wrong. This is my choice and it's my pleasure," Dr. Swann purchased the dress and she wore it out of the store. "You'll need something else to go with it, like shoes, and gemstones or something shiny," said Dr. Swann.

"No, you've done enough," said Vala.

But the doctor would hear no more of it. He took her across the street to a jewelry store and bought her a starstone necklace, a real starstone necklace! Vala had never owned a real starstone in her life and now, suddenly, she had a whole string of her own. He also bought her a hair comb so she could wear a proper Alduran hairstyle. Then he bought her shoes to match the dress, a bottle of top-quality Alduran perfume, and earrings to match the necklace.

"You look wonderful. Perfect for tonight. And please, no more thank-yous, I've heard too many from you already."

All Vala could do was smile, she felt like the queen of the galaxy. "How can I thank you? What can I do to repay you?" she asked.

"Nothing. You need to know that you are valuable and that you deserve to have happiness. You don't always have to stay living in the shadows."

Vala broke down and cried and they hugged for a moment before she pulled herself together. Next, Dr. Swann took Vala to one of the finest and most expensive restaurants in town. Vala was overwhelmed, she could not take the smile off her face. When they were offered a drink, Dr. Swann asked Vala what she would like. She thought for a moment and then told him what her favorite was from Aldura.

"Would you like an appetizer?" asked the doctor.

"No, I don't think so," replied Vala.

"Are you sure?" Vala thought for a moment, she only had appetizers at formal dinners on special occasions. "Well, maybe just a small one." Vala fit in easily as if she was one of the ladies that would dine here regularly. Her court etiquette and posture were perfect. As a handmaid for Senator Callista, she was expected to know these things so she had no problem fitting in. After appetizers, they chose the main course.

"What would you like for dessert? And don't tell me you don't want any, I know you Aldurans like your desserts," said Dr. Swann.

Vala smiled again and gave in. She chose a dessert she liked. There was soft music playing and an open floor for dancing in the restaurant.

"Do you like dancing?" asked Dr. Swann.

"Of course I do, I'm an Alduran," replied Vala.

"Well then," said Dr. Swann getting up, "shall we?" He held out his arms and Vala took his hand and they began.

Vala was a sight to see. She danced very well and carried herself gracefully. She was a light and beautiful mover and Dr. Swann was impressed. Being considered the best dancer on the floor was something new to Vala, she had always been overshadowed by Ariella's exceptional skill. It was true, Vala was a very good dancer.

"You're a wonderful dancer," Dr. Swann said after they finished.

"You could probably be just as good with lots of practice," she replied.

"Haha, maybe," he said.

After the dinner and dance, they wandered outside to an adjacent garden. Dr. Swann plucked a red rose in full bloom and gave it to her.

"There is one more thing I would like to ask to you about, but not here. Would you like to go to the fountain gardens outside my living complex?"

"I would," Vala replied.

It was a short walk to the fountain gardens which were just outside the luxury apartments where

Dr. Swann lived. Rain clouds had been gathering over the evening, but the beautiful lights in and around the fountains brought cheer to the darkness. Together they strolled side by side past the artistic creations of lively water, brought to life in the lights of the night. For a moment, there was nothing but the beauty of the park and what silence could be offered by a busy city. Then Dr. Swann broke the silence.

"Vala, would you be willing to stay in my life?"

Vala gave Dr. Swann a pleasant smile. There was no one she loved more and for her, there could only be one answer. In her mind she began to form the word "yes"...but then her memory got the best of her. That voice and the words it spoke... "I would love to...but I can't. I have to stay where I am. I can't share my life with anyone else."

"I'm not entirely sure I know what you mean, but I'm sure we can work things out."

"It's not just what you're thinking...it's...it's just past experiences; it couldn't be possible."

"Then why have you been leading me on this way for so long? I thought you really loved me."

"I did love you...I do; but I realize now I should end it. I've been such a fool. I'm sorry, so sorry I didn't stop sooner. I just had such a wonderful time that I forgot about my circumstances. I want to thank you for tonight though. I really felt like someone special. I suppose it was a big waste though."

"It was not a waste. Like I said, you need to know that you are valuable. That doesn't change regardless of what our relationship ends up being." He paused and then continued. "So you really want to end it then?"

"No, but I feel I have no other choice. Anyone who is close to me is in danger and I don't want you in danger. I'll leave now before I cause any more harm." Vala's heart was heavy and she was deeply despondent. The weather seemed to reflect her mood as a light rain began to break out.

"I'll take you home," said Dr. Swann in the midst of his confusion.

"No, I'd rather go myself," replied Vala. It was getting late, dark and cold, and the rain had begun to fall harder.

"Are you sure? The weather's getting bad and it's not smart for a lady to go out alone, especially at this time of night and in this city."

"I'll be fine. I'd rather be alone. Besides, I'm trained for this."

"Well… I can't force you if that's what you want, but I strongly advise against it."

Vala took her leave without a second glance and as she turned away, tears ran from her eyes and joined the raindrops as they fell to the ground. Dr. Swann watched her depart into the gloom. Vala walked swiftly and miserably through the rain, staying in the more public and well-lit areas. As she walked, she observed others carrying on with their happy lives. She could never have someone special like they did. She would not allow herself to. As her thoughts went on, she felt more and more regret for leaving Dr. Swann. Then the capture of Ariella by the Roecatans came to mind. She thought she had surely lost her, but then she returned safe and unharmed and was still alive and well. And April; she was in no greater danger than she had put herself in. Maybe things were changing; maybe there was nothing for Vala to worry about now. She stopped and stood still in the rain, thinking everything over as she watched others enjoy themselves. Then she made her choice: a choice that would not only change her life but the course of the galaxy's future, though she herself had no idea at this time. She turned and ran all the way back to Dr. Swann's living complex. At the entrance, she saw a rose on the ground. It was the one he had given her. She must have dropped it. She picked it up. It was wet, but undamaged. She quickly made her way to his door and knocked. He opened it and was surprised to see Vala.

"I've changed my mind. I don't want to leave you. You bring me so much joy and I love you."

"Are you sure you're not going to change your mind again?" he asked

"No, I made my choice. No matter what comes, I won't be separated from you. I'm ready to love again," she handed him the rose. "Trust me."

He took the rose and they both smiled. Dr. Swann invited her inside. The apartment was luxurious but small. He could obviously have one much bigger and even more grand, but he had no reason for it.

"You're wet," he said.

"It's the rain," replied Vala.

Dr. Swann turned to look outside the glass doors of his sizable balcony. The lights of the city shone softly through the falling rain. "All of a sudden, it looks beautiful out there."

"Does it?" replied Vala.

"Of course, now that you're here," The doctor replied.

"Then go out there, I dare you!" said Vala playfully. Dr. Swann smiled at her. "Alright, if you insist."

He opened the door to the balcony and went outside. He laughed a bit. "Come on out, the water's great!" he said with a smile and Vala ran out with him. They laughed and smiled at each other.

"Do you really mean what you said? Are you positive?" asked Dr. Swann. "I don't want you to make the wrong choice for yourself."

"Yes, yes I am positive," replied Vala with a bright, joyful expression.

"Then," said Dr. Swann, drawing Vala close, "Ms. Vala Stella, will you marry me?"

Vala's Choice

Vala was thrilled and trembled with excitement. She paused for a moment to take in what had just happened, then broke the suspension as warmth and joy flooded in. "Yes!" she exclaimed.

"You've made me so happy," said Dr. Swann.

He took out a starstone ring and placed it on her finger. She was overwhelmed with joy and put her arms around him. She would not let go. She thought to herself that there were so many other young women in the galaxy. So many others more beautiful, more attractive, and more desirable than her, and being a wealthy, handsome young doctor, Dr. Swann could easily have chosen one of them and yet he had chosen her; plain simple her.

"I don't know what to say. I don't deserve this," she said.

"Of course you do. You are far above all jewels this galaxy knows," replied the doctor. "How soon do you want it? The wedding I mean?"

"Oh, so much to think about! I suppose at the beginning of the year after things have settled down. That reminds me! Next week we're going back to Aldura for the winter ball at the palace and then we'll stay for the new year. You should come, there are many types of people to meet. The senator's going which means I have to go. I've never gone with a partner, but I am allowed to take one. You could go with me."

"I'm not so sure. I think I'd feel too much like an outsider."

"But they're all friendly. They'd love to meet you and they would certainly do their best to make you feel comfortable. You'd get used to it and have fun!"

"Well, I guess it won't hurt."

"Good! I'll arrange it for you." Then, suddenly recalling the time, Vala exclaimed, "It's late! I'd better go."

"I suppose you're right; are you sure you still don't want me to take you home? I could give you a ride and get you there sooner, and drier," said Dr. Swann.

Vala smiled. "This time I'll gladly take up your request. The sooner I can get back, the better."

When Vala entered the senator's penthouse after her new fiancé left to return home, she was greeted by Amara.

"Vala! You're here late. It's past midnight! And you're soaked! Where did you get that jewelry? And that dress?"

"Shh. I've had a wonderful time! And...will you keep a secret?" replied Vala in a lowered voice.

"I will," said Amara.

"I'm engaged!" exclaimed Vala in a low voice, showing her beautiful ring. Amara's jaw dropped in shock.

"What?! I could tell something wonderful was up, but I didn't expect this! It's such a surprise!" exclaimed Amara in a loud whisper.

"I know it's a shock, but it's true! But let me tell the others tomorrow when I'm ready," said Vala.

"I can't believe it; how could we not have known? Is it Dr. Swann? Does that mean you'll leave?" asked Amara.

Vala explained to her how it happened and what her plans were. Then she left Amara, who was still stunned, and went to bed.

As the end of thee year approached, the capitol was opened to travel again and there was excitement in the air when the senator and her companions received the news that they would be able to return to Aldura for the winter break. This meant it was time to prepare for the winter ball. As was a common Alduran custom for holidays and other special dances, Ariella had a dress specially designed and constructed for the winter ball. This year, her dress would be white with some gold accents. She had not been able to attend the summer and autumn balls due to the events at the capitol, so this winter ball would be the first Alduran court dance she would attend this year. It was also April's first dance at the palace, and she was very excited; she had never experienced such an extravagant event before. Dr. Swann was unable to attend the winter ball but would join them for the new year.

They arrived a few days early so Ariella could meet with the queen and other officeholders in the Alduran government. During these days, Vala, April, and Amara had more time to themselves and spent it on their enjoyment. Because Vala and April worked for the Senator of Aldura, they were considered employees of the Alduran court and though their priorities were to Ariella, they were encouraged to provide some assistance to the palace servants whenever they stayed there. Vala was acquainted with the staff responsible for arranging the winter ball and when she and April were found loitering around the palace chatting and laughing, they were asked if they would like to help with the decorating. They both gladly obliged. Preparing the ballroom for the event was the best way to get into the festive spirit. When the night of the dance was finally upon them, fresh food and flowers were delivered to the palace, new dresses were unwrapped from their designer's packaging, the best jewelry and hair accessories came out, and excitement mingled with tense nerves. Vala and April did their job to make Ariella appear stunning and then quickly rushed off to prepare themselves. By the way young, enthusiastic April was carrying on about it and anticipating it, one would have guessed she was the most excited of all. Corin and Amara wore their ceremonial Alduran uniforms, this was the last dance they would wear them at before receiving a new design for the New Year ball. The ballroom was beautifully decorated with garlands, flowers, lights, and ice sculptures, as well as several other ornaments. There were also refreshments on a large, long, beautifully decorated table. The table had a white cloth and was decorated with the same decorations that covered the room. Lights and colors reflected off the floor. Ariella and Corin made a beautiful scene as they danced together across the floor and caught the eyes of many. As they danced, their expressions and the way they gracefully flowed made them appear to be one with the music and with each other and everyone marveled. April went all out as much as she could while retaining the humility, modesty, and respect that was expected of her position. She went around getting to know many of the guests in the best way she could while keeping in line with the palace protocol and became quite popular. She seemed to attract the attention of many young men as well, leading Vala to watch out for her and make sure she didn't carry herself too far. The night was beautiful and festive and when it was over, Vala stayed behind with the event staff to help clear and clean the ballroom. They would leave the beautiful winter decorations as they were until it was time to prepare for the New Year's dance.

 The next day, everyone slept in after dancing late into the night. As they prepared for the day, Ariella and April began an excited conversation about the dresses they would wear for the New Year dance. April chose to wear a black dress with accessories of the best starstone look-alikes she could afford, and Ariella described the glittery gold dress that had been designed and constructed for her.

"What is your dress going to be like Vala?" asked April.

"It's a surprise. I'm not letting anyone see it until the night of the dance," replied Vala. She seemed to be harboring a calm, reserved excitement about the dress, but no one could get anything out of her.

"It must be something amazing if you're keeping it a secret," said Ariella. "I can't wait for mine; it should be delivered any day now!" she exclaimed.

Vala was glad to see Ariella in high spirits. Ever since Corin had rescued her and she returned to the galactic capitol, Ariella always seemed like she carried a heavy burden and didn't often smile. "Dr. Swann should be arriving any day as well," said Vala with a smile. "He'll have quite a bit to learn. April, would you like to help?" she continued.

"Sure, I think it will be fun," replied April, cheerful as always.

When Dr. Swann arrived, he was warmly welcomed and introduced to Alduran culture. Vala and April took him to the palace ballroom every day, which was seldom in use otherwise, and taught him about Alduran social dance culture. Vala began to explain some of Aldura's dance culture.

"Besides the usual universal etiquette, there are other things we need to make sure you understand. For some events, guests may be expected to use a dance card, but for this event and most dances in our more modern society, dance cards are often not used. Instead, guests will simply ask a partner for the next dance they wish to dance to. Guests may also request songs. At casual dances, recordings are typically played but for this dance, the music will be performed live. There are songs for every kind of dance so the more types of dances you know, the better off you are. Historically, balls would start off with songs for medium speed dances, then move to fast dances, and end with slow dances. This was to give the ladies enough time to have their dresses altered for the different styles of dance as necessary. Say, for example, you want to wear a long flowing dress, but you also want to dance some fast songs. A long flowy dress may not work for all those dances, so tailors were hired to attend dances and expertly create stitches and seams in the dresses to alter the shape and length for the fast dances, and again for the slow dances if long skirts were desired. Advances in clothing construction have been allowing us to break out of that system; now you'll more likely see an even mixture of all the different dances throughout the entire night. Some songs have routines, but the majority are freestyle. There are songs which are danced in pairs - which make up most of the ball - and a few songs which are danced in large groups. Solo dancing is also perfectly acceptable. Then there are the fast dance competitions. These are where your knowledge of every different step and move is helpful. The host or hostess will choose a song and whether it will be danced in pairs or by individuals, and also a judge to handle any disputes and make sure everyone plays fair. Then he or she will announce whether the competition will be done to a set routine or steps, or whether competitors will dance whatever steps they choose. Then, the song will start off slow, but the tempo will increase as the song progresses. Competitors will have to keep up with the tempo until they miss a step, mess up, lose connection with their partner, lag with the music, or until they're too tired to continue. Once that happens, they drop out to the side and watch the rest of the dancers until the last individual or pair remains. It's very fun, though I suspect I know who will win," Ariella and Corin came to mind as she said this. "We often throw other competitions into a dance, but the fast dance comp is the most popular and is the one you need to understand. Jam circles are also highly popular, and you will see them at least once at pretty much every event. It may seem like a lot to learn, but once you experience it, you'll catch on quickly," said Vala.

"We'll demonstrate it all too to help you understand," said April.

"And then we'll have you practice with us," said Vala.

"Any time you're not dancing, you're a spectator. If spectators are really enjoying watching a dance, they might clap and cheer or clap with the beat," said April. "And it may sound like a lot, but once you're thrown into the event, you'll catch on quickly. It's not that difficult," she finished.

The two handmaids helped Dr. Swann practice almost every day and when they were not practicing, Vala gave him a tour around the capital and described their customs, culture and way of living, including education.

"Here, our goal for education is to set up the younger generation for success and to help them become smarter and wiser than the previous generation. We have public and private schools, though many children are taught at home as well. There are also tutors and instructors for hire if parents wish for their children to learn at home but are unable or don't wish to teach themselves. Senator Callista learned some from her parents but had tutors for many of her subjects. Dance and politics were her primary subjects of interest and her parents strived to find the best instructors they could afford. I think it served her well. You have only to look at her on the dance floor to see how impressive she is, though much of it is also natural talent. Every year, children are evaluated to make sure they have met the minimum education requirements. Once children reach their final four years of schooling, they can choose to specialize in a certain area. They can choose if they want to apprentice or prepare to go to a university. Students can apprentice for any career, all they have to do is apprentice and learn for four years, all year long. At the end of the four years, if the occupation requires it, they must demonstrate their skills and knowledge to experienced professionals and pass an examination. If they pass, they get a certificate proving it. If the profession requires any additional certifications or tests, the student can then test to be certified. If they pass it, they can begin their new career. The alternative is getting a degree at a university or college and then passing the same certifications and tests. There are a lot of youth organizations and programs as well. The most prestigious one is the cotillion ceremony for youth who have reached adulthood and are beginning their new careers. It's an old tradition that dates back many years and was originally reserved for the young ladies from families of the court, and sometimes the wealthy, but has changed over the years. The tradition has evolved over time with society and only recently became what it is today. The change also opened the event to young men as well as women. It encourages young people to work hard, achieve goals, and be involved with their community. It used to function as an event to introduce the most eligible virgins to society but has evolved into an event that exhibits the most promising individuals for the future of various industries and allows the young people to make contacts with some of the leaders in their chosen industry. Because it's open to all youth on the planet and the amount that can be accommodated is limited, those who are interested must submit applications. The ones chosen show a lot of talent, hard work, achievements, community service and most importantly, good recommendations. Those who are chosen get to tour the capital, meet the elected king or queen, and several other officials, be presented to society, choose to do one or more presentations of their skills, and attend a ball and dinner. The young people can also choose a companion to accompany them to the ball. It's a fun event to see. All the skills, achievements, volunteer hours, interests, and hours spent working towards the goals of the accepted applicants are usually made available to the public unless the applicant requests that they be kept private."

The New Year

The new year quickly came upon Aldura and festivities started up again, or perhaps never stopped. The palace ballroom was decorated with flowers, fabrics, glittery substances, garlands and lights to celebrate the occasion. April looked elegant in her black dress and Ariella was radiant in her glittery gold dress. Amara and Corin once again wore ceremonial uniforms but this time they had new ones. Vala's dress was finally revealed when she stepped out of the room she shared with April. It was a bold glittery red dress with her hair pulled back and styled to look like a rose. She never wore bright colors that attracted attention, always more conservative colors or pastels. She preferred to stay hidden and not stand out in the crowd. Tonight however, she was feeling different. She was feeling joyful and passionate and very much in love; and she showed it in the dress she wore. When those who knew Vala saw her in her dress, they marveled. She looked ravishing. She and Dr. Swann took each other's hands and began the first song together. During the event, Dr. Swann was introduced to several of the guests, including Abigale Mirella, an Alduran doctor, and Queen Jasmine Selina of Aldura. As Dr. Swann, Vala and Dr. Mirella were standing to the side conversing, Vala suddenly recognized the song that began playing.

"This is one of their favorite songs," she asserted with a smile, nodding at Ariella and Corin. "They have a few songs that they only like to dance with each other and this is one of them," said Vala as Corin and Ariella began their dance.

Ariella and Corin moved so beautifully to the music with both their bodies and even their facial expressions. Their connection with each other was beyond exceptional and their passion for each other showed in this dance more than ever before. They were such an amazing, beautiful sight that slowly, all the other dancers paused their dancing to watch. Corin and Ariella were so caught up in the dance that they hardly noticed the change in the floor. Everyone was silent as they watched the two together. It was so beautiful, nobody dared make a sound. Only the music played. There was applause when they finished the dance and Ariella and Corin realized they had been the only ones dancing. As they exited the floor Ariella approached Vala.

"You were so beautiful! That's the best I've ever seen you dance. Everyone loved it," said Vala.

"So it seems," said Ariella, trying not to look too pleased. She had enjoyed it, but she didn't like having attention drawn to her and Corin as they danced.

"If you two were in fine arts instead of politics, you'd be rising to stardom!" exclaimed Vala.

As the final hours of the old year approached, the guests and some of the staff began gathering outside on the lawn where they would witness an outstanding fire and light performance. There were refreshments placed outside and the whole palace was beautifully decorated like the ballroom. There were sparkling tall glasses of several different kinds of drinks, large confectionary fountains and all sorts of fruits, desserts, and appetizers arranged beautifully into towers, sculptures, and designs. The refreshment tables were decorated with flowers, petals, glitter, ribbon, candles, and even lit fountains with petals, glitter, or candles floating in them. Each little dish, drink and food item was carefully decorated. It was a beautiful sight. Ariella, Corin, Vala, and Dr. Swann walked outside together. April was already outside enjoying social interaction and the beautifully decorated drinks and desserts while Amara was preparing for a special role in the New Year celebration. As they walked out, Vala explained to the others what she had heard about this year's celebration performance.

"They're going to have some sort of show with horseback archers shooting arrows with fire. They may be doing some horseback gymnastics too, I caught a glimpse of some of the costumes when I was helping with the event preparations. At the end of the show, one rider is supposed to deliver a torch to the archer, who will be Amara. She'll use the fire to light her arrow and shoot it through a small ring. When the ring catches fire, it triggers the release of fireworks and confetti and other creative things they came up with. Everything is supposed to be timed so that the arrow passes through the ring just as midnight strikes. Amara said there will be several rings lined up behind the first one that releases the fireworks and confetti. Each ring is smaller than the one before it. The last one is just small enough for the arrow shaft to fit through. The goal of the archer is to see if they can shoot the arrow through the last ring where it gets caught by the fletches after going through. I'm excited that Amara was offered this opportunity. She's been practicing all week and visualizing the whole shot. I think she'll do well."

When midnight was almost upon them, Amara took the ceremonial bow and arrow she would use. The riser of the bow was gold, and the vanes of the arrow were also gold. The bow and its arrow were carefully tuned for her, she had been working with it the last

The New Year

few days. She took her place a few minutes before midnight and waited with her equipment ready. When she heard the light thundering of hooves approaching, she dipped the arrow point in oil and took a deep breath. This was an exciting and important shot, and many eyes were watching from near and far. She had to stay calm and put all worry and excitement away if this was going to be a good shot. It was just her now, shooting the same shot she had made physically and mentally so many times before. As the horse and rider drew near, they jumped the hedge that formed a circle around where Amara was standing. They approached her and the rider held out the torch. She calmly lit the arrow tip on fire and nocked the arrow to the string. She placed one finger above the nock and two just under it and gracefully lifted the bow as she had done thousands of times before. She drew back and aligned herself, keeping her eyes on the target the whole time. Confidence and commitment were key. She continued her movement while stretching her bow arm towards the tiny ring at the end of the line and suddenly, she released. She continued to follow through with the shot, it had felt strong and beautiful, and the arrow flew true. It passed all the way through to the ring and set off the celebration right on time. Amara smiled; she had done it; it was the new year. If only Captain Adwin was here to see me, she thought to herself. Fireworks shot up and exploded and glittering confetti mixed with thousands of flower petals flowed down.

There was cheering and excitement and celebration all around.

After the initial celebration, Dr. Swann and Vala wandered off to the palace garden. After walking for several minutes, Dr. Swann noticed Vala seemed to be heavy-hearted.

"What is it?" he asked.

"Nothing. It happens every now and again."

"What does?"

Vala didn't want to answer, what was the point in talking about it anyway?

Dr. Swann pressed on gently. "Let me help you."

Vala began to lower her walls. "It's just memories that the new year at the palace brings back...It's broadcast every year and my sisters and I used to enjoy spotting all the different fashions and analyzing their construction every time we watched the broadcast. I can't help thinking of them and how they would love to be here. I can imagine them watching tonight's broadcast and maybe catching a glimpse of me. They would really be proud." Vala was silent, her sadness suddenly filled her. "And now they're gone. My friends, my family; all of them." Her head was bowed to the ground, and she stopped and stood still.

"I'm very sorry. You never told me exactly what happened. I know it's always been a pain point for you."

"I know... I just couldn't...bear to bring up those memories." She stood stern and sorrowful and refused comfort. Then her bitterness and anger began to surface. She picked up a stone and threw it as hard as she could. "Why?! What reason was there? What did I do to become so hated?! If I ever find him, he will pay! He deserves justice!" She turned away.

"Vala, please tell me what happened," said Dr. Swann gently, wrapping his arms around her.

She remained cold. She didn't change her embittered expression and looked away into the distance. "He murdered my family and friends when I was fifteen years old. I don't know who he is or why he did it. The only way I could know him is by his voice. He called me hated child and..." she turned and looked at Dr. Swann fearfully, "He said I should think twice next time I begin a close relationship."

Dr. Swann considered Vala's last words carefully. "So that's why you almost ran out on me...But then you changed your mind. Are you still afraid he might hurt us?"

Vala remained still as her many thoughts and emotions turned and swirled in her mind. "I don't know... I ... I don't even know who he is or if he still exists. Sometimes I am afraid, but right now I'm so angry that I wish he would show up, then I could bring him to justice." She paused and seemed to be processing more of her thoughts. "Are you sure you still want this? This relationship, even if it could cost you your life?"

"Vala, you must know something. You are precious to me, and I would rather die and have lived a short life with you than live a long life without you; even though it's going to be quite an adjustment to work with your lifestyle as a handmaid. And I don't think we are in as much danger as you fear." They gazed at each other in silence for a moment, and then Dr. Swann spoke up again. "You seem to have a lot of pain that's been tormenting you for years. What if you release it and let it go? Maybe it's time you start letting it go and just spill it out and process it rather than holding it in and allowing it to fester."

Vala was still, battling with the choice to keep her bitterness in as she had been for so many years, and the desire to find peace and comfort. Finally, after what seemed like a long struggle, she gave in. She put her arms around the doctor, and he tightened his around her and patiently listened as she spoke more about her feelings and her past, and cried the sorrow away. For the first time in many years of her life, she allowed herself to find comfort in someone else rather than hardening herself and burying the emotions. She softened up and began to find some healing, though the memory was still there.

The respite on Aldura was far too short. Just a day after the new year, the senator and her companions made their return to the galactic capital. They were quite refreshed after the break on Aldura, though as weeks passed, tensions and pressure rose again.

The New Year

Since the president had died, there seemed to be no more advancements on the investigations into Roecata. Eerily, Ariella could get no answer when she asked about updates on this matter and when she checked in with the president's office to see how the investigation was going. Her relationship with Casimir Blade was changing too, especially with the controvorsey over Roeacata. More and more, Ariella began to suspect that Casmir had something to do with the mystery of the Roecata investigation and additionally, his small party seemed to be getting their way over many issues. It began to cause Ariella some concern. On the outside, she and Casimir were still cordial to each other but internally, there was pressure and tension building between them and their trust in one another began to weaken. Yet, through it all, Casimir did not try to distance himself from Ariella but instead, seemed to be seeking a tighter hold on her. Ariella's companions and those close to her began to notice this change in their relationship, but either could not convince her to listen to wisdom and distance herself from him, or felt it was not their place to speak up about it. On the outside, however, others suspected she and Casimir Blade had some sort of close relationship going on. There were even rumors passing around in the shadows that they had some sort of affair. No one knew the true state of Ariella's heart, however, as she refused to share it with anyone, not even those closest to her. In the third month of the year, Vala and Dr. Swann were married in a small private ceremony with a few friends, and some of Dr. Swann's family – his parents, grandparents, cousins and their parents, and his sister who Vala had got to know well as the wedding approached. Vala had no desire or reason to make the wedding celebration big. Nevertheless, they were wedded at one of the most beautiful venues in the city with a fine dinner and elegant decorations. Vala wore a beautiful white dress and a crown of white flowers from an Alduran fruit tree that carried a beautiful scent. So she could continue her normal duties while living with her new husband, Vala and Dr. Swann bought an apartment close to Senator Callista's. One early morning while everyone was still asleep except Corin, who was guarding the premises, Vala got up to come over to the Senator's complex. This morning there was a lot to be done and Vala wanted to get a good start on the day. As she entered, she met Corin.

"You look tired," she said.

"I've been up all night on watch," he replied.

"Yes, but that's part of your normal routine, and something looks different. I think there's more to it," said Vala.

"Something's on my mind. It's Ariella. I feel like I don't understand her. It's like she becomes a different person when we're here than when we're on Aldura," he said.

"I could agree with that. What's the trouble?"

The New Year

"When we're on Aldura, she seems so light and free, but here, she seems to be hard and shut off. And something's going on with her and Senator Blade. I'm sure you've noticed. She seems to be hiding something and doesn't want to open up to me about it. I asked about her thoughts on furthering our relationship and she avoided the conversation. She seems afraid to address the issue. There's something going on underneath the surface that she refuses to talk about, and she seems overburdened...I guess in the end, though, all I really want to know is if I truly have her heart."

"On that you are correct. Unfortunately, I don't think I know much more than you do, but what I do know is that Senator Blade is either after Ariella's affections, or else he wants to control her and use her for something. Honestly, it could be that both are true. He asked her to consider marrying him before you and she met. As far as I know, she's neither told him yes or no, and he seems to be willing to hold the situation out for as long as it's been going on, but has been pressing her a little more as of late. I believe she's uncertain of what to do with the situation. She clearly doesn't want to tell him yes, but she hasn't said no which means she must fear what would happen if she did refuse him. Or perhaps she believes she has some sort of advantage or bargaining power over him as long as she says nothing. I don't agree with her choice. I think it's dividing her and destroying her life and happiness. I always wondered how this would play out when you entered the scene. I had hoped and truly thought that that would cause her to tell Casimir no right away, but apparently not. I know that she really does care for you though, and if she had to make a choice, she would choose to run away with you rather than stay and play charades with Casimir Blade. The fact that she even developed a love for you shocked me. For many years she has been strongly against forming any kind of romantic relationship. The fact that you were able to break in and cause a spark in her is truly exceptional. I think you should try to win her over so this game of usury can end."

"I certainly will, but I may need your help."

"You will have it then. And if it were at all possible, I think it would do her good to get away from all this, I think the two of you need a break and some time together."

The next day, Dr. Swann slept in after a long late night shift and when he finally awoke, he saw he was home alone. He got up and prepared himself for a quiet, relaxing morning with some tea and journal reading. Then, just as his peaceful day started, he heard some shooting coming from below. Suddenly, Vala rushed through the door with a small firearm in her hand and slammed it shut.

"I'm on it!" she exclaimed in a small communication device. "Oh, Galen, you're awake! Just in time!"

"Just in time for what?" asked the doctor, looking very disoriented.

"The invasion. There's a small band of soldiers, or assassins of some sort, outside launching an attack on Senator Callista's apartment. It looks pretty bad; we may have to get out of here. Take this!" she tossed him another firearm. "Take these too," she said, giving him a communication device and a knife, "they may be useful." She spoke into her communicator. "Husband's awake and armed Captain."

"Excellent," came Corin's voice over the communicator. "Amara?" came Corin's voice again.

"They'll be up there any second," came Amara's voice.

Vala took a rapid-fire gun out of a corner.

"Since when did we have that in our home? And what exactly is going on?" asked poor Galen, still frozen in shock and bewilderment. This was not the kind of life he had ever imagined living; it was something just for stories.

Vala took the gun to the closed door. "We're going to have to fight. These assassins are after us."

"I don't think they're after me. What am I even doing? I'm a doctor. I'm supposed to heal people, not kill them. How did I get myself into this mess?"

"You married me, remember? If it bothers you too much, then just try to temporarily immobilize them. You're a doctor, you should know how to do that. And one last thing," she turned and looked at him, "I love you so much." She turned again and pushed open the door and began firing at the attackers with the rapid-fire gun.

Corin, Amara and Vala soon had the attackers cornered between them and quickly overcame them.

"We've learned there are more coming," said Corin, "and no one is responding to our distress signals. Not the government security, not the police, not the military, no one. I don't know what's going on. Are you ready to get out of here if necessary? "

"I'm ready," said Vala.

"Good, take April's place and she will load what is necessary onto the ships to prepare for evacuation," said Corin.

"Trouble?" asked Dr. Swann.

"Yes, we could all be in danger. We'll have to be ready to escape. Will you come with us?" replied Vala.

"I don't think they have any reason to get me. Besides, I can't just disappear from the hospital without warning."

"I think you should come. Once they know you live here, you'll be a valuable source of information and they'll come for you. You'll be safer on Aldura, come with us. Besides, they like you back there and the spring ball will be coming up."

Dr. Swann thought it over. He didn't like this spontaneous change for their lives but considering the danger, it was probably the best option. "Well...of course I'll go with you."

"Good. Pack your bags and stay in touch on that communicator, I need to go. I'll see you soon." They quickly embraced and Vala ran to Ariella's side.

It was quiet for a while but sure enough, the second wave of attackers approached since the first had failed. The second wave was more organized and more difficult to hold back. Corin and Amara did all they could but were eventually pushed back. Finally, when there seemed to be no hope of defeating the attackers, Corin took Ariella by the hand while they were all fighting.

"You must get out of here Senator, there's nothing more we can do."

"But I can't leave, we're still in session!"

"If you stay, you'll get killed!"

"What about the others?"

"They have their orders; they'll leave too, now come on!" Corin looked at Vala. She nodded and showed a faint smile. Corin grabbed Ariella who refused to leave, threw the unyielding senator over his shoulder, and as she protested, took her to his ship which they kept at the capital as a backup.

"Where are the others and why are we using your ship?" asked Ariella as soon as they were onboard.

"They are taking your ship; we are taking mine. You'll be much safer and unnoticed this way."

"But I-"

"Just don't worry! We'll all be fine."

Ariella had reservations about leaving, but Corin had already taken off and was flying away. There was nothing more she could do. When Corin and Ariella, accompanied by Cosmo, were safely departing, the others began to retreat. When they had the chance, they rushed to the senator's ship with Seren following along. When they were all inside, Amara quickly took off and set course for Aldura.

When Corin and Ariella arrived, they did not go directly to Verona, Aldura's capital. Instead, Corin flew them into Florina.

"Why are we going here? Why are we not at Verona?" asked Ariella.

"I'm not taking you back there until I get a straight answer. Are you worth my time or not? Do you genuinely love me and want a future together or not? I have no reason to tolerate living amongst politicians so if you don't truly love me and desire for us to live the rest of our lives together, I'm going to resign and say gooddbye."

"So that's what this is! You had it all planned out! Well, I will not give in to your trap! I gave you my answer."

"Well I'm not satisfied with it; and the escape and attack were not planned…well, not completely planned."

"I will not give in to threats."

"Then why have you not refused Casimir Blade? Why do you continue to give into him?"

Ariella turned sharply. "How do you know?!"

"It's becoming obvious."

"Well...that situation is different. As long as there's a hope for him, and this picture he wants to paint of us is maintained, it gives me leverage and inside information. And it helps me to know my enemy...I believe he's hiding some things from me and I want to make sure Aldura is not harmed by him."

"I know you don't trust him and as you said, he's hiding something so why do you continue with this charade? Is it really helping you? Anyone observing closely might say the opposite. It looks to me as if you're no different than any other conniving politician."

"I've had enough of this! I'm taking your ship and leaving this place!"

"Go ahead and try, but I think you'll find it won't cooperate for you."

"What?"

"I programmed it so that it responds only to me and Cosmo, but how it works that way I won't tell you."

Ariella was frustrated. "Cosmo, go start the ship for me."

Cosmo stared at Corin and then at Ariella. He didn't move.

"You can't try to use him either, he's too loyal to me."

"Well...then I'll walk back!" replied Ariella, very frustrated.

Corin still stood in his place almost ready to laugh as Ariella began walking in her fury. He found the whole thing rather amusing. Then he began to stroll alongside her. "So, we'll go for a nice long walk. A good choice for a date."

"This is not a date!"

"Fine, call it what you want but I still say it's a date."

"I despise you sometimes."

"You're not yourself. Something's wrong and you won't confide in anyone. No one knows what's really going on in your mind."

"Alright, I am not myself. I'm stressed, suspicious and a little afraid. How does Casimir's party seem to be controlling everything and why am I, as well as some other senators, being attacked and not being defended or helped?"

"Afraid? That's new for you."

"Please don't joke about it."

"Sorry, I don't mean to make light of the situation. And I do agree, the situation is not right, it's very strange." He paused for a moment, noticing that Ariella still looked very tense and unhappy. "It seems like you're not taking well to Vala's idea of getting some time away. "

"Vala's in your scheme too?"

"Forget I said anything. It's just something she mentioned to me in a brief conversation. Don't have any bad feelings towards her."

"So everyone is plotting behind my back?!"

"No! It's not like that! I just think a rest from that poisonous atmosphere will do you good. Don't you trust us?"

"And leave Aldura without representation in the Senate?"

"There's nothing you can do there right now."

"Then..." Ariella paused with a frustrated look on her face. For the first time, she didn't know what to say because Corin was right, there really was nothing she could do, and it bothered her so much. "I'm worried and I don't know who to trust. I feel so helpless." She began to cry a little and Corin held her close.

"How about you start with some rest? Disconnect yourself from what's going on for a few days and show me more of your home planet. And then after that, maybe you should have a talk with Queen Selina and your councilors. That's what they're there for. As much as you want to do everything on your own, involving others will benefit not just you, but them as well. There's a reason for their offices as you know better than I do."

Ariella agreed.

After she calmed down, Corin spoke. "In that case, we can take my ship instead of walking. You name the place, and we'll go there...and about the ship responding to only Cosmo and I, I was just bluffing."

"What?! Why you...in that case, I can take it and strand you here!" exclaimed Ariella, taking off towards the ship with a smile.

"Not if I get there first!" replied Corin, running after her, smiling. They both raced to the ship laughing, with Cosmo following behind.

During their break, Ariella showed Corin some of Aldura's mountains and they visited the vineyard regions. They went through some of Aldura's farmlands and natural areas and then to the beaches. Ariella loved the sand, the view, and riding the waves. One day, she sat down alone and began to think to herself. The words Corin had spoken a few days ago when they first landed on Aldura had not left her, and day by day, she could tell that he was serious. There was no bluffing in his words and actions. Every day she had been thinking about it, and the fear and realization that he might truly leave her was becoming more real. All the hidden issues of her heart were beginning to come to the surface, and it seemed there was no more hiding it. She could no longer keep one foot in and one foot out, she had to make a choice and go all in. She would either have to lose Corin or lose the connection she had built with Casimir Blade and her reservations about commitment to a relationship, both which were a means of self-protection.

The following day, they explored another region with rivers and mountains. One particular mountain they visited had water at its foot and there were smooth slide-like carvings going down which had been naturally formed by the water running down the mountain. Some of these cut outs were safe enough to slide down into the water below, which made it a popular place for adventurers to visit. They took ropes and grapples and climbed up the mountain's surface to the top where there was a ledge coming way out from the mountain's side. The view from the ledge was a beautiful sight and well worth the climb. Below the ledge at the base of the mountain were sharp rocks. Next to the ledge was another carved slide, but this one was a dangerous one and not safe for sliding. It ran down to end under the ledge above the sharp rocks. They climbed up to the ledge and paused a while to take in the view. When they had seen enough, they began to go down and suddenly, Ariella slipped and fell down the dangerous water-carved cut out. The rushing water pulled her down and kept her from getting a good grip.

"Helllp Coriin!" she cried.

Corin took one rope, quickly grappled it onto the ledge, fastened the other end around himself, grabbed the other rope, and jumped down using free-fall to reach the end of the water-carved slide before Ariella did. Corin swung the other grapple and it caught onto where the slide terminated. He used this rope to draw himself to the end of the slide and secured himself there. Then he saw Ariella approaching as the water carried her over. He held out his hands and caught her as she reached the end of the slide. Ariella took hold of him, and he used the ropes to lower them both to safety.

"You always manage to place yourself in danger, Senator," said Corin.

"I guess I really do need you," said Ariella, still recovering from the fright, but relieved. In this moment, Corin's arms felt the safest place to be. In fact, there was nowhere else she would rather be. She began to remember the misadaventures she and Corin had been through, and how she felt in those moments. She would have been willing to give up her role as a senator to pursue a life with him. She had cared nothing about the consequences. What had changed? How did she get to where she was now? "Let's go to the river, the part where it's narrow and slow," she said. As they sat down, Ariella began to say what was stirring in her heart.

"Corin..." she began. There was an unusual softness and a genuineness in her voice. "I've been thinking...I am so sorry for what I put you through. It must have been horrible for you. I feel horrible. I had no right to lead you on and tell you yes, I wanted a relationship, but to wait and push you to the side... and keep you in the dark as to why I was behaving the way I was. The truth is my love for you is genuine and there's no one who makes me happier. But I'm also afraid of what will happen if I fully commit to you, and what Casimir might do if he finds out. I don't know how much you know, but he's kind of been courting me since before I met you and I haven't refused him because I've been believing that as long as I don't say no, I'll have more leverage, and I don't want to find out what will happen when I do say no. And also..." she seemed to struggle letting the next words come out. There was a deeper truth that she had kept hidden from everyone, and this was the true root of her struggle with her relationship with Corin. "The thought of committing to a relationship, and marriage especially, makes me a little afraid. When I was younger, many of the young men in the court sought my affections and tried to pursue me when I just wanted to be left alone and focus on my assignments and my future. I feared that they wanted me for some reason other than just for who I was. That began putting me off towards men my age and having an interest in a relationship. But there was one friend who was my age who was loyal and seemed more trustworthy than the others. I opened my heart to him and he began courting me. We thought the relationship was going to build into to something life-long, but then he failed me and proved that like the others, he was not a good fit. In the end, he was controlled by other fears and agendas. There was a bill in the legislature that brought heated division among the youth. I sided with the unpopular opinion and held firm to my convictions about it. One day, this boy I was in a relationship with and I were confronted by two of the other boys opposing our view. They spoke awful, hateful words against us and began to threaten us. My suitor could not stand under the pressure, especially when they seemed ready to do us physical harm once the debate got heated. Rather than standing up for me, he backed down and gave into them, leaving me abandoned to fend for myself and heartbroken. I ran off and after that, it wasn't just over with him, it was over with all men because they just seemed too soft and not trustworthy. I decided it would be better to stay a single woman and have no one to depend on but myself. That seemed to be the safer way to live. And so here I am, afraid to make any commitments… and now I suppose I've become no better than those boys in the way I've been behaving towards you and Casimir. How far I've fallen…" She held back her tears as she continued. "You've been good and faithful to me, and I have not been the same to you. I don't deserve you, so if you don't want me, I understand. But if you do, I'm going to make a choice, and there's no turning back. I chose you above all else. I cannot keep living the way I've been living. If you'll still have me, I desire to be with you the rest of my days, fully and completely. No more indecision. I'm all in." A few tears streamed down her face.

    Corin saw the deep humility and sorrow in her, and she looked more genuine than she ever had before. He knew this was real, there was nothing feigned in her speech. His heart was warm towards her. He took

Ariella, his beloved, in his arms and she embraced him tightly. Nothing more needed to be said, their actions were all that were needed. Finally, Corin broke the silence. There was one important question that still needed to be answered.

"So...what I'm hearing is you're offering a proposal."

"Oh!...I guess I kind of am," she said and laughed a little.

"Well, let me make it official. Ariella Callista, I desire to take you as my bride, and to run across the galaxy wherever life takes us. Will you accept my proposal?"

Ariella laughed in delight and smiled at him. "Corin, it would be my greatest delight to accept your proposal and join you on a life-long adventure together."

After the river, they visited fields, forests and islands; then they went to a special place hidden on Aldura, a garden.

"This is called The Garden. It always stays trimmed, watered and without weeds. It is kept up perfectly and the plants never die but how is a mystery. No one is ever seen working here and yet it is kept immaculate. This garden is full of mystery and wonder. It's as if time stays still here, yet it is ancient," said Ariella, marveling and wondering over the beauty and mystery of the vast garden. "I've only been here once before; I was a girl. You leave this place with awe. Once you come, you don't ever want to leave. It's very peaceful. It leaves an imprint on you for the rest of your life. It's so beautiful, so mystical...a leaf never drops, a flower never dies. The fruit is always ripe, it never ages or falls to the ground. It's captivating."

The garden was full of flowering plants and fruit trees. In the center was an open space surrounded by a grove of great trees, towering high into the sky. Their circumference was beyond that of any tree on Aldura, it was as if they had been growing from the beginning of time. In the open space was a rock and underneath it, a spring that welled up to water the garden. On top of the rock, in plain sight, standing by itself, was a tree. Unlike the rest of the trees in the garden, this one was dead. In fact, it was the only dead thing to be seen in the garden, and yet, this was where the life giving water flowed from. The area surrounding it was where the most exotic and most beautiful plants grew. There were trees with gold and silver interlacing through the bark and leaves, other trees had leaves that were a normal green with a thin line of gold or silver trimming the edge. Other trees were almost entirely a gold or silver color, boasting silver or gold leaves and smooth silver or gold bark. The fruits of these trees were beyond description. Many flowers surrounded the spring and many of these flowers had the same gold and silver colors of the trees. All around the forest were colorful plants, delicious fruits of unimaginable flavors, and delightful scents. It was indeed too wonderful a place to simply leave, so they stayed all day and into the evening before leaving.

    The next day, Ariella spoke to Corin. "You know, we should probably speak to my parents about what just happened. That we're engaged."

    "Oh...yeah, you're probably right," said Corin, so together they flew back to Ariella's childhood home. They vacationed there for several days while Corin and Ariella's parents were able to get to know more about each other. Thankfully for Ariella, they were happy to welcome Corin into the family. During their visit, memories from childhood were brought back to Ariella, and Corin learned more about her past life. Ariella had always been a good dancer and had always loved it. As a child, she learned almost every style of dance. She had also been musically talented and played a few instruments. She lost her interest in music, however, when she got older and more involved in politics and youth political programs and had not made a note since. During her last four years of education, she paged for senators and representatives and learned all she could from them. Though she could have easily chosen a path in professional dancing and had become an exceptional athlete in ice dancing, it was politics and the well-being and freedom of her people that interested her most. Keeping up with dancing was simply a fun past-time. Her youthful charm and beauty had become quite renowned over the years as she grew into adulthood, and it had not been uncommon for others to encourage her to compete in beauty contests or choose the path of a celebrity. Ariella simply had no interest in that kind of life however, and sometimes wished more people would leave her alone.

    One day when she was seemingly alone, Ariella wandered around the house and found her way to the music room. It was spacious with chairs, tables, mirrors, music stands, and was equipped for dance practice. It had large windows and a door that opened to a large balcony. She came across the instruments she used to play and gently touched one, then played a few notes on it. The touch and the sound of the instrument brought her far back to another time. Back to the days of youthful innocence when life was good. She decided to stay here for a while. She opened the balcony door to allow the late spring breeze to blow in, then she fingered the instrument again and cautiously began to play. It had been years since she made any music and though she was a bit rusty, she still had the skill. As she continued on and let her guard down, she fell into a world of her own and began to enjoy herself, first playing one instrument and then the next. Corin was outside and heard Ariella's music. He looked through the open door of the balcony, she looked so fresh and rested and beautiful. All her stress had completely vanished. Her music was beautiful too. In that moment, she looked enchanting and captivating; like a perfect princess out of a story, the desire of many men, but devoted only to one - that one being Corin. Corin climbed up the balcony to her. Ariella almost jumped as she was startled out of her world of music when he suddenly appeared. She immediately stopped.

"Where- how did you-?"

"Don't stop," interjected Corin. "That was beautiful. You didn't tell me you were good with instruments."

"It just never got out. I don't do it anymore."

"Why not?"

"I don't know. I suppose it's just a lack of interest or motivation or time, but I will admit I did enjoy it those many years ago."

"And did you enjoy it those few minutes ago?"

Ariella paused a moment, she felt so happy and refreshed. "Well, I can't hide or deny that I did." She looked around the room. "You know, I also used to practice dancing here. All the time." She paused and looked up at Corin "How did you become such a good dancer?"

"Well, I picked it up in the streets and in joints I'd pass through. Anyone who was brought up in a place like this might think it unimaginable, but there are really good dancers who live on the streets in the places I grew up in. If you know where to find them, there are holes in the wall that host regular dances. It's a great past time for some, and a great place to socialize and have some fun. I learned all I could from the best ones who were regulars at the joints I was familiar with."

While Corin and Ariella were away, the others enjoyed their stay on Aldura too. The palace would be holding its spring ball soon, but Vala guessed Ariella and Corin would miss it. Vala volunteered to help set it up, as one of her favorite parts of events was the behind-the-scenes work. She loved seeing it all come together and getting to be a part of it all, it put her in a festive mood. During their stay, Vala also took some time to teach Dr. Swann the basics of Aldura's favorite activities: archery, horsemanship, more dancing, and a bit of ice dancing. It would also be beneficial for Vala to maintain her skills in some of these things, as well as her physical fitness. By tradition, most of those in Aldura's police and military forces knew how to ride dressage and jump a horse or how to shoot a bow if not both, and Vala, being a bodyguard, was also expected to keep up with these things as her position allowed. She also trained in the use of weapons and attack and defense strategies. One activity that Dr. Swann and Vala grew to enjoy doing together was riding. The climate of Verona, Aldura's capital, was temperate which allowed for cool springs with many new colors emerging from the re-growing vegetation. The week after the spring ball, the cotillion ceremony was held for the young men and women who had received the honor of participating. Often, professionals and prominent figures from many industries would come to seek or observe new talent and some were invited to speak to the young people who were just beginning their new lives with a new career; and of course, the media would be there to broadcast this famous once-a-year event. Vala was now well known to several of the capitol staff and was asked to assist the young ladies during their time at the palace, as well as witness some of the presentations for the skills she herself was fluent in. Vala was very delighted and gladly accepted the position. After arguing that it was completely unnecessary, she was also given a specially designed dress to wear for the ball. Vala had a wonderful time watching, helping, and meeting the young ladies and some of the young men too. She loved doing these sorts of things. The final day was closed with a ceremony where the king or queen would bestow on them a token of honor and ended with a magnificent ball. The following day, or the day after the following day, the young individuals would go home or to a venue where their families would hold their own private celebrations with friends. In order to participate in the event, the men and women would learn and practice etiquette of the court which had been preserved from the original tradition. They were expected to know and follow all the rules, but Vala was more than happy to help and advise the young ladies since she was familiar with it all. Vala did not wish to attract the attention of others or the attention of the media, so she kept to the side, enjoying everything and taking it in. It was all about the young people anyway. This last day was the most formal of all and Vala made sure both she and the young ladies she counseled were well prepared. The dinner and dance were always a spectacular event, and everyone was eager to see what fashions the attendees wore. Typically, most of the young men and women present at this ball had their clothing specially designed and constructed. One of the highlights of the event was to get a good look at the latest fashions as each one entered when their names were called. It was almost on par with a fashion show. Being back on Aldura, enjoying free time in the open air with someone she loved, and participating in colorful, lively events such as this had begun to change Vala. She was living a new kind of life, and she was finally smiling and laughing again. She had something she never thought she'd have again, something she was too afraid to pursue or even dream of ever again. Vala was happy, very happy.

When the event was over, Vala and Galen took some time off to visit the fields outside of the palace complex where their horses grazed. It was a beautiful mid-spring day. Vala liked to watch the horses graze; their lips were so big and strong, yet so gentle, dainty, and nimble. She watched as they pulled up the grass with their incisors, and how they used their lips to push aside the weeds they did not wish to consume and single out what they did want to eat. Today, she and Dr. Swann both decided to ride bareback with no bridle. They mounted their horses and began their ride. As they cantered across the field, Galen's horse ran on some rough ground, tripped, stumbled, and almost fell to the ground, taking him with it. Galen fell to the ground, but the horse regained its balance, shook off, and began to graze nearby. It seemed to be fine. Vala quickly made her way over when she saw that her husband did not get up.

"Are you all right?" she asked, a bit frightened as she rode up. She came right alongside him, still on top of her horse.

He sat up and with a mischievous smile, grabbed her and pulled her, startled, off the horse onto the soft ground. "Yes," he said.

"You lousy scoundrel! That's the last time I look after you," said Vala sarcastically.

They both laughed as they lay in the grass among the horses. Life felt so good right now.

"How about a short cross-country ride?" asked Vala, suddenly getting up.

"I think that's a better idea," said Galen.

With that, they prepared their horses and took them out on a ride in the empty lands outside the palace. Towards the end of the ride, it began to rain, and they raced back, enjoying the run, and made it back to the dry barn lightheartedly to take care of the horses. When the rain passed and the sun shone once more, the plants - now with plenty of water to allow for the transfer of more xylem and an increase of surface area in the leaves - began maximum production of phloem and oxygen. The excited chlorophyll shone out brightly everywhere and dominated the outdoors with a beautiful, overwhelmingly vibrant green on the freshly washed ground. As she gazed at the beauty of nature, Vala suddenly was suddenly inspired to see more.

"We should go to Solana; it has a very nice climate. It's dry and cool and the temperature stays relatively steady through most of the year. The weather and the city there are beautiful, I'd love to see it this time of year. Flowers grow in the city all year long because the weather rarely changes. And the beaches are beautiful too. They're cool and more rocky, different from the ones in the Florina region."

"Well, since we seem to have some free time, let's do it before Ariella returns and you're called back to duty. I'd love to see more of Aldura," said her husband.

So they made up their minds to go to the city of Solana and it turned out to be a wonderful vacation. There were large mountains, beautiful beaches by the cool ocean as Vala had said, and beautiful native and non-native flowers and foliage were planted everywhere in the city. As Vala had said, the weather was very nice and cool compared to that of Verona and

Florina where they had stayed earlier. It was certainly not as humid either.

When they returned to Verona the following week, Vala received a message from Corin relaying his and Ariella's news. They had agreed to have their wedding the next month and keep it small with the quick time frame. Vala was beyond excited. When Ariella and Corin joined the others, Vala and April jubilantly offered their congratulations and help for the ceremony.

"Please don't mention it to anyone without our permission, the wedding is going to be small, and I don't want it to be publicized or attract attention," Ariella told them; and so they kept it to themselves.

The wedding was held outdoors on a late spring day, and they decided to hold it in Florina at Ariella's family's country house. They decorated with lots of flowers, petals, draped fabrics, and little lights. Ariella wore a beautiful white dress with lace and embroidery and accessorized her hair with a few blossoms of a late spring-blooming flower. It was a little white flower that grew on vines and carried a strong, beautiful scent. The wedding was a small, private ceremony with just a few friends and family. When Ariella and Corin finished their vows and exchanged rings, all eyes watched in anticipation to see what they would do next. There was a pause, it was impossible to read Ariella's thoughts as she looked into Corin's face. There was a mix of exuberance and serenity in her expression, though she seemed to be hesitating. Finally, Corin broke the pause "I'm not waiting any longer," he said as he drew his bride closer and kissed her for the first time. Ariella returned the kiss with passion, more so than anyone would have ever expected of her. It was intimate and genuine. Once Corin and Ariella were officially married and finished the ceremony, Vala and April could not resist having them showered with petals and glittery confetti and even released butterflies around them. The refreshments were kept simple but were still finely decorated and that night, they all danced under the stars.

Sunshine and the Darkness

Ariella and Corin's marriage was kept a secret to the public because the senator feared what her enemies, and Casimir in particular, might do with the knowledge. A few weeks after the wedding, they all returned to the galactic capital, as Ariella was anxious to return and not miss anything new that might be happening. The small imperialist party had grown significantly and some of their ideas seemed to veer away from what the Galactic Union had been founded on. Ariella wondered how such a small party could have gained the majority. It was possible for this sort of thing to happen, but very unlikely. To make matters more concerning, Casimir Blade was running for the presidential office and was doing surprisingly well. She worried what would happen if this party gained control, and tried hard to change the stances of those moving to the imperialist party. Sometimes she succeeded but more often, was unsuccessful. Everything seemed to be coming under the imperialist party's control and Ariella began to wonder if it was worth it for Aldura to stay in the Galactic Union. When she arrived back at the capitol with Corin and Amara at her side, she made plans to speak with Senator Blade. She was not going to play games with him anymore and he needed to hear it clearly. When she arrived at his office, his security guards stepped outside and closed the doors behind them. Amara and Corin also remained outside waiting.

"Senator Callista, you're back. This is an unexpected and pleasant surprise. You never seem to make invitations or requests of me. It's truly a delight to see you here."

Ariella wore a bold and bright expression. "I'm glad you see it that way," she said. "I am going to take things straight to the point and not waste any more of our time. I've come to officially say that any sort of relationship I might have with you politically and otherwise, is now broken off. And I never had a desire or plan to be your bride, so even though going years without giving you an answer to your proposal should have made it clear, I am now going to plainly give you my no so that there is no more confusion." Ariella held her bold gaze as she and Casimir looked each other in the eye.

Casimir responded with a threatening look. He was taken aback by this sudden confrontation from Ariella, but he kept it hidden. "Be careful what you decide. If you choose to go against me, you may very much regret it. I think you can see who has the upper hand in this legislature now, and I will continue to grow stronger, it's inevitable."

Ariella felt the temptation to give into fear, but she held her place. "My mind is firmly set. I must stand for what I believe is right, no matter what happens to me."

"Are you saying you're going to fight against me?"

"I do not wish to start a fight with you, but if it comes to that, yes."

"Even if it costs you your life and the lives of those you love?"

"Is that a threat?"

Casimir did not respond to her question. "I think you'd better consider your stance some more. If you refuse to run alongside me, you will no longer be safe, and you're running out of time. It will be over soon."

Ariella grew very suspicious. Now she knew he had to be behind some of the recent events that had placed senators in danger. And what did he mean by it would be over soon? "I don't know what you're scheming, but I will not compromise on what I believe to be right. If it means I die, then so be it!"

"In that case, let the battle begin, and when I win, you will be my greatest prize," Casimir cooly replied.

"I'll see you out." He got up and opened the door, appearing to be cool and cordial. Ariella held a fiery demeanor as she walked out and gave him one more glace before departing with Corin and Amara. She walked swiftly back to her office with the two tailing her, sensing her agitation. When they arrived and Ariella locked the doors behind them, Corin asked what had happened. "I think Casimir is at war with us. And there's some scheme he's got going on, and it's not good. He's getting dangerously close to having control over the entire legislature, and I don't like it." She related to them what he had spoken to her in his office. "Don't speak of this to anyone, but I believe Aldura may have to be ready to exit the union before things get uncontrollable. If Casimir's after control of the entire union, for the good of our people, we'll need to get out before damage is done. We'll need to watch Casimir and his party very closely." Corin and Amara responded with grave, thoughtful looks and after their conversation, became more watchful and alert than ever before in their everyday tasks.

As the year progressed, Ariella continued to notice subtle changes in the legislators and their their behavior. It seemed to be increasingly easier for Casimir to get what he wanted, and it infuriated her. At the end of the year, her worst fears were realized as Senator Blade won the election for the next term's president. Outbreaks and rumors of isolated battles in various parts of the union began to break out. Several weeks later, she returned to Aldura again, wishing to discuss the latest situation in the galactic senate with Aldura's government. She traveled with her usual companions while Dr. Swann stayed at the galactic capital to continue his work. He and Vala would not see each other for about two months until he came to Aldura to participate in the winter and new year celebrations. While on Aldura, Ariella discussed how the third party had grown so powerful with Casimir Blade at its head and how the opinions of many senators of several other planets had changed, many rather suddenly and seemingly without reason. Many who had once opposed Casimir and his party were now supporting him. She recalled her past conversations with Casmir to the queen and how she felt everyone was losing their power. She urged Aldura's government to consider whether they should remain a part of the union or become an individual state if things were to continue in the direction they were headed. Of course, they would also have to gauge the public's support while trying not to draw any attention that would bring the union down upon them. It helped that there was already some talk of secession passing between some of Aldura's citizens.

    Vala and Dr. Swann as of yet, had no permanent residence on Aldura, so Vala was offered a guest room in the palace for hers and later, her husband's stay. They both had become quite well known by the current queen and the palace staff. When the winter ball finally began to approach, Dr. Swann joined Vala on Aldura. Dr. Abigale Mirella had become a friend of Dr. Swann and Vala and offered to give them a tour of the hospital in Verona upon his arrival since Aldura's medical technology was some of the most advanced in the galaxy. She showed Dr. Swann how certain tests could be easily run and occasionally illustrated them while Vala eagerly volunteered to be a test subject for demonstration. Abigale took them to the lab to demonstrate some of the test techniques and let Dr. Swann try them for himself using Vala as a sampling subject.

"Do you see anything that stands out?" asked Dr. Mirella, casually after one particular test.

The expression on Dr. Swann's face was one of unbelief. "Maybe you'd better look to confirm because what I'm seeing is a high level of these particular hormones which would suggest a pregnancy.

"You're certainly right," confirmed Dr. Mirella casually after checking for Dr. Swann.

Galen turned to face Vala, stunned. He was speechless and then, could only come out with "Have you been feeling sick recently?"

Vala could hold it back no more. "Yes!" she exclaimed excitedly, throwing her arms around him.

"She's almost in her third month," said Dr. Abigale.

"W-why didn't you tell me?" asked Galen.

"I wanted to surprise you. And I asked Abigale to confirm it first, that's the real reason we planned this day. You sure look shocked, are you all right?" replied Vala.

"Well, what can you expect? What can you expect me to think when all of a sudden, I find out my wife's pregnant?"

"That you're a father," replied Vala.

"We need to get him to treatment; I think he's going into shock," teased Abigale.

"Oh, I'm in shock alright, but not that kind. I can't believe this; this is almost ridiculous; you two surprising me this way. If this is a joke, you've really outdone yourselves."

"It's not, it's really true!" replied Vala. Dr. Swann took a few minutes to collect himself and then happiness and the reality of the situation flooded in.

The winter and New Year celebrations were bright and enjoyable this year and Ariella and Corin both demonstrated their dance skills once more. This time they were married and were as impeccable in their dancing as ever and both were the last ones left in the fast dance competitions. In the solo competitions, the two were highly competitive with one another. Sometimes Ariella would win and sometimes Corin would. They both kept track of how many of these competitions each had won since they came to know each other and always tried to get more wins than the other. During their stay on Aldura, the union's elections had finished. To Ariella's displeasure, Casimir Blade had become the new president of the Galactic Union. After the celebration for a more brooding year, they all returned to the capital where Ariella felt a threat looming.

The following months grew colder and darker in mood but briefly lightened up as spring appeared. As the spring passed and summer approached, Sunshine Swann was born and delivered at home by her father. She had red hair like Vala's. Life was changing for Vala. When she returned from her maternity break, she found it challenging to keep up with her work as well as care for Sunshine, but with the help of Galen and the others, she was able to do it. Sunny was a bright child and was loved by everyone, but no more than by her own parents. She was light and joy in the midst of the dark changes. New laws were being put into place and certain freedoms the people once had were being restricted. War seemed imminent, since there was still apparently an unknown faction hiding out in space, though since they had captured Ariella some years ago, they seemed to have retreated from the offensive and withdrew into hiding. What they were doing in the shadows, no one seemed to be able to find out, but it was rather worrisome and caused much concern in the capital. Sometimes, Galen would have dreams about losing Sunny. Though they were just dreams, he did worry over her while Vala tried to reassure him. When Vala accompanied the senator back to Aldura, she took Sunny with her, and Dr. Swann would join them when he could. He and Vala now owned a small house on Aldura so they could have a place of their own for their new family whenever they traveled back to Vala's home planet. The few trips they made to Aldura were a bright but much too short respite from the anxious capital. The beginning of the next year in the capital was not a pleasant one. Even the weather seemed to take on the mood of the feelings that were swirling around. It was cold and dark and misty most of the time and the inhabitants were slowly beginning to change their views and ideas, some almost seemed to be controlled. During the second month, Vala had Sunny with her as she was out on the street running errands. Even though this was the safe part of town, she was a little uneasy and felt like she was being watched as she returned home. As she walked along the dim streets, still overcast from the weather, she noticed a girl with short red hair staring at her. Vala couldn't help but look back at her, a bit confused. There was something familiar about the girl.

"Mother?" said the girl in a low voice almost as if to herself. Then she spoke again. "Trust him, you must trust him." The girl was solemn and then turned away into the shadows.

Vala was confused, had what she had just seen and heard really happened? She looked down at Sunshine who was in her arms, then she walked on. Suddenly, a dark figure jumped down and confronted Vala, it had been following her in the shadows. She turned to face it; its cover was blown.

"Give me the baby!" the assassin demanded, pointing a weapon at her.

"No!" cried Vala.

She took out her weapon and dogged a shot from her opponent, then fled, with the assassin following. She managed to lose the attacker and hid in fear, she could be discovered any minute. Then a young man with deep black hair approached her.

"Come here quietly," he said in a whisper. He was a stranger to her, but there was something in his eyes that spoke peace and safety.

"Why? Why should I trust you?" asked Vala.

"I'm here to help," he replied. "Come around this corner where they won't find you."

Vala was hesitant but made her weapon ready and cautiously followed him. When they were around the corner, Vala saw a ship but it was an odd design she'd never seen before.

"Vala Stella, Vala Swann. I see you have the precious little Sunny with you too. This is certainly a day of wonders for me, but also one of urgency. I need to take her before it's too late, I'll keep her safe."

"Why should I give her to you? I don't even know who you are."

"You wouldn't know who I am, not at this point in your life. My name's Marcel Astro. If you want Sunny to survive, if you want Aldura to survive and freedom to endure, you must send her with me."

"That sounds like a rather far-fetched story to me. Why should I trust you? How do you know our names and where will you take her? Will I ever see her again?"

"I'll take her to the future where she will be safe and acquire the skills and knowledge she needs to help Aldura."

"I don't believe you."

"I expected nothing less of you. I've just come from the future where there are two kind foster parents waiting. This ship is no ordinary ship, it travels through time."

"Prove it to me, and prove to me that I should believe you."

"Very well." Marcel made note of the time and stepped into the ship. He departed and then returned within a few seconds.

"Well?" he asked, stepping out of the ship.

"Well what?" replied Vala.

"I showed you."

"I didn't see anything except you leaving and returning."

"Think back further. You saw someone in the shadows. A girl."

Vala thought for a moment and remembered the girl she had seen. Unbelief and wonder came to her face. "You're saying that was-that was my Sunny?"

"Familiar, right? And the only reason she was there was because her mother made a hard decision: to send her off to safety many years away. You willl see her again but if you refuse to give her to me this may be the last you will ever see of her and your galaxy as you know it could fall into darkness. Of course, you still may not be fully convinced, so I brought this with."

Marcel untied a leather lace from around his neck and as he pulled it out from under his outer garment, revealed a ring the lace was strung through. He placed the ring in Vala's hand. Look it over carefully, I don't think you can deny what this is. You gave it to me for this purpose. Vala looked it over carefully. It was her engagement ring. The same design, the same material, a little worn, and it possessed the same unique engravings. She handed it back to Marcel who was looking to her for an answer. Vala was hesitant. The ring could have been forged, but not likely since she kept it safe at home, and what was the chance of anyone knowing about it? She remembered what the girl had said and somehow in that moment, she felt it was the best thing to do. She didn't know why, but she had a strong feeling that she needed to trust this man. She looked at Sunny lovingly with tears in her eyes and then gave her to Marcel.

"I know how hard this must be," said Marcell with care and compassion in his eyes. "There's nothing like the love of a mother. There are several people waiting for her who know her name, but her code name for our operation will be Squimba. Perhaps if you have not already, you will hear of the legend of Squimba from which we chose the name."

He took Sunny gently in his arms as though she were very precious. Vala noticed that Marcel exhibited a deep love for the child and just a hint of sadness. He seemed to know her quite well as he gently took her in his arms; she was rather mystified by it.

"Dear little Sunny, so small, so young," he said lovingly, and disappeared into the ship and left.

Vala stood alone for a moment, feeling empty inside. What had she just done? Was this even real? As she turned to leave, the assassin suddenly dropped down on Vala, stabbing a small knife into her chest. Vala cried out and almost instantaneously, the assassin barked:

"Where's the child?" Vala was stunned for a minute as she sat on the ground clenching her wound with her attacker standing over her.

"Gone. She's safe, somewhere where you can't go."

"Did the dark star traveler come? Did he take her from you?" Vala didn't answer, she was struggling with the emotions of having just lost her child and the pain of her wound.

"Answer me!" said the assassin, coming down on her.

"I don't know!" replied Vala, starting to cry out loud a little.

"If you don't want to tell me, then perhaps you would like to meet the boss and tell him. I'm sure he will be very delighted to speak to you, after what you and your family did to him!"

Vala's eyes opened wide with fear. She kicked the assassin and bought herself enough time to quickly draw out her firearm and shot her attacker dead. Then she slowly stood up, shaking from the pain, fear, and blood loss. She winced and cried out a little as she pulled the knife from her chest and used her cloak to cover the wound as she applied pressure to it. Then she walked off, fighting back tears, and headed home. When she arrived, she opened the door to find her husband, who had just come home, sitting back and reading over something. When she entered, he turned to look towards her. His relaxed expression quickly changed to one of alarm. Vala was disheveled, clutching a bleeding wound, with tears in her eyes, and there was no sign of their daughter. He got up and rushed to her.

"What happened?" He asked.

Vala did not say anything and fell into his arms and began to sob. Throughout the night, Dr. Swann did his best to patiently figure out what had happened and where Sunny was while he tended to Vala's wound. This was not a problem that could be fixed overnight. Vala had lost another loved one. Her enemy was still out there, moving against her, and now Galen was caught in the middle of it and was now sharing in her pain. Dr. Swann recalled his dreams. So, they were true...

That night, when they laid down to rest, Vala was silent. In fact, she had not said much at all since she came home, except to answer her husband's questions.

"Are you sure you still want to be with me?" she asked suddenly. "Because it seems that I can't have a normal life and now you're stuck living it with me. I thought things were getting better and that I was passed this curse or whatever it is. I'm sorry I brought you into all of this."

Dr. Swann reflected on Vala's question for a bit. Then he responded. "Don't think you're the only one to blame. I could have done more to make sure our family was kept safe. I could have had the foresight to suggest you consider leaving your position working for the senator, or that we leave this city completely, but I didn't want to ask you to stop doing something you seemed to love; and I didn't think this place was as dangerous as it appears to be. But...know that I will never leave you. You are still the love of my life. Your pain is my pain, but I will also get to take part in the joy that you'll have when this is over."

"I don't know if it will ever be over..." said Vala.

Sunny was taken to a good home. Her foster father was a scientist, and her foster mother was an archeologist. Their primary research focus was time technology. They had to work in secret, as time travel technology was not to be known or made available to anyone because of the threat it could pose if used by the wrong people. The reason they were working on it was for a special operation: one that would change their fate, the fate of the once beautiful, bright, and thriving Aldura that had existed back in time, and the freedom of the galaxy. The galaxy had been in darkness for many years, and they wished to change it all. Sunny's foster parents also had children of their own, but they grew to love Sunny just as much. It was an exciting but sobering task to raise someone who would become an important historical figure, and they made sure she was well trained. Sunny turned out to be an incredible genius. She showed great interest in math, science, and weapons, and began learning chemistry, astronomy, physics and advanced mathematics early in life. She was also trained in combat and the use of weapons by a native of Kairah and became a powerful and skilled warrior. She never had many friends, however. Her interests were always different from those of everyone else her age, but she still had her adopted family and certain others who were involved in the operation for company. Among her friends was an interesting man named Marcel. As far as Sunny could remember, Marcel would always drop in and out at various times. Sometimes he appeared older, other times he was younger but as a child, Sunny didn't notice much of a difference. She grew solemn and kept her bright red hair cut short, about one or two inches above her shoulders.

It was not easy for Vala and Galen to recover after the loss of their beautiful daughter but they found comfort in each other. Ariella and April were very accommodating to Vala's wound and her grief and gave her time to recover, often checking on her and doing what they could to make her feel loved. The following month, a new bill was brought before the senate. It would allow the Galactic Union, or rather, its president, to place soldiers on all the planets in the union. The reason stated was that it would allow the union to better monitor the people and enforce security measures to ensure everyone was safe from invasion and hidden enemies. The sponsors articulated that it was especially important with the attacks that had been going on the last few years. After reading it over and listening to the debates, Ariella knew there was another reason behind this bill. It would allow Casimir Blade to have complete control of all the planets in the union and he could easily crush the freedoms of the individual planets. She called for her councilors to meet with her as soon as possible so she could discuss the bill with them. At Ariella's request, Councilors Betulace-cay, Valencia and Tiro promptly joined her at the capitol where they had a private discussion about the bill. After Ariella's visit two years ago, at the end of the year, Councilors Valencia and

Tiro had taken it upon themselves to secretly gauge the public's opinion of secession using their positions, and they had managed to put together a report. Now, during this secret meeting, they gave their report which favored the actions Senator Callista planned to take. They all agreed it was the right choice: Aldura would not stand for the passage of this bill and they would do whatever it took to keep from falling under its power. Ariella threatened Casimir and the leaders of the Imperialist Party with a filibuster if they continued to support its passage or refuse to rewrite it. They were confident in their power, however, and promised her she would have no chance because cloture would be invoked. After speaking once again with her councilors, Ariella secretly contacted the Queen of Aldura and urged her to gather the planet's congress to consider what their actions would be if the bill should be passed and whether or not they should secede. At home, the Alduran government had been monitoring the issues of the Galactic Union and talk of secession had already been floating around for some time. If this bill passed, most of Aldura already agreed secretly that separation should happen. The queen agreed to Ariella's appeal and called a special session to take place behind closed doors. The congress debated the matter rather swiftly and without taking too much time, they agreed to leave the corrupted union if the bill should be passed. When the time came to debate the bill at the union's capitol, cloture was indeed invoked and time was limited. When she was recognized, Ariella spoke her mind.

"Why don't we just give aid to the individual planets who need it and allow them to handle it their own way rather than forcing everyone to come under the control of one individual? I don't like this idea of sending soldiers onto all our planets, this power could be easily and heavily abused; it sounds dangerously close to the beginnings of tyranny. Many of us have our own armies, I suggest we send the Galactic Union's soldiers only to those planets that need aid. Aldura will not tolerate this. We will not be occupied by the union's army; we can defend ourselves! I fear there is more to this bill than just protecting planets. If you vote for this bill, you don't know what you are getting yourselves into. It will give the union's government and president too much power! Aldura will not stand for this! We would sooner leave the union than give in to this! I yield my time to the minority leader."

There was a great commotion after she finished and it took some time for the vice president, who had decided to reside over the senate for this particular debate, to bring the chamber back to order. Once order was restored, a senator in the majority party spoke up. Ariella noticed this disregard of order. The minority leader should have been given the rest of her time to speak rather than this senator. She tried to call for a point of order, but no one would acknowledge her. The senator began.

"I suggest Senator Callista be careful with her words, we don't want to start a civil war."

Ariella was irked and grew defiant of the rules her opponents were not playing by. She cut in. "I take back nothing I said! If this bill goes through we will not stand for it! I meant what I said!"

The vice president stared threateningly at Ariella. "Will the sergeant at arms escort Senator Callista out of the room? Speaking out of turn without being recognized will not be tolerated."

Ariella resisted with resentment. She glared at the vice president as the sergeant at arms took her. "So this is it then," she replied malevolently.

She was escorted out and the doors were shut and secured behind her. The debate continued. In the end, votes were cast and the bill was passed. Ariella retreated to a private chamber to talk with Councilor Betulace-cay.

"This is it. We're leaving the union. One of us has to let the queen know, and as soon as Casimir knows we've seceded that will likely put us in danger. You should leave right now. I'll stay behind and do the dangerous work and inform the union of our choice," said Ariella.

"Are you sure you want to do it? Even without support?" asked Councilor Betulace-cay.

"You have a family, they need you. Besides, you know me. Apparently I'm good at putting myself in dangerous situations. I'll be fine. You should leave now while it's still somewhat safe."

Councilor Betulace-cay finally agreed though he insisted Ariella leave too. She was resolute, however. The next day, Vala helped Ariella dress for her announcement of Aldura's secession after she contacted the queen about her decision.

"So this is it, the end of an era," said Ariella. "Are you ready Vala? Ready for the danger ahead?"

"I am," replied Vala.

"You all should leave, don't wait for me. Corin can get me out. You should go while it's still safe," continued Ariella.

"We won't leave you, we will all share in your danger while we still hold our positions. We're not going to make ourselves safe until you are. I refuse to leave you, as do the others," Vala replied.

"Well, I suppose I can't get rid of you, but be ready. I have a feeling we'll need to get out as soon as I'm finished," said Ariella.

Vala finished Ariella's hair, it was braided and pulled back in a simple style. Ariella looked at herself in the mirror, she was dressed in black and some dark grays. "Are you ready?" she asked Vala again.

"Yes."

"Well then... here comes the last senator from Aldura."

She paused to catch a breath before walking out the door where Corin and April were waiting to escort her to the senate chamber. Once she was recognized, she announced boldly to the Galactic Union Aldura's choice. After her announcement there was quite a commotion as Ariella began walking out, knowing she was now in danger. Suddenly, Casimir Blade appeared, walking swiftly towards her as she made her leave.

"Senator Callista, I strongly advise you and your planet to reconsider. It's not wise to leave such a strong, powerful republic."

Ariella paused and turned to face him with a cool, lofty expression. "A republic? I know your plans, Casimir, I've suspected them for years. I believe it is a wise decision. We are a neutral state now, we wish for no war and we are a superpower in the galaxy. You know that and that's why you want to control us. Be warned, and don't you dare touch us," she replied with some fire beginning to light in her eyes.

"I see this as an act of treason! If this is what you want then be prepared for war! However," his voice softened, "even now, I would not have you personally harmed. My offer of marriage, or even partnership still generously stands, even now."

"Even if I still remotely wished to consider it, I am in a position that would make it impossible."

"You don't know what you're up against, I will pursue you and your planet until I have possession of you both!"

"I will see that others get the information and proof they need to know what you're doing and the threat you are. Your empire will fall, Casimir."

Ariella departed and left Casimir standing in the vestibule of the senate building. She walked out of the beautiful capitol where she had spent so many years. It was a sad parting, but she must move on, and quickly. Everything was loaded on board the senator's ship as she had requested. Corin and April accompanied her to and from the capitol and after their escape, the three of them met Amara, Vala, and Dr. Swann who were waiting at the ship.

"Let's go, I don't think we're wanted here," said Ariella as she approached them.

They all boarded the ship and left for the last time. The parting from the once glorious capitol was one of mixed feelings. "Well I guess this is it. I suppose we'll be parting ways after this, now that you all are officially relieved from duty. I will miss you all," said Ariella.

"I won't part from you. Even if you require my services no more, I'll still keep in touch. And I think we can all agree that until we reach Aldura and are formally dismissed, we are still in your service. The trip's not over yet," said Vala.

"You're a wonderful friend Vala," replied Ariella.

The others followed Vala's example and agreed they would keep up with one another and maintain their friendships though their paths might take them different places. All their adventures had brought them close together.

"There's a blockade up there. They'll let us through if they know what's good for them," said Corin.

As they drew near, they waited for the ships in the blockade to finish their scans. There seemed to be a delay.

"This doesn't look good," said Corin as the silence lingered on. "We may have to make a run for it."

Finally, they received a message. "Senator Callista, you may not pass."

"We've always been able to pass here before. You would be wise to let us pass again," responded Corin.

"You have declared yourselves to be rebels and traitors to the President, you may not leave. Prepare to be boarded."

"The audacity!" exclaimed Ariella. Then she replied. "I am an important official of Aldura. We are a neutral planet, but a superpower nevertheless. I strongly advise you not to perform an act of war but instead let us pass."

"I have my orders. And you are the one who's performed an act of war," came the response.

Corin shut off communications. "I guess we'll have to fly our way out of this," he said. Amara took control of the defense systems and Corin began making his way through the blockade. The ships began to fire at them and Corin began flying quickly through a maze of fighters, ships, and turrets. It was a struggle and took some incredible flying skills but they finally made their way to freedom. Just as they made their escape, however, a large cable reeled them back in, followed by another and another. The ship was taken inside one of the large ships and held securely below.

"Well, here we are again," said Amara, "only this time I don't know how we'll get free."

"Well they're not going to keep me here, I'm getting away," said Ariella.

"How?" asked Vala.

"Corin, you got me out once before, can't you figure out a way to escape again?" replied Ariella.

"Getting out the first time was easier. You and your friends created a diversion and there was less security at the time. I don't know how to get out safely, but we'll try to figure out something. I wonder what their intentions are."

Cosmo was busy tinkering with the equipment he often carried around. He found something of interest on the screen he was using and insisted that Corin take a look at it.

"You were able to get information off the enemy ship?" asked Corin, "It appears they are taking us somewhere...to your friend's base, Ariella," he said.

"What friend?" she replied.

"The president."

"He is not my friend! I despise him, now more than ever."

"Well, it appears we're really captives this time. All we can do is wait and see what opportunities we run into," Corin replied.

"I think we should use the situation to investigate. If we're going to an enemy base, perhaps we could gain some valuable information. We can split up into two groups, we'll also try to figure out how to free the ship," said Ariella.

"It's a long shot and it doesn't seem very safe, and it will be almost impossible to separate once they come for us," said Corin, thoughtfully.

"Since when have you ever cared about risks? It's not like you to consider the danger involved," said Ariella.

"I don't have a problem with it. I'm just making sure everyone else knows what our situation is before they make a decision they regret," he replied.

"We'll be in danger anyway, we might as well try it," said Ariella. "Is everyone with me? You don't have to do this, I'm just asking you to."

All the companions agreed to help, they were not going to go down without a fight. When they finally arrived at the location the large ship was transporting them to, it was decided that Amara, Vala, and April would go out first. Seren was shut down and hidden and Ariella stowed Seren's remote in her garments. The ship had been transported to a secure hangar in a secret base. To their surprise, all the ships and soldiers at this base wore the same emblem as the ones who had captured Ariella some years ago.

"I don't believe it. Or maybe I do..." said Ariella. Perhaps Casimir has been behind this faction all along."

As soon as they were seemingly alone, Amara, Vala, and April crept out through a small emergency evacuation hatch in the senator's ship. As they got out, they saw armed forces coming their way and quickly took cover. The soldiers came to the ship and took the weapons from the others who were still inside and escorted them off.

"We'll have to free them," said April quietly; she was handling the situation rather well.

"Let's go," said Amara.

"You two can go, I'm going to look around and see if I can find any information on what's going on here and how we can escape; someone has to do it," whispered Vala.

"Are you sure you want to do that by yourself?" asked Amara.

"I'll be fine, I'll try to keep in touch," replied Vala and they parted ways quietly.

The others, including Cosmo, were taken to a chamber where to their surprise and horror, President Blade was already waiting for them. This time there was no cordial speech between them.

"Where are the others?" Casimir asked.

"We didn't find anyone else in our search of the ship," replied the captain of the guard escorting the three captives.

"They escaped long ago," said Ariella.

"I'm not fully convinced. I want another thorough search of the captive ship and a search around the grounds. The senator may not be giving us the whole truth," said Casimir, directing his comment toward the guard and another captain beside him. His orders were immediately carried out, then he turned back to his captives.

"You were quite brave almost escaping, but now you're in my hands as enemies and I must say: it will make it much easier for me to get what I need from you."

"You won't get what you want from us!" replied Ariella.

"I think I will. You have all I want, all I need to know about your planet. And I think your captain, being entrusted with certain secrets about your planet and its security, has all the knowledge I need."

"If you want information, there are others who know more than him, take me for instance," Ariella replied.

"I think what he knows is satisfactory. Besides, I don't want to damage you," replied Blade.

"You'll do nothing of the kind!" fiercely snapped Ariella. Corin, almost simultaneously, exclaimed, "I'll tell you nothing!"

Sunshine and the Darkness

Dr. Swann and Cosmo were held off to the side, clearly they were not considered important at the moment.

"We have ways of getting information out. You, Captain, can be one of our first subjects in finding out how effective our new method works," continued Casimir, "You might say it's a form of hypnosis or mind control. When I'm through with him, he'll tell me all I wish to know. Unfortunately, some of our test subjects lost much of their memory after the procedure, but that does not concern me. We will begin now."

Ariella was horrified. It appeared Casimir had been up to much more than she had realized. The captives began to struggle but to no avail. Ariella managed to grab Corin's hand and gazed upon him with fear and longing before they were pulled apart. Casimir's men took a tighter grip on Corin as two scientists prepared to administer a drug.

"I'll save you, I'll get you back...and I love you," said Ariella in a lowered voice with tears welling up.

Corin was taken to an adjacent room where Casimir and his scientists attempted to extract information from him while the others were taken to a private cell. When they were finished with Corin, they escorted him to the cell with the others while a few more guards came to take Ariella, Dr. Swann, and Cosmo. Ariella thought Corin looked empty with no emotion.

"Corin?" she asked, hopefully.

He did not reply. Ariella was distressed and frightened. Not knowing what else to do, she stayed close to Dr. Swann for comfort. Dr. Swann had been carefully observing the scenario. When Ariella got close enough to him, he whispered to her.

"I've heard of this type of process before, but I've never seen it practiced until now. It's a new idea. There's still a chance to bring him back, given the right supplies and knowledge, but we can't wait too long. If they continue with those drugs, he may not survive," he continued in an even lower voice.

"That will be enough speaking to each other," said Casimir, approaching them. "Take them and lock them up, no one must know about this," he commanded.

"What do you intend to do?" asked Ariella.

"I will figure out some fate for each of you traitors, but I have something special in mind for you. You know you've earned quite a reputation as the most beautiful woman in the galaxy and I have no doubt it's true. I admire you and your strong will very much, even though we are enemies. By the laws of my culture, I intend to make you my wife."

"But that's impossible! Even in your culture! I am already married!"

"Well, I can soon change that, Miss Rebel. I have been digging into the old laws of my culture and the laws of war for the union. Because you are now my prisoner of war and a non-citizen, I have the right to make you my wife as soon as you have been bereaved;

and legally you have no say in the matter. I will dispose of him when I get what I need. Lock them away!"

Ariella was stunned. As she was being taken away, she managed to brake one arm free and punched Casimir's face harshly. She boldly looked him in the face with a defying, scornful, and fiery stare that made him so uneasy, he stepped back; even he could not endure her expression.

"Be warned Casimir, this isn't the end. I will keep fighting, you haven't seen the last of it!" she declared as they were taken off. Then an officer came to give Casimir a report.

"My Lord President, we have detected unauthorized movement in the secret chambers."

"I'll go myself, take the Alduran captain to be transported back to the research fortress, and have the others taken aboard my ship, I want them to stay separated. I think it's time we left this place," commanded Casimir.

Ariella, Dr. Swann, and Cosmo were taken away and Casimir departed in another direction. As they were being escorted, Amara and April stumbled upon them and began a skirmish with their captors.

"Don't bother with us, get out of here, now! Get the ship ready for escape! Or any ship!" exclaimed Ariella.

Amara and April gave each other a questioning look, but they finally backed down and got away before they were caught.

"I guess we head back to the ship. She must have a plan," said Amara to April, who agreed.

Meanwhile, Vala had discovered one of Casimir's secret labs on her search. She quietly crept around, taking all sorts of things that looked important, and placed them in a pack. As she was sorting through the contents of the lab, her heart jumped as she suddenly noticed a figure in the dark enter through a door. She ducked and remained absolutely still and silent.

"I know you're in here," he said.

Ariella, Dr. Swann and Cosmo were taken to a passage that led to a hangar. Their escorts had relaxed their hold on them and Ariella found a moment to briefly free both her wrists. She clapped them together as soon as she gained the freedom of both of them, and two serrated blades shot out from under the cover of her decorative wristbands. In reality, these harmless bands were bladed weapons. She quickly stabbed the two guards escorting her and took their weapons. She and Dr. Swann turned the tables and took their captors as their captives. They quickly tied them up and locked them in a closet on the side of the corridor after getting what information they could out of them.

"Let's go find Corin while there's still time!" insisted Ariella. She took a small device out of her sleeve. "Good, they didn't find his tracker, I can get a signal. Come on!" She ran off and the other two followed.

They raced on, following the tracker's signal, and were brought to a nearby hangar. "They have him on board that ship!" Ariella exclaimed. She ran closer but it began to take off. She fired heavily upon it with a stolen weapon. It was all in vain, however, and she knew it. It flew off and her heart sank.

"We have to get out of here!" insisted Dr. Swann as enemy soldiers were running towards them.

Ariella pulled herself together. "We have to get back to my ship, and quick! The others are probably there already."

They took off running again and as they neared the hangar where the ship was held under guard, they ran into Amara and April.

"Why aren't you at the ship? And where's Vala?" asked Ariella.

"The whole place is locked down; we can't get in and it will be difficult to get out. They know we've escaped, and Vala went to look around," replied Amara.

"She went alone?" asked Dr. Swann, looking concerned.

"Well let's go see what we can do about it, we have to get out of here," replied Ariella.

When they reached the hangar where their captive ship was held, they found that it was just as Amara had said: sealed off.

"Cosmo," began Ariella, "this is very important. Corin is captured and we're trapped here. We need to get to the ship to rescue him, but we've been locked out. Do you understand? We have to get in."

She looked desperately at Cosmo as he stared into her face. She hoped he understood her and would do as she requested since he normally only did something if Corin told him to. To Ariella's relief, he seemed to get the message. He began working on overriding the controls to the closed door to open it. Soldiers approached the group and began firing to stun. Ariella, Dr. Swann, Amara and April fought back. Cosmo continued his work and finally, the door opened. They all rushed through the door and into the ship, quickly fighting their way through. Ariella was the first to reach the ship.

"Hurry!" she said as she ran to the cockpit and started up the engines. "We need to figure out how to get out of here and fast!" she exclaimed.

Once they boarded, Amara joined Ariella and Cosmo in the cockpit as they awoke Seren and analyzed their situation and surroundings to figure out the best escape. They weren't free just yet. April took it upon herself to attempt to track Vala in the meantime.

While the escape was taking place, Vala was confronted.

"I should have known the senator would plan something like this. Surrender now; you cannot escape."

Vala remained still and silent.

"Don't think you can hide," continued the voice of Casimir, drawing closer. Vala held her weapon at the ready; then Casimir stepped right up to her and she jumped back, pointing her weapon at him.

"Hand over the stolen items and no harm will come to you, I see you're just a young, scared companion that the senator sent to perform this duty and you have done well so far."

Vala did not respond.

"Maybe I can make you an offer. You give me the stolen items and some information, and I will reward you. Surely you must want something more, being nothing but a servant I suppose. I can give you wealth, power..."

"I desire nothing from you."

"Then I shall have to take what's mine by force!"

Vala shot at Casimir, but the shot was deflected.

"Oh, that's right...you can't kill me that way." said Casimir, looking delighted with himself.

Vala began to back away in fear as Casimir drew out a sword. Then she was struck with a thought, a memory from her past.

"I know your voice. I know what you did, murderer!" She drew the only weapon she had that was not a firearm: a knife.

"I don't quite understand what you mean, but then I suppose I have upset a lot of people recently," replied Casimir.

"What do you mean you don't understand? You know what I speak of! What did they do? What did I do to receive your wrath those many years ago?! I'm going to give you the justice you deserve!"

Casimir truly looked confused but remained cool and Vala almost wondered if she was mistaken. But she couldn't be. He was the one who had killed her friends and family years ago.

"I know nothing of what you speak of, but I will reclaim what is mine." He thrust himself at Vala while she simply backed off and defended herself, waiting for the opportune moment.

Casimir fought gracefully and full of pride with a sword while Vala fought fiercely, but continually had to back off. As Casimir and Vala passed through a small passage, Casimir donned a terrifying mask; a mask Vala remembered well. He pulled a lever and gas filled the passage. Vala choked on it and quickly backed out through the opposite end. She was soon forced to the edge of a platform that opened out to the atmosphere; there was quite a drop from the edge to another platform underneath.

"I have the upper hand now, give over what you stole, and you will live," demanded Casimir.

Vala looked him in the eyes. Fear and unsure feelings had been growing inside her since she breathed in the gas, but she managed to bring up just enough bravery and boldness.

"No!" She struck Casimir hard and injured him. In anger, he knocked her over and she lay just on the edge of the platform.

"Then be destroyed!"

"I will not!"

Vala, seeing it as the best option in her troubled, poisoned mind, pushed herself off the edge and fell down below. Casimir looked down and scoffed, then called for aid. A few men came and reported that the captive ship had just escaped.

"Send ships after them. Get them back here, but alive," commanded Casimir as he and his men departed.

Vala lay on the platform below in pain and distress. She suddenly remembered her communicator and took it out. She called weakly and desperately for help. As they were escaping on the ship, Ariella received Vala's incoming plea.

"Vala's finally contacted me! She's in trouble!"

"We're on our way right now, just hold on. I'll follow your tracking signal," Ariella reassured Vala.

They quickly made their way to Vala and Amara brought the ship alongside the platform. Dr. Swann and Ariella rushed out to the platform and quickly carried Vala into the ship on a stretcher. She did not look well at all. As they boarded the ship, fighters came about, and Amara began evading them. Vala was brought to the small medical bay on the ship and Dr. Swann began examining her. He asked her a few questions, but she did not answer. She was moaning, despairing, and almost hyperventilating. She felt afraid and insecure and was also in pain. It was clear that she was very anxious, and Ariella and Dr. Swann did their best to comfort her.

"I-I feel terrible. What's happening to me? Will I ever be well again?" complained Vala, starting to cry.

"You're fine, all you have are some bruises and a broken tarsus and metatarsus, it's nothing to be too anxious about," replied Dr. Swann gently.

Ariella was moving back and forth between the sick bay and the cockpit, updating herself on both situations while Amara was doing her best to get free of the ships attempting to capture them once again.

"Corin did some modifications on this ship, if I can figure everything out, I should be able to achieve a higher velocity so that we can outrun them all," said Amara, who was busy working on the ship and employing the help of Cosmo, when she could, Seren, and April.

"It feels like more than just broken bones, I feel like I'm going to die," continued Vala in her distress as she clenched Dr. Swann's hand, "please stay with me." She was panicking irrationally and was still breathing hard.

"Ariella," said Dr. Swann sharply.

Ariella quickly made her way over to the doctor and Vala.

"I can't get much information out of Vala but something's wrong. She wouldn't act this way simply from a fall, no matter how bad it was. She was in Casimir Blade's lab and could have been exposed to something. Do you have any kind of lab on board?"

"We have a small one set up for basic analyses," she replied.

"Can we do a blood test?"

"Yes, with certain limitations."

"Draw some of Vala's blood while I work on her injuries."

Ariella did as she was told and used the lab instruments to analyze it using just about every test available; the Alduran lab instruments were easy to use.

"I have the analysis," she said as soon as it was finished.

The doctor quickly looked over the results. "It appears she has some foreign compound...a drug, in her system. Vala, this is important, were you exposed to anything at the base?" he asked.

"Gas-it was gas," replied Vala still in fear and distress.

"That must have been it. We'll finish treating her and use a tranquilizer, that's the best we can do for now until we can do a more thorough test. Hopefully there's not much harm done other than causing panic. Sleep a while Vala," said her husband.

Ariella helped Dr. Swann with the rest of the treatment.

"Don't leave me," said Vala, starting to fall asleep. "I won't, I'll stay here with you," reassured Galen as Ariella returned to the cockpit.

"I think I've gotten everything figured out," reported Amara, returning to her seat in front of the main controls.

"Good, show us what you've got," replied Ariella.

"It will be very fast, we'll need the compression suits; unfortunately, that includes Cosmo," said Amara, giving Cosmo a discontented look.

"I'll let the others know, then I'll see what I can do about the monkey," said Ariella.

When they had all quickly prepared themselves and Cosmo had finally allowed them to dress him, Amara thrust the ship forward and they made their escape.

"We'll need to take a quick stop before we continue the pursuit; let's stop here," said Ariella, pointing to a small friendly base on the map.

Casimir was furious at the loss of his captives. "Do we still have the other prisoner?" he asked.

He received a "Yes" in response.

"Good, we'll use him for bait, she will come for him."

When Ariella and her companions reached the safety of the base Ariella had located, they all rested and refreshed themselves and Dr. Swann was able to give Vala a more thorough analysis and treatment.

Chemical Weapons and a Mystery Girl

After she had been cared for at the base and the compound from the gas wore off, Vala felt much better. It turned out that what Vala had stolen from Casimir's base was more useful than she had realized. When Ariella and Dr. Swann looked through it all, they were able to find the same drug Casimir used on Corin. Fortunately, there was a small lab on the base they had sojourned at, a few lab technicians, and a biochemical engineer. With the help of the lab and contact with a few experts on Aldura, who Ariella trusted, they were able to create a counter-drug that would inhibit and overpower Casimir's. Of course, it had taken sleepless nights and a lot of work spent on considering the feasibility, safety, biological effects, kinetics, thermodynamics, and solubility with several chemical formulas. The longer they stayed, however, the more anxious and disconsolate Ariella grew. She did not want to wait any longer. Her companions comforted her and assured her they would go with her to rescue Corin.

"Vala, are you sure you want to go?" asked Ariella, as Vala's recovering injury limited her mobility.

"Of course, I want to help in any way I can. Besides, I don't know when there will be a transport from here to Aldura. I don't know how much help I can be since I'll have to depend on a crutch and my doctor will always be around reminding me to be careful," she gave Galen a slightly sassy look, "but I'll find something useful to do. I don't want to stay behind while the rest of you go off on a dangerous adventure. I insist on going. This is my life now."

So it was decided that they all would go. As soon as they were ready, they boarded the ship and followed Corin's tracking signal. Ariella, Corin, Amara, April and Vala all had secret trackers so that if they were lost or in trouble, they could be found. The trackers were kept safely hidden, but could easily be removed by the wearer. So far, nothing had happened to Corin's. By following the signal, they were led to a planet near Steelar-Romlin. It appeared to be desolate.

"Be careful, find a safe place to land; somewhere where we're least likely to be detected. I don't trust this place at all," said Ariella.

Chemical Weapons and a Mystery Girl

They landed safely in an area that looked secret and unused and cautiously exited the ship. They crept around, looking for signs of the enemy. Everything looked all right and there was no sign of anything threatening so they continued to follow the tracking signal. Their trek continued through the quiet wilderness without a sign of hostility. Despite being seemingly safe and unnoticed, the party grew a bit restless, feeling that they may be walking into a trap. Amara was particularly alert. They took a few more steps when Amara, who was in the lead, halted and put her hand up. The others promptly stopped and remained silent. Ariella gave Amara a questioning look and she gestured to her with signals, telling her that she had heard people with weapons not too far from where they were standing. Dr. Swann in return, gave Vala a questioning look since he was the only one who didn't understand all the signs the others used to communicate. Vala whispered the message into his ear. They all prepared their weapons and crept forward, waiting for Amara to signal when and what their next move should be. After continuing along for some minutes, Amara quickly beckoned them into the trees and they followed her, hiding themselves as best they could and readying their weapons again. Soon enough, the armed troops Amara had heard earlier appeared. The soldiers did not seem to notice them as they continued to walk straight past the hidden group; but, when roughly half of the soldiers passed by, they stopped. It seemed they were using a device or communicating with their base to find the small band of intruders which was composed of the senator and her companions. Amara was already ahead of them. The soldiers hardly had time to stop before she was upon them and gave her signal to fire on them. The skirmish continued but the amount of soldiers seemed to be a manageable number for them, until their enemies were joined by air craft that brought reinforcements. It was now clear that not only were they outnumbered, but that this ambush seemed to have been planned out as if they had been observed the whole time. It was no good now, there were too many soldiers to fight back so they surrendered to their new captors who handled them rather harshly.

"Be careful with her! She has a broken leg!" demanded Dr. Swann, referring to Vala.

"Who are you to give us orders? Be quiet!" replied one of the soldiers.

Dr. Swann protested, but to no avail. He found it hard to believe that someone would disregard another person's sickness, regardless of who they were. They were taken aboard one of the aircraft units and flown to the planet's center of civilization and to Casimir Blade.

"We meet again, and this time, it appears I have all of you. I suppose things worked out better for me that you escaped. This was too easy," he said in a delighted voice.

"I'm not through with you!" replied Ariella.

"I'm sure you're not. And I see you have with you the young lady who stole my secrets and escaped with them. She's also the one who gave me this scar. For that and her defiance, she will die!"

"You'll have to get past me first!" exclaimed Dr. Swann.

"That will be no problem, seeing as I'm the one who has the authority here. She will be executed and you and the rebellious senator can watch your beloved friend die. Take the other lady and the Kairahn, make sure they are completely disarmed, and lock them away!"

His orders were quickly carried out.

"Don't think I am in the dark as to who you all are and what you've been doing. I am very resourceful and I've been studying up on each one of you. I know exactly who you are and your relationships with each other. I am told that last time, Mrs. Rebel," he scoffed at the mention of Ariella's new surname, "you escaped because of secret weapons concealed in your clothing. I will have some of my women give you a change of clothes so that it will not happen again…and I will grant the doctor some time with his wife," he gave a mocking pitiful smile, "her execution will start as soon as everyone is prepared. I think the people here are really looking forward to an exciting show."

Casimir finished and they were all taken away for their designated fates. Vala and Dr. Swann were taken to a small arena where the execution would take place. A few locals and soldiers began to gather. The last to arrive were Casimir and his personal servants and guards, with Ariella. Vala and Galen stood awaiting the commencement of the execution.

"You don't look too scared," said Dr. Swann.

"I'm not afraid of dying. Once it's over, I will no longer have to endure the pain and cruelty of this life; I will go to a beautiful, wonderful place. In some ways, I rejoice inside. I'm not afraid. Will you be alright? Once I'm gone?"

"No, but I'll get by," replied Galen.

"Find our daughter, then you will be," said Vala. The guards prepared to take her and she held Galen tightly. "I love you," she said.

They embraced one last time, then Galen, with one arm around Vala, took her left arm and slid his hand gently down to her wrist. Vala flinched as she felt something prick her. Galen continued to hold her.

"You'll be fine," he whispered as they looked into each other's eyes.

Two soldiers came and took Vala.

"Please be careful with her broken leg, she doesn't have much longer to live so you could at least give her that," said Dr. Swann.

The soldiers respected his wish and took Vala. As she was taken out to the open, the crowds roared and she held her head high and proud, showing no fear. As she continued to walk, she suddenly began to feel sick and seemed to get worse and worse. She started staggering and began losing consciousness. Suddenly, she collapsed. The guards tried to pick her up and make her continue, but it was useless. She dropped to the ground, unconscious, and they began examining her.

"What's this?" came Casimir's voice.

"She just dropped dead," responded one of the guards.

"Have a medic take a look and if she is dead, I want a report!" commanded Casimir. His command was promptly obeyed and it was determined that she was dead, but the cause was yet uncertain. Then Dr. Swann stepped out into the open.

"Please, if she is dead, let me take her."

Everyone was silent, anticipating a response from Casimir. He was silent, pondering the situation. Then he spoke up.

"We have no use of the corpse, give him his precious bundle. But you may not leave, I have yet to decide your fate," he said to the doctor.

Ariella was standing close to Casimir. "Please, let him live and allow him to go back home and bury her," she pleaded in her innocent feminine voice as she inched her hand towards his weapon.

"Perhaps I will consider it, for you," he replied gently, then he realized what Ariella was doing and changed his tone. "But if you move your hand any closer, I will order for him to be shot."

Ariella paused and stared him in the face with a daring expression.

"Not if I get you first!" she replied as she snatched the weapon and held it to his head before he could give a command or anyone could stop her.

She had learned from Vala that if he was shot where he wore armor, it would be deflected. "Now, the doctor goes free. You will take me to the rest of my companions and free them or you will die. One false move and you're dead. Now, do as I say!" demanded Ariella.

Casimir had no choice but to do as she said, so he commanded everyone to lay down their weapons and showed Ariella where the others were. Dr. Swann took Vala in his arms and quickly rushed her back to their ship. He immediately carried her into the medical bay, started her heart and respiration, and quickly brought her to life. When she came around, she was a bit confused.

"Don't worry about the others, they should be here shortly. I just had to kill you to let the rest of the action take place and save your life," said Dr. Swann.

"What-what happened? What did you really do to me?" asked Vala.

"The last time we were on Aldura, the senator and I were asked to go to a research lab while you were busy working on some things at the palace."

Chemical Weapons and a Mystery Girl

"And?" replied Vala, impatiently.

"We were given secret drugs, only to be used at the utmost need. They suppress all your vitals to make you appear dead. Often they even bring your heart to a stop or very near it, so they have to be used in the right circumstances with the right people. I had to get you out quick before you really did die."

Vala looked amazed. "Why didn't you tell me about it?" she asked.

"I was given strict commands not to tell a soul, so I didn't. I'm sure you of all people would understand," said Dr. Swann.

"I do..." she paused as a smile formed on her face. "You're so wonderful, you crafty murderer," she said lightheartedly.

Ariella first freed Amara and April and they joined her. Amara handed Ariella a syringe, each one of them had been carrying one but Ariella lost hers with the change of clothes. Then Amara and April departed, knowing they would have to lower the planet's defenses if they were to escape. Amara also took Casimir with her at Ariella's bidding. The ex-senator thought he would be more useful and less troublesome with Amara and April, especially since she would have Corin to deal with. Once Ariella learned where Corin was, she went to find him. When she reached him, Ariella injected him with the antidote

Amara had given her. It seemed to help, but Corin still didn't know who she was. Ariella took Corin's hand, and she ran along, leading him behind. Corin was confused.

"What's going on? Where am I?" he asked.

"We're taking you to treatment; you're a sick man, Corin," replied Ariella.

"Who are you? How do you know my name?"

"I'm your wife as you don't seem to remember."

"Wife!? Since when was I married!?"

"Since about two years."

As they neared the ship, they slowed down. They would have to wait for April and Amara, so Ariella decided to take her time. She brought Corin on board and walked him to the medical bay where Dr. Swann and Vala were waiting.

"He's better, but still not himself," she said.

"It will hopefully just take time," replied Dr. Swann.

As they spoke, Amara and April returned in haste.

"We need to get out now! Casimir escaped us. We did manage to destroy the defense systems and the communications system, but we're still in danger," said Amara, rushing to the cockpit and starting up the ship; preparing to get them out of the atmosphere. Amara escaped some fighters that approached them and soon they were on their way back to Aldura.

Once on Aldura, Corin began a slow recovery through his treatment while he and Ariella stayed in her parents' summer home in Florina. It didn't

take long to recover his memory, but his encounter with Casimir had left other effects on him that began to emerge. He began showing an occasional apprehension towards his wife and more and more frequently, would be awakened by bad dreams.
His apprehension towards Ariella developed into a greater fear that deeply concerned her. She sought out the best doctors and was referred to a specialist who was also a professor at Florina's university. After discussing the situation with the doctor and arranging an appointment, she went to sleep that night worrying about Corin and the nightmares he might have again that night, but also hopeful that he would finally be cured. The mixture of her troubled and hopeful thoughts kept her awake for a while until her mind finally shut down as she drifted off to sleep…

 Suddenly, Ariella awoke with a start, her heart pounding with fright and confusion as Corin held two knives to her throat.

 "Corin!" she exclaimed, looking shocked and fearful.

 Corin seemed to be hesitating and Ariella regained some of her composure as she gazed at him with concern, though fear was still lingering in her eyes. Something suddenly seemed to snap in Corin's mind and he withdrew the knives which they kept close out of habit. His eyes showed that he felt guilt and contempt. Then he regained himself.

"I can't stay with you. I'm supposed to protect you but now I'm trying to kill you. You're not safe with me."

"I won't let you leave, I am going to stay with you and help you through this. I can defend myself."

"You seemed rather helpless just now, and this isn't the first time I've had thoughts of attacking you, they've come up before. Only before they were easier to subdue. It's getting worse and I won't risk it."

"Well, I will."

"I've always admired that spirit, I want to keep its owner safe. I think I should at least stay in another room for now," he said as he got up and walked towards the door to leave.

"Corin…"

But there was nothing more Ariella could say. She didn't want him to leave her, but she knew she would not be able to convince him. He was doing the more sensible thing for her safety. He left the room and Ariella turned back to her pillows and cried before sleep took her once again. Corin's fear and hostility towards Ariella did not cease. Though Ariella was not entirely looking forward to it, as she expected, Vala contacted her the next day from Verona to find out how Corin's recovery was going.

"It's really not going well," replied Ariella as she braced herself against breaking down into despair and shedding some tears, "he's regained his memory… but…" she paused and braced herself again, not wanting to show any signs of how upset and desperate she really was, "he's growing more fearful and aggressive towards me. We've been working with Dr. Henley, but so far we haven't found any success. The drugs he was exposed to are still being researched more thoroughly."

"Oh Ariella, I'm very sorry. How are you? You don't look very good," said Vala.

Ariella hesitated again. If she answered, she would surely break into tears, but there was no getting past Vala's question and she could not be fooled either. "I... I don't know," she said as a few tears leaked out, "I'm afraid for him and the two of us. I don't know how long it will be before he is cured; and what if he can't be? He says that he doesn't want me to be in danger from him and wants to leave for my protection until we find a cure. I don't want him to leave though, I can't live life without him," she began to cry a little.

Vala looked deeply sympathetic, "I'm coming over, you need some support."

"Vala, you don't need to go out of your way for me."

"But I can't let you go through this yourself, you need someone to support you."

"Vala, I'm not a senator anymore which means you're not my handmaid anymore and you're no longer obligated to look after me in any kind of way. You shouldn't have to leave your home and life for my sake."

"But I'm a doctor's wife now, and more importantly, your friend, which means it is still my business to come support you. I'm going to do it. I'll see you soon."

The day after Ariella's discussion with Vala, Corin was again not himself. This time, he drew another weapon upon her while she was carrying on with normal business around the house, and pinned her to the wall.

"Why are you doing this? Why are you trying to kill me?" she asked.

Corin stared at her as if she were one of his greatest enemies, then he finally spoke. "Because you're the enemy of the people in this galaxy. You're the reason for the suffering of all those people, both in the union and resisting the union. It's because of your defiance and rebellion. You're the reason the war is going to escalate and not come quietly to an end. It's you who are responsible for the suffering of people already hurt by the war and many more to come. And...you're the one who caused my suffering. How can I know that you just didn't use me to achieve your own desires and plans?"

Though she knew he didn't mean it, Ariella was hurt and heartbroken to hear this and couldn't suppress a small bit of doubt and guilt over his answer. Could what he had said really be true? Was the start of this new war all her fault? She didn't have much more time to consider the matter, however; she was still under attack and had to move quickly. Her mind raced as she analyzed her best move of defense and what Corin's response would be, she knew him well enough to anticipate his reactions. She could go for the knife in her sleeve, but Corin would grab it with his free hand and pin it to the wall. She could then kick his legs out of position so he would lose balance, but he might anticipate this and maintain a strong stance. She could take her free hand and grab at his armed hand and push it away, but it might very likely end in a draw or his victory. Once he resisted her attack, however, he would not be able to move forward with his attack. She had no time to give any further thought to the situation however because Corin was making his first move. Ariella went for her knife and she and Corin both played out their moves as they had both predicted. Ariella was desperate for an escape and though she could hardly bring herself to do it, having no other thought immediately occur to her, she lifted her foot and kneed Corin in the gut, followed by another kick that knocked him back, giving her just enough time to escape. Corin didn't chase after her, however; he was still laying on the ground. Ariella stopped and noticed he had dropped his weapon. She turned to him and as she approached him slowly, she saw he had a mournful, resentful look on his face. The heartache Ariella had felt the last several days returned. She walked to Corin's side and sat down on the floor with him from where he had not moved.

"Are you all right?" she asked with deep concern and sadness.

"The blow you gave me didn't do any damage if that's what you're talking about." He paused and drew a breath. "But I can't go on like this, I can't let you be in my presence while I'm such a threat to you. I can't stay any longer. I love you and I don't want you to be hurt or killed."

Corin paused and Ariella gently touched him. He continued to speak what was on his mind. "I said something to you, it's fading from my memory, it was something negative...like an accusation wasn't it?"

A twinge of guilt surged through Ariella. "Yes, you said that the reason for the new war and for the suffering of others...and you...was my fault."

"You know I didn't mean any of it."

"I know, but it's made me think. What if it is my fault? What if I am the one to blame? My leadership in Aldura's secession not only turned the whole union against Aldura, but it also encouraged others to attempt to follow in our footsteps and break away from the union. That's the reason the war is escalating. And having you and the others follow along with me during the secession only put all of you in danger; now look at what's happened to you and Vala. Maybe I even provoked Casimir by letting our relationship grow stronger, only to betray him in the end. Maybe we should never have left the union at all, maybe it wasn't the right thing to do."

"You can't blame yourself for everything. Whether it was the right thing to do or not, Aldura is more well off now than before because we seceded, and by the way things were going, I'm sure there would have been war, unrest, and rebellion anyway. And you can't take the blame for what happened to Vala and I, you gave us the choice to go our own ways to safety and we chose not to. You're guilt-ridden and I'm...well, I'm not entirely sure yet. It seems we're both broken and in need of healing."

"Yes, but can we ever be fixed?" Ariella paused and then brightened up just a bit. "...I will not let this pull us apart, I will not let him separate you from me. At least stay for Vala, she'll be coming to stay with us for a while. With her around, you won't have to worry so much about my safety."

The following day, Vala arrived. She never carried the same positive energy that April did, but she brought comfort and refreshment with her. Ariella's and even Corin's spirits were lifted a little. It was almost the time of the spring flower festival and though it seemed unlikely that Ariella and Corin would partake in the usual festivities, Vala persuaded them to at least let her help them decorate the house for the occasion; so Vala and Ariella began work on unpacking old decorations which were stored in the house as well as putting together new decorations. To create a livelier atmosphere as they worked, Vala put on some music that lifted Ariella's spirits all the more. As she was working on the decorations, Ariella began subtly moving to the music. She could not resist it and finally called for Corin.

"What is it?" he asked as he descended the stairs to where Vala and Ariella were putting together decorations.

"I'm dying to dance; it's been way too long. Will you accompany me?" she asked.

Corin looked uncertain. Vala replied to the look on his face. "You've been down too long Corin, you should let yourself have some fun. I know it's been a challenge dealing with the after-effects of what Casimir did to you and that you're constantly worried over Ariella's safety because of the state you're in, but emotions and mindset as you should know, influence your health. We may not know how to cure you yet, but maybe enjoying yourself will help."

Corin considered her words and with a bit of reluctance but a willingness to try Vala's advice, partnered up with Ariella. They began dancing together to the music playing in the background and as they continued, their sorrow and pain vanished from their minds. For once, they were happy again. Vala smiled to herself and continued to work on the decorations, there were paper and silk flowers to be made, live flowers to be replanted into decorative and hanging pots, and garlands of real flowers to be made. She began unwinding irrigation lines which were made to hold small flower plants or cut flowers and channel water and nutrients to them. These lines were used to make long-lasting garlands of real flowers. Over the days of Vala's stay, she planned horse rides and other activities to bring some more simple enjoyment into Corin and Ariella's lives. Through the enjoyment Vala had thrust upon the two, Corin's anxiety seemed to lessen. A week later, after Vala's departure, Ariella and Corin were left in a more hopeful and confident state. Nevertheless, Corin was still not fully recovered and there was nothing new from the doctors at the university. After another event that had caused Ariella and Corin to drift apart for the rest of the day, Ariella began wandering down the road leading from the house, silently crying a few tears. When she approached the end of the road, she stopped and sat down, mourning her situation. As she sat, a man suddenly appeared. Ariella had not noticed him coming and she was startled at his sudden appearance. She looked up at him and tried to conceal her tears. He was wearing a plain hooded cloak but there seemed to be a gentle kindness and knowing in his eyes.

"Why are you sad?" He asked.

"Oh, I... I... "

Ariella paused; she had almost spilled her personal sorrow to this stranger. This was something she was always cautious to avoid but somehow, this stranger didn't seem so strange. He felt safe. It was as if they knew each other.

"It's… it's…my husband is unwell…in his mind. We're trying everything but nothing seems to be working. And our relationship is starting to suffer as a result. I'm terrified, I'm heartbroken, and I'm angry. I don't know what else to do. I'm at the end of myself."

"It sounds like you need a healer," replied the stranger.

"Yes, if only one could be found. I'd do anything."

They were both silent, then the man looked down at Ariella with an inviting smile.

"Go to the Garden, you'll find the Healer there."

"The Garden?" replied Ariella, a bit confused.

She hung her head down in thought as she tried to understand what he meant by that. Then she raised her head back up to ask him, but he was gone. She turned to look for where he went but could not see him. Was the encounter real? Or did she just imagine it? She got up and walked back to the house, thinking about the conversation she had just had. The Garden… was it THE Garden? The one she and Corin had visited years ago? When everything was so light and free? She had never heard of a healer there. She had never seen anyone there. But somehow, she felt they should go.

"Corin!" she called when she returned home. She walked around the house calling his name. Finally, she found him wandering out in the fields.

"Corin!" she cried out, as she jogged toward him.

"What is it?" he asked in a dull tone.

"We have to go the Garden."

"The Garden?"

"Yes, the Garden. The one we visited when I first showed you around Aldura."

"Why?"

"I know it doesn't make sense, but just trust me. A man came and told me to find the Healer in the Garden. I just have a strong feeling we need to go."

"I don't get it. Who was the man?"

"I don't know, but I trust him."

Corin looked very skeptical.

"What's it going to take for me to convince you? Or do I have to drag you there?"

Corin didn't seem to know how to respond. He stood still, silently thinking it over. "Well, it doesn't make sense, but I'll honor your crazy gut feeling since I've followed quite a few myself. I am concerned for your safety though; what if I suddenly turn on you during the trip?"

"We'll make it work," said Ariella thoughtfully.

"You know how to fly my ship, and we can use it and take Cosmo to help us. Just lock me in one of the chambers on the ship and let me out when you've safely landed," said Corin.

"Corin, I don't-"

Corin interrupted her.

"I insist. I'm not taking any chances on your safety."

Ariella was against the idea, but Corin was right, it probably was the best thing to do considering his current state.

"Alright," she said. They quickly prepared for the flight and without delay, carried out their plan and departed for the Garden.

When they arrived, Ariella landed the ship with Cosmo's help and then let Corin out of the chamber he had been locked in. They walked out of the ship carefully, hand in hand, in awe of the Garden. They stepped through the entrance and began walking through it. Just as before, it was silent and peaceful, but no other person was to be seen. They continued on, following the small creeks upstream until they reached the spring that was the source of all the water. Everything was quiet, but there was already peace flooding through both of their minds. They looked around in wonder and anticipation, looking for someone, but whom they knew not. Then, as they turned back to face the spring, all of a sudden, a man was there, sitting on the rocks where the spring bubbled up.

"You're looking for me?" he asked with a pleasant smile.

Corin and Ariella faced him. His appearance was plain and there was nothing overwhelmingly desirable about it, and yet there was something beautiful about him that drew them in. He was simple and pure, and it was as if he was the embodiment of peace, life, and love. His eyes were fiery yet kind, gentle, and loving, and it was as if he was reading every thought they had, and every moment of failure and victory, piercing right into their souls. But there was no condemnation, just a welcoming love, with understanding and sorrow for their brokenness. They were captivated, and together, drew closer to him.

"Come, rest and drink," he said, beckoning towards the spring.

Corin and Ariella accepted his invitation and sat down to take a drink. The water was cool and refreshing, restoring life to their minds and bodies. Already, the weight they carried inside their hearts was beginning to lift.

"We're looking for the Healer," said Ariella, "do you know him?"

"I know him well," replied the man.

"Where is he?"

"Well, he's right here."

"You? You're the Healer?"

"Yes, that is one of the names I go by."

Ariella's emotions began bubbling up now that she had found the one – perhaps her last hope – who might be able to help. "Can you help us?" she asked.

"I can." The man looked into their eyes. There was peace and love in his expression. He gestured to the dead tree. "You see that tree? I poured out my life there to make this place, and every good thing that flows from it, accessible to you." Then he turned to

Corin. "Corin," he said. Ariella was surprised that he seemed to know their names. They had not introduced themselves. "Do you forgive those who hurt you?"

Do I what? Thought Corin. *After all they did to me? Casimir especially, he doesn't deserve forgiveness.*

The man maintained a steady gaze with Corin's eyes. It was almost as if he was reading Corin's mind. In his gaze, Corin couldn't keep his bitterness and unforgiveness in. Something was welling up deep inside his soul, calling him to do what the man was inviting him to do.

"He has caused you much pain. It was unjust of him. But you have continued to carry the pain he put upon you. Don't you want to let it go?"

"Yes," said Corin. The names and faces of those who had hurt him, and those he had been offended by, began to come to his mind. "I forgive them."

He said the words.

Suddenly, something broke inside of him, deep in his soul. He felt the burdens caused by the pain begin to lift off. The man looked at him with love in his eyes and touched Corin's head. A wave of peace filled his mind and heart. It was as if all the pain and all the mental torment was being flushed out and replaced with a deep sustained peace and joy. His mind cleared up, clearer than it had been since before he could remember, and the pain was gone. It was too good to be true. Tears began to well out of Corin's eyes, but they weren't tears of sadness. They were tears of relief, tears of experiencing something so good, it didn't seem possible, and yet it was true. Ariella looked at Corin. He never cried. She had never seen such a deep expression of emotion from him. Something had changed. Something had radically touched him and changed him. He sat in silence, enjoying the peace and freedom of his mind. Ariella was observing in awe. Then, the man turned to Ariella, with the same look of love and compassion, and a hint of fire in his eyes.

"And to you, Ariella, I give strength and peace." He touched her forehead and she fell into a dream-like state. She rested there on the soft ground in complete peace, a deep peace she had never experienced before. She could feel the life of the Garden flowing through her, giving her rest and strength.

When Ariella and Corin finally got up, they had no idea what time it was. In this place, it was as if time didn't exist. All they knew was that they had both experienced something so wonderful and so beautiful, it was hard to believe it was true. But it was. They had felt it, they had experienced it, and they were changed. Corin's mind was set free, and the burdens on Ariella's heart were gone. It was miraculous.

After they returned home and Ariella became herself once more, her concerns about the state of the galaxy surfaced again. Things had changed, as several other planets had been inspired by Ariella to stand up for what they felt was right and to leave the Galactic

Union as well. Ariella grew restless over the rising conflict and the battles Casimir was beginning to wage on other planets and decided to visit Queen Selina to discuss the matter; the two knew each other quite well. After a light discussion of various other subjects, Ariella began sharing her feelings about the current situation with Casimir.

"I can't stay here, not while Casimir Blade is out there ruining lives. Many of my friends are out there either being controlled or fighting him back and in need of help. They are all out there fighting while we sit back and do nothing. Casimir has even declared war against us and still we do nothing!"

"It is true," replied Jasmine Selina, "but I see things differently. As long as we are not invaded or attacked, I find it pointless to spend lives and resources. Our armies are for the defense of our own people. Could you send many men and women out into space to fight and die? To where, perhaps, they may never see their home again? I won't."

"I can understand your reasoning, but I still feel differently about it, the whole galaxy is at stake. If we don't act now, our enemies will grow stronger, and then when they come to invade us - which is inevitable - will we still be strong enough to hold them off? I am willing to speak to the representatives and senators in our legislature as well as the people to persuade them to adopt an opinion contrary to yours. Everyone

Chemical Weapons and a Mystery Girl

knows I'm a powerful speaker and can win people to my side."

"It is true you are a great motivator and a powerful speaker, but I am the queen and I have the authority over the military and my mind will not be changed just because others' are. You may do as you wish, I will not stop you; but sometimes, I believe, you are overconfident in your abilities and act far too recklessly, expecting everyone to jump in and support your ideas. I am advising you as a friend to be careful what you get yourself into."

"Suppose I go out there myself and help the others who are fighting against Casimir Blade. I can't do it myself, but if we could offer them aid or weapons, I would do what I could."

"What would you say they need most? We don't lightly give out our most advanced materials of war and you know it won't be easy to send money, it will take long debates."

Ariella paused and considered. "Casimir uses chemicals and biological agents as his main weapons right now. If we could send them agents that could counteract the ones Casimir uses, it would be a good start."

The queen paused to consider this request.

"That seems reasonable, but it will take time and resources to produce them."

"I will help, I will do all I can to help get there. If you are willing to do this and need the support of the congress, I will certainly lobby in your favor. I suppose we'll have to make allies and begin relationships with other planets and systems now that we've seceded. I will even personally visit the others and deliver the resources we can offer them myself."

"I'm surprised to hear you volunteer yourself as a lobbyist, seeing as you dislike most of them yourself." Queen Selina fell into silence as if deeply considering what her answer to Ariella's request would be. "I'll see what I can do and let you know what you can do, just be patient. The items Vala took from Casimir Blade will be very useful, I'm sure. I don't advise you to go out on your own or with whatever companions who go with you but if you do go, as a friend, I hope you return safely."

As time passed, Ariella's request was finally met and the material aid was produced and ready to be transported. Ariella told Corin, Amara, April, Vala and Dr. Swann of her plan and though she didn't expect anyone other than Corin to come with her as they did in the past, she wanted to let them know and would welcome them if they did decide to accompany her. Despite the risks, they all decided they would accompany Ariella, though Dr. Swann was against Vala coming along as she was in her first trimester expecting another child. Vala did not want to be left behind, however, especially when the others' lives could potentially be in danger and she would let no one stop her from going. Ariella wasn't the only one who wanted to help other planets in the fight against Casimir, several Aldurans who were more passionate about the matter had volunteered their services to the newly forming war. Among those volunteers was Dr. Mirella, who wanted to use her skills to help those injured in battle. Even people in the heart of the union's capitol joined the fight against Casimir. This group of people included Dr. Swann's sister Camelia who took up a position in secret intelligence operations. Ariella, Corin, and the rest of their companions departed Aldura and went to visit other planets that had seceeded and were at war with Casimir Blade and the union which was losing its freedom to him day by day. Many of the planets were the home worlds of some of Ariella's past friends and colleagues, people she had grown to trust and who had taken her side many times. She helped them in what ways she could, and Dr. Swann volunteered to educate them on the chemical cures and weapons she brought to them. With Casimir's mind-altering chemical weapons, his main weapons of war, the aid Ariella brought from Aldura turned out to be very useful. Casimir's enemies grew stronger and soon they had a fighting chance. President Blade, Emperor Blade as some of his enemies called him and rightly so, soon discovered who was curing his victims all over the galaxy and spared no expense on pursuing the former Senator Callista. Corin and Amara were able to safely evade their enemies but during a particularly difficult escape back to Aldura at the start of the new year, they crash landed on a harsh planet. This planet primarily consisted of frozen lands and deserts. It was, however, charted and inhabited in some areas. There were also small bases here, some were friendly, but others were not. The silver ship crash-landed in a cold snowy region.

"We'd better take all the supplies we can if we are going to survive this weather," said Amara.

The ship was beyond repair so their best option was to find the nearest place of civilization where they could find transport. It was windy and cold as they stepped out, not nice weather to begin walking through; but the sooner they started, the sooner they would reach safety. There were also enemies to be cautious about so it would be important to leave no signs and take as little time as possible if they were to safely reach a town or base before they froze.

"It will be best to refrain from using fires as well. We don't want to be discovered," said Corin.

They put on thin heating pads underneath their coats and loaded themselves with what they could comfortably bring along and began a long walk through the snow, ice, and wind. After walking most of the day through nothing but windy, icy wasteland, most of them began slowing down.

"We're freezing and tired, can we please stop?" asked April, beginning to shiver, and she and most of the others stopped as well.

Amara and Corin, however, did not think it a good idea and with the aid of Dr. Swann, convinced them to keep walking. As long as they were moving, kinetic energy would form heat and they would stay warmer than if they stood still or sat down.

"Besides," said Amara, "it's not necessarily safe out here, we have to reach safety as soon as possible. The more we walk, the sooner we'll reach a more comfortable environment."

Thus, she and Dr. Swann were able to convince the others to keep going. When night came, the temperature dropped, and the wind continued. They stopped to rest and bundled up with everything they had but the environment was so bitter, most of them could not sleep. After those who were tired enough to sleep had a short rest, they continued on. When the sun came up the next day, the wind began to die down and the new day brought more warmth than the previous one had offered. The weather was still cold, but the wind chill was gone, and April began to regain her spirits. She grew excited at all the snow and began throwing snowballs at her friends. Slowly, everyone joined in the fun and there was laughter in the air. They continued to move along while frolicking in the snow, forgetting their weariness and the cold when suddenly, Amara stopped them.

"Something's coming," she said.

"What should we do?" asked Ariella.

"We can try and take cover...only there's not much out here, it's all flat. I suppose we'll just have to have our weapons ready," said Corin.

As they continued cautiously, with weapons at the ready, a small party approached them, transporting loads of supplies. When they drew near, the travelers noticed the company with the monkey.

"Who are you and what is your business out here?" asked one of the travelers as he and the others with him stopped with their weapons pointed at the small, cold party.

"We mean no harm; our ship crashed many miles from here and it's beyond repair. We're stranded. We hope to find shelter and a place where we can acquire a new ship to return home," said Ariella.

"How can we be sure you have no secret intentions? Our home world has seen many operations recently by both sides of the war. We don't easily put our trust in strangers."

"You must believe my story, it's true. You can search us, but you will find nothing. You wouldn't refuse to help four ladies, one being with child," she motioned to Vala, "out in the cold?"

The man who had been speaking paused for a moment, then made a decision. "You can come with us. If your friend really is pregnant, she would have no business in some sort of war mission; at least I would hope not. We are taking supplies back to our town. We will meet a schooner that will take us there."

Chemical Weapons and a Mystery Girl

They joined the travelers and at the end of the day, reached a tiny frozen dock where a small schooner was waiting. They would have to cross a small sea to reach their destination. It was very cold, and chunks of ice floated on the surface of the water. Dr. Swann thought back to many years past when he had learned about the unique properties of water that made it less dense in its solid state than in its liquid state, allowing the ice to float rather than sink. This was due to water's unique molecular structure and the fact that it expanded in the solid state. The travelers loaded their supplies on the ship, and everyone went aboard. As the sun faded, snow began to fall. It was cold and bitter, and everyone remained silent, but some not without wonder for the snowflakes. Not one snowflake was the same, every single flake had been created with a different pattern. The trip would last the night and they expected to reach the town early the next morning, so they took shelter and made themselves comfortable inside the ship. They were exhausted from the last two days and having very little sleep the night before. The night was cold and quiet, and the snow stopped for a while to reveal the bright stars in the clear, cold, dark sky. The sea was calm and almost as smooth as glass and reflected the light of the stars as well as the lantern light from the schooner. About an hour later, the snow picked up again and the sky grew darker and colder as a storm rose. The harsh weather remained for most of the night. About an hour before sunset, the schooner approached the shore where it was to land. Everything was packed and the boat's occupants were ready to go ashore. The weather was very hard now and the sailors could hardly see what lay ahead. Ariella and Vala were standing on one side of the schooner waiting to go ashore. Then, out of the darkness, Vala saw a large ice chunk on the side, and that the boat was being pushed towards it by the wind. "Quick, move!" exclaimed Vala, pushing Ariella out of the way just as the boat hit the ice. Just as Vala saved Ariella however, she was tossed over the side as the boat hit the ice. As she fell into the freezing water, she hit her head against the ice. She was not unconscious, but was dazed and not in her normal state of mind. Ariella cried out Vala's name as she fell overboard. The others quickly noticed and Dr. Swann made for the damaged edge of the ship as if to jump. Ariella was also determined to save Vala.

"I'll get her," said Dr. Swann, turning to Ariella.

"Be careful," she replied.

He jumped into the water after Vala, ignoring the temperature of the water, while Ariella prepared to rush off the ship as soon as it was docked. The water was freezing but Dr. Swann didn't give much thought to it. He reached Vala who was struggling in the ice-filled water and brought her to the shore. As soon as the schooner docked, Ariella jumped off with coats, blankets and medical supplies and rushed to where he was bringing Vala to shore. She helped him bear her

Chemical Weapons and a Mystery Girl

onto land and then wrapped them both in blankets and coats. They were both shivering but Dr. Swann paid no attention to himself so Ariella ensured he was warmed and recovered from the ice as well. The others slowly joined them with the rest of the supplies.

"Is there a place we can stay?" asked April.

"We'll take you to the inn," said one of the travelers.

Once they arrived at the inn, they were warmed and relieved. There were fires blazing and initially it was almost too much heat for their frozen extremities to handle. Dr. Swann cared for Vala and after some rest, both she and the baby she carried were fine.

"I guess now all there's left to do is get some rest and find a ship to get back home," said Ariella, relieved. Or so she thought...

Dr. Swann opened his eyes. A bright, hot sun was beating down on him. He was lying in the sand, out in the desert with no water. With nothing but his clothing, in fact, left to die. He was in a dream-like state and thought he saw someone fair and beautiful, resembling Vala, come to him. She encouraged him, and told him not to give up but to keep going. They were depending on him. He slowly awoke and came to full consciousness, then a horse stepped up and nudged him with its nose. It had a saddle and bridle. Then he remembered. He had been riding a horse earlier, this same horse in fact. It was a desert breed. Its kind was small but strong, full of endurance and spirit, yet gentle and very smart. It was beautiful, nimble, and majestic; a king among horses. For these reasons, Aldurans used this type of horse as one of the symbols of their people and valued them highly. The horse seemed to have taken care of itself. How long Dr. Swann had been lying in the sand, he did not know, but the sun would set in a few hours. He remembered he had been riding somewhere...to accomplish something. He slowly got up with the strength he had and climbed up onto the horse. Then he remembered. He had been riding to an enemy base that had been discovered. He was still on the same planet that was full of snow and ice but also had vast deserts. He remembered being told that a small party had gone to the base to retrieve new secrets of the enemy. His sister had been a part of that party. All contact with the group had been lost and he had insisted on joining a team that would ride out to search for the missing party, who were likely to be in danger. He wanted to do all he could to ensure his sister Camelia remained alive and safe. He had left Vala, now in her final trimester, at sunset to go find the enemy's whereabouts and the missing party that had been sent to it. He had refused to let her go along with him because of her condition. Something had happened, however, some sort of darkness, and he could not remember anything else. The rest of his party was nowhere to be seen. He didn't know what had happened to them. He was very weak and dehydrated but he rode on, hoping to reach the enemy base. When he finally reached it, the sun had disappeared, and all was dark under the moonlight. He made his way secretly into the base and to his surprise, it was scantily guarded. He dismounted and quietly crept around, looking for signs of the others who had supposedly breached this same base. As he stealthily searched around the base, he saw no one until he came across a woman who was bound. He approached her but she was still and silent as if there was no life left in her. He moved closer and checked her pulse. She had one, but it was faint. Then she stirred and he saw her face.

"Camelia," he whispered. She looked wearily up to see her brother.

"Galen? What are you doing here?" she asked.

"I came to help you all."

"Then you have come too late. I fear all the others are dead. The enemy found us, as you can see."

"Then I'll get you out."

"Wait. Before you do anything else, listen to me." She beckoned for him to move closer. "It's important that you know and remember this," she whispered. Then she made her voice as quiet as possible and whispered something into Dr. Swann's ear. "Remember it and get out of here, fast," she continued to whisper, after delivering a word to him.

"Not without you."

Dr. Swann was cut short as suddenly, lights came on and a man approached.

"We have an intruder," the man said with interest. "What has she told you?" he asked sharply.

"Nothing," replied the doctor.

"I don't believe you...But if you speak the truth," he grabbed Camelia and held an evil knife to her, "then she will have to die. I can't let her tell anyone."

"Wait! She did tell me."

The unknown enemy took his knife away from Camelia and looked at Dr. Swann. "She did, did she?" Then he turned back to Camelia and stabbed her.

Dr. Swann stared in disbelief as he watched the life of his only sibling leave her.

"Camelia!"

Grief and anger rose up inside of him, she was gone, and he couldn't save her. A thought flickered through him, a small hope that she wasn't really dead. She just needed some immediate emergency care and she would be fine. But it was unlikely. If this man wanted to kill her, he would have done a thorough enough job of it. Dr. Swann turned his attention and anger towards the man who had just stabbed Camelia.

"Why!?" he exclaimed.

"I didn't need her, she was near death anyways and anyone who knows that secret must die, including you."

Dr. Swann drew a weapon he had taken from his horse's saddle and in desperation and fury, used it to subdue his enemy. "I will bring you to justice," said Galen to his captive.

The captive, however, was smiling and snickering to himself. "Very well, but you cannot leave without this place going up in flames that will consume you. If you try to move, you will be destroyed. You must die." He gave an insane laugh and pushed a button hidden on his arm.

Galen did not expect what happened next. The whole base exploded, and he passed out once again.

Vala stood in the desert dwelling that had been her home now for several days. Those last few days seemed dark and distant; she could hardly remember them. She did remember some time ago that Galen had left her to go on a search mission. She had wanted to go, but he wished for her to stay behind after all that had happened to her, on top of being pregnant. She had reluctantly agreed to his wishes. She had stood in the sand as the sun set, watching him ride off. It was sunset again and she had strange and uneasy feelings, and a certain longing to see him return. Something was going on. She was worried about him. She thought of him as she stared off in the direction in which he had left. Somehow, she had a sense of fear, she felt he was in trouble....She had waited far too long. Then she made a decision. She would ride out.

"What are you doing?" asked Ariella as Vala prepared a horse and mounted with a bit of a struggle.

"I'm going to find Galen; I feel he's in danger. He's been gone too long without contact."

"It's dangerous out there."

"I know."

"But you'll go? Alone?"

"I can't stay here; I can't stand it. Waiting around."

"I'll go with you."

"No, I only just brought you here to safety. I don't know what it is she gave you to protect or what she told you, but I know it's important. I think you should stay here."

"Alright, but make safe moves, err on the side of caution." Vala gave Ariella a glance and galloped off.

It was night and once again, and Dr. Swann found himself lying in the sand. He was only slightly conscious and in exceeding pain. On top of that, he could barely see. Everything was a blur. This time he was sure he would die. Then he thought he saw Vala as she approached on horseback. The moon was shining behind her. She quickly dismounted and came to him with deep concern and love on her face. Galen felt soothed by her presence but as she knelt down over him, he faded out of consciousness once more. After having some other business in the area, Amara had found Dr. Swann just before Vala arrived.

"Vala, what are you doing here? Especially in your current state?" asked Amara.

Chemical Weapons and a Mystery Girl

"What happened?" asked Vala, ignoring Amara's question.

"This base exploded; he is apparently one of the victims. I'm amazed he's survived so far," replied Amara. "

"He needs medical attention immediately, is there anyone or anything around here that can help?" asked Vala.

"No, I'm afraid not."

"Then I'll take him, I'll go back to the base," said Vala as she, with Amara's help, lifted Galen and placed him on the horse she had taken.

"Are you sure you can get there on your own? It's dangerous," asked Amara as she helped Vala mount the horse behind Galen.

"I can do it, I have to."

"Then may you be safe and swift, go before the enemy finds you. I'll stay here and hold them off if they approach your direction." Amara took out a weapon and Vala raced off.

Enemy skirmishers were reported to patrol this area which made it dangerous and just as Amara feared, several of them suddenly appeared. They began pursuing Vala while Amara kept some of them occupied. Vala noticed her pursuers and urged her horse into the swiftest gallop it could take. Of course, it wasn't quite as easy with two riders, one being unconscious and the other pregnant. The attackers were fast and Vala desperately raced to safety. After a few miles of running a race in which she seemed to be losing, Vala came upon what appeared to be a neutral encampment, but she dared not stop with the skirmishers right behind her. She didn't think she would make it in time but might have to stand and fight. Then cloaked riders suddenly appeared out of the shadows behind the skirmishers. They had various weapons, and many had bows. They hunted down Vala's pursuers as she approached the camp. The riders bore a mark similar to that of Alduran soldiers on their shoulders, though it was darker than the normal yellow she was used to seeing. They offered her their help and accompanied her as she made her way across the desert to the base she was escaping to. Though the arrival of her allies gave her time to slow down and rest, time was of the greatest importance to Dr. Swann's survival, and she had many miles to cover yet. One of the more able-bodied riders came to help and supported Dr. Swann on a spare horse. With a few riders accompanying her to hold back the enemy, Vala continued on all night at the quickest pace the horses could safely take until dawn appeared. As the sun came up, more skirmishers approached Vala and the band accompanying her, and they were thrown into flight once again. The base was now in sight and Vala was more desperate than ever to reach it. The riders accompanying her hunted down their pursuers as she arrived at the gate of the base. A few others came out of the base to help her and some of the cloaked riders followed behind her. Vala came to a halt and with some help, gently took Galen off the horse and shed a few tears of desperation. One of the cloaked riders who was somewhat smaller than the rest, and who seemed to be their commander, stood by in the shadows of the gate watching. She seemed rather grave at the sight.

Flames

The base was not so much of a military base, but more of a refuge for friendly war victims. A few Aldurans as well as other allies against Casimir worked and volunteered at the base. As Vala entered the medical facilities with Galen and one of the riders to help her, she had the unexpected pleasure of finding Abigale Mirella as one of the volunteer doctors of the medical facility. Dr. Mirella and a few nurses were quick to care for Dr. Swann while Vala waited anxiously. Finally, Abigale brought her news.

"We've saved him. He's alive but barely responsive."

Vala gave an expression of relief.

"That's not all though," said Abigale gravely, "will you be patient enough to hear me out?"

The Senator From Aldura

Vala, now a bit worried, agreed to listen. "He's suffered a lot of wounds, but we're confident most of them will heal without a problem. He did, however, receive some damage to his eyes and was most likely blinded. There's a chance we can save his sight with surgery, but we don't have any specialists here and with the recent changes in the war over here, it is not likely we will be able to send him back to Aldura any time soon. We will do our best to establish contact with Aldura, however, and get all the help we can from a specialist. Even so, there's no guarantee the procedure will be successful, and it will be very difficult for him, especially because he's a doctor. His life will be completely different. He's asleep right now, but when he learns what's happened to his eyes..." she paused. "I'm sure you know as well as me that he will quickly deduce what's happened to him if we don't tell him. He will need a lot of consolation. And there's more. Because his mental state may possibly be compromised, he may not have the will to survive much longer. I spoke to the leader of the riders who saved you. She explored the area where you found him. You remember that sort of blackout or memory loss we all experienced on this planet?"

"Yes."

"It was the result of a chemical dispersed from that base. It appears that Galen did get into the base, but it exploded. We found that he was also infused with another drug, one that seems to give its victims a negative outlook on life, even moving them to the point of no longer wishing to live. It's similar to the one you were gassed with when we first discovered what Casimir was doing. The rider's leader, a girl surprisingly, says she studied the drug and the site of the base. She thinks it was still being tested and was not yet intended for use. She believes it was set loose in the base's vicinity because of the explosion and that's how he ended up with it in his system. We also discovered that his sister, along with others who tried to get information from the base, died. If Galen knew his sister died, that combined with the knowledge of the damage done to his eyes might increase the effect of the drug. There was information of great importance at that base as you probably know and if he was able to get it, he is the only one who can pass it on. That in itself may make him a higher priority in the war effort which should make it easier to get the immediate help we need. We need him alive, but unfortunately right now we are losing him because he already does not wish to live."

"Couldn't you try to synthesize a drug to counteract the effect?" asked Vala.

"We don't have the mechanisms or supplies here to do it," replied Abigale, "and it would take more time than we can afford."

"What about the girl? The rider's leader? I hear she's very knowledgeable; could she help?"

"I don't think so, she had to leave."

"Did she give you a name? I've been hearing about her, but I know nothing of her."

"She did not, she's very secretive."

Who was she? Wondered Vala. This was not the first time she had heard of the mysterious girl. While they were staying in the icy village, a few days after their crash, they had discovered a few allies in that area. The mysterious girl was supporting the allies and was there on some business. Ariella and Corin had been summoned to speak with her and as they met, Vala learned that the enemy was searching for them. With this information, Vala went to warn them and they all escaped just in time and raced to the desert where they sheltered. There they all stayed in hiding and dressed and lived as the tent dwelling locals, waiting for a safe opportunity to leave.

"Can I go see him?" asked Vala, referring to Galen.

"Of course. You may be of more help to him than us," replied Abigale.

"I'll make sure he lives; I won't let him die," said Vala, feeling very determined.

When Galen awoke, with bandages around his eyes, Vala was right beside him and just as Dr. Mirella predicted, he was in a very despairing mood. The first thing he asked about was the fate of his sister and the news Vala gave him made him no better.

"What about my eyes?" he asked, "I can't be fooled, I know something's wrong."

"Yes," said Vala slowly, "but there's no need to despair yet. Dr. Mirella says they are going to perform surgery on them."

"Yes, but those surgeries aren't always successful. It may very well fail, and then what is my life? Even with implants, I still won't be able to see like I used to. All the education and training I went through will all be in vain! The life I built will have come to nothing. If the surgery goes bad, and if implants don't work out or aren't an option, then what good will I be? I'll have nothing left, just a ruined life."

"But you'll have me, and I'm sure there are still many things you'll be able to do. Even if all the medical procedures fail, I'm sure we could still get support, and I can continue to care and provide for our house."

"But how could you possibly do it? How can you look after me and the baby and work all at the same time? It would be too much for you. I think it would be better if I just died."

"Don't say that, not to me. I lost everyone I ever loved once already, don't make me go through it again!" replied Vala, now fighting back tears. "You're my world, my joy. If I lost you, I would be devastated. Don't you dare give up your life over something petty like this, don't you dare! It's far too precious! You are more than your education and your work; those are just things you do. They do not determine your value! I'll do everything I can to look after you and keep you alive; I am not going to allow you to die."

Every day, all day, except for a few breaks, Vala stayed with him. She made sure he was as healthy as he could possibly be and did her best to talk to him. They had very few conversations, mostly because he was asleep. When he did wake up, he would not speak much and when he did, it was often his same complaining about how his life was over. Then Vala would speak encouragement to him. She cared for him relentlessly and even came for an hour or more every night. When the doctors were ready, they performed surgery on his eyes with success and finally, he awoke to his conscious, more normal self; though with dressings covering his eyes so he couldn't yet see. Everything that happened previously was difficult to remember and felt like just a dream. Vala was not there when he awoke, however. She had fallen asleep in her own small room after staying up late. Abigale Mirella was checking on him.

"I'm glad to see you alive and doing well," she said, smiling and a bit surprised at his sudden recovery.

"There was someone watching over me when I was unconscious, someone keeping me alive...like an angel. Who was it...who was...she?" asked Galen.

"I will bring her in to see you when she is available."

"What about Vala? That caretaker...reminded me of her. I thought I had dreams about her."

"Vala's sleeping, she's been working hard. I'll take her to you when she wakes up, I know she'll be glad to see you conscious and well," replied Abigale as she left.

Abigale woke Vala and told her the news. Vala was delighted and eagerly accompanied Dr. Mirella to Dr. Swann's room. When they arrived, Abigale told Vala it was time to take the dressings from Dr. Swann's eyes and let him see. She told Vala she could be the one to do it. Then she walked into Dr. Swann's room.

"Your caretaker is here to see you; she's going to remove your dressings. Here she is; I'll leave you two."

Vala walked in and Abigale departed.

"So...who are you, mystery nurse?" asked Galen. "You did so much. There was someone stern and relentless, but also someone gentle and encouraging. Were they the same person?" he continued.

"Yes," replied Vala.

Dr. Swann replied, "I know that voice."

"You do? Then shall I uncover your eyes so you can confirm it for yourself?"

"I don't need to see to know for certain who you are: the one who was hard but kind, the one who never gave up on me." Then he paused "but I would like them uncovered just to be able to see your face."

Vala laughed and removed the dressings from Galen's eyes. When he could finally see, his eyes first fell upon Vala who was right beside him.

"You're a beautiful sight," he said.

"So are you," said Vala, beaming.

"You're so wonderful, how would I have survived without you?"

"I'm glad to see you've revived, you cost me a lot of grief and lonely hours," Vala said, heading for the door.

"Hey, are you leaving already? Will you stop by again soon?"

"I have a patient to tend to…I'm just getting you breakfast and a few other things. Now that you're conscious, it's about time you had some whole food instead of those fluids that have been going through your system. We even got some fresh fruits from Florina, I'm going to juice some. Of course, I'll be back soon!"

All that morning Dr. Swann's spirits grew but then he remembered his experience at the enemy fortress some time ago. Now that his mind was back to its normal self, he wanted to know for sure if his sister was truly dead. Vala told him it was true and stayed with him as he mourned. She had only seen Camelia a few times, but had come to love her nevertheless. Camelia had always had an interest in adventure and intergalactic politics. When the war began, she decided to take sides against Casimir and went off to help the forces allied against him. There had been little contact from her for a while and now it was obvious to Dr. Swann and Vala why.

Flames

Some weeks later, Corin was still looking for a good ship to take them back to Aldura when he, Amara, and Ariella were called to an urgent meeting. The meeting was held by one of the commanders stationed at the base. Amongst others, the mysterious girl who went by the code name Squimba and a man named Marcel, whose identity and position were unknown to all but a few, were present. When they were all assembled, the commander began.

"We've had some grave news.. and I'm sorry Amara, I've heard you're a Kairahn. It appears Casimir Blade has amassed a huge army and employed a Kairahn to help him. His name is Shaan Katana Vanhi…" Amara gasped at the name as the commander continued, "…and he has recently moved up as Casimir Blade's second in command. Blade feared the mighty Kairahn people and gave them a choice: Join him or die. They refused to join him, so he sent the whole of his army and his weapons to wipe out the planet's population, and Vanhi, with the knowledge of some of their secrets, turned against his people in favor of Casimir and led the conquest. Apparently, he used the planet Kairah to test a weapon. We're unsure of the damage that has been done to the planet, but we do know the Kairahn population was pretty much wiped out, though there are some survivors out there."

Amara was aghast and grieved. She knew the name of the murderer; she knew it well. Her thoughts trailed off while the commander continued.

"Now Blade is sending that vast army in our direction. It is believed that he is sending it to Aldura."

Ariella was horrified at the news that had been shared and almost just as horrified at how much power Casimir now had over the galaxy. It was hard to imagine after knowing him for so long as just a senator. "We must get back; and Aldura must be warned," she insisted.

"A warning has been sent. Whoever wishes to leave this place may do so and will be provided with transportation. Many of us are volunteers anyway." The commander continued again. "We've also learned that Vanhi has just landed on this planet, we could be in a lot of danger. He is alone as far as we know, so we'll send a small attack group to take him and destroy him if necessary."

Amara suddenly jumped in. "Don't go, don't try it. It's too dangerous." She continued on, "Vanhi's a Kairahn, but he's also a Kalipyrah."

"I thought the Kalipyrah were only a people of legend," said someone.

"No, they are real. They've just remained secret for many years. I suppose you've heard the stories that they are a people of fierce anger; that a fire burns within them and when provoked, can become some of the most beautiful creatures in the universe, but also rage in fierce anger that makes them almost unstoppable. It is a terrible and beautiful sight. It creates a deadly foe. Long ago, Kairah was ruled by these people. They were prideful, prone to erupt in rage, and sought power and dominion. They were very beautiful too, and none more so than the ruling family. No one dared go against them, they were too terrible and undefeatable. Finally, the people of Kairah agreed they did not want to be ruled by these fierce people, so they came up with an elaborate plan to overthrow them. After much bloodshed, they defeated the Kalipyrah and over the course of several years, they developed the current structure of government we've been living under. They made sure all the Kalipyrah were destroyed. But a few remained and their descendants still live today, though there are not many of them left. They don't often make themselves known because they fear persecution. You can't win against him, let me go instead."

Then Ariella spoke up. "But Amara, from what you say, it sounds like even you won't be a match for him; even if you are a Kairahn. If he's a Kalipyrah, he's bound to win. I don't want you to throw your life away, my friend." Ariella's eyes pleaded with Amara.

Amara remained cool as ever and replied. "But that's just the point. It's my secret. I am a worthy opponent, the only worthy opponent here at least. I too am a Kalipyrah and a descendant of the old ruling family from long ago."

Everyone was surprised, but none more than Ariella. Only two people in the room remained cool as if this was no surprise to them, the two who were surrounded in mystery: Marcel and the girl whose code name was Squimba.

"What? I never even suspected..." said Ariella, trailing off.

"My mentors taught me to control my emotions. When I came here, I told only Captain Camara what I was. He also taught me how to deal with the fire and the anger and to keep it from appearing. I suppose Vala is the only one who has witnessed my wrath and even then, it was not at its full strength. When Captain Camara was slain, I ran to him and in my fury, struck down everyone in my path; but I reined it in as I reached him. He had been such a wonderful mentor; I didn't want to let him down in his last moments. I must go to Vanhi, I'm the only one who stands a chance against him. Besides, there's something between us. Something I wish to discuss with him. If he knows I'm here, he probably wishes to see me as well."

"Be careful Amara, keep your communicator with you. We'll pick you up or offer you help if you need it. I hope all goes well," said Ariella.

They quickly finished up the rest of the meeting but Amara barely paid attention, her thoughts were elsewhere. When they were through, they parted ways and most of the non-natives prepared to depart the planet.

Flames

"I pray for your safe return," said Ariella to Amara as they parted.

Amara wished to leave right away and said only a simple goodbye, she was too worn with other burdens. She went off on her own to find Vanhi and it didn't take her long, intelligence knew his location and that was where she found him. She approached him at his location, and they met.

"Kaida," he said.

"Vanhi. What brings you here?"

"You."

"Me? Why me?"

"You left. How could you do that to me? I thought you were beginning to love me."

"I only did what I judged was right. I loved you, but I had to put an end to it. It wasn't allowed and you know it. I couldn't go on; I still loved you and I couldn't stay because of it. I left, but I never forgot you. I thought that perhaps someday we would meet again."

"Well, here I am; finally."

"Finally? I know what you did. How can you expect me to still love you? How could you do what you did?"

"It was for you. I lived many years wishing you were still on Kairah, but you weren't there. You never came back. I hated our people and their laws. I was always told what I could and could not do and when the time came, I had to marry the wife who was chosen for me. I hated it, I hated them. All I ever wanted was you, and more freedom. Yes, I killed them. I'm a Kalipyrah, I had the power and the right! It is my place and my inheritance to be above the rest of those commoners. A man named Casimir Blade befriended me when I was still young and when I grew older, he offered me command over his armies. When he wished for me to destroy our people, I gladly did it. Do you remember Priya?"

"Yes."

"She and I were matched together, we had to marry each other. I killed many, including her! I despised them! Now the Kalipyrah have power again! And we can both reclaim the throne that once belonged to our families thousands of years ago."

Amara broke out in tears. "Shaan, how could you? How could you do such a terrible thing? And it's because of me?! If you're asking for my love, you don't have it. I can't love you anymore, not after this. You killed many people, OUR people! Many of them were my friends and family!"

"I came all this way, did all this for you, and now you dislike me?" Anger was building up in Vanhi.

"Because of the choices you made and the murder you committed. Because you've changed." continued Amara.

"Kaiya Amara. Always following the rules and disciplining yourself, I see even your escape to freedom and the rest of the galaxy has not changed you. You are a Kalipyrah and yet you remain cool and submissive as ever. Tell me you still love me!"

Flames

"No!"

"Then what have you come here for? Do you seek to kill me like the rest?!" Now he was raging within.

"I have come to learn the truth and it grieves me. I have no choice now. I must stop you and bring you to justice."

"If that is the way you'll have it...then you will die too, just like the rest!"

"I didn't want to do this, but it appears now I have no choice," replied Amara.

Vanhi raged forth, dark and beautiful, fiery and powerful, as he drew his Kairahn sword. He would be too tough for Amara to take in her normal state. She had controlled her feelings so well for many years and had learned to put the rage aside. Now she could think of no other way to face Vanhi than to do that which she had trained herself so hard not to do. She was certainly upset with Vanhi for what he did. She unleashed her Kalipyrah power, and a fire and immense beauty shone forth. Her hair was the darkest, deepest black and her eyes were terrible with a fire burning in them. She drew her gold-coated Kairahn sword, and she and Vanhi began their dual. It was a sight to see if anyone had been there. There they were, two Kairahns with their exceptional reflexes and senses, moving so quickly that any normal human could hardly keep up with their movement. Added to this scene were also the power, strength, and magnified skills of the Kalipyrah.

Ariella, Corin, Dr. Swann, Vala, April, Seren, and the monkey were preparing to evacuate along with some of the other volunteers. Some of Casimir's soldiers had approached the base and were now attacking it. Most of its occupants had already left but a few remained. Corin had finally found a decent ship and that was where they were headed. He led the way to the ship through the flames of the falling city with Ariella and the others following behind, firing weapons at the soldiers who pursued them. When they finally neared the ship, Vala gasped and held her side.

"What is it?" asked Dr. Swann as they began to board the ship.

"I've been shot," replied Vala.

"Let's get in quick!" He replied. He brought Vala in and sat her down as Corin began to take off. Dr. Swann examined Vala's wound. "It's definitely a puncture, a solid bullet must have been used; and what worries me most of all is the location it hit, it could be very serious if it went deep. Did you see the weapon Vala?"

"Yes, just a glimpse; it was a powerful one," she managed to say.

"Does anyone know if this ship is equipped with medical supplies?" asked Dr. Swann, somewhat curtly.

Ariella and Corin had previously made themselves familiar with the ship and Ariella showed Dr. Swann and Vala to a small medical chamber.

"I don't know what supplies we have on board, but I hope they're adequate," she said.

Vala was groaning. "It's very painful, something doesn't feel right."

Dr. Swann quickly checked the vital signs of Vala and the baby. "This isn't good at all. I need to be able to see what damage has been done internally, what do we have available?" he asked, tending to Vala.

Ariella searched around. "There's not much... here's an old medical scanner."

"That will be fine. Can you set it up and get it ready?"

"I think I can manage."

Ariella made it ready and Dr. Swann used it to examine Vala in more detail.

"It's just as I feared, the bullet ripped the placenta. That was quite a weapon; and shot. Under the circumstances, I think the best thing to do is to begin surgery. The baby is due soon anyway. Have you had any experience in situations like this?" he asked Ariella.

"Just a little," she replied.

"Good, help me prepare and set up. The sooner the better. If anyone is available, we could use another set of hands. Do it fast!" ordered the doctor.

"I'll go get April, maybe she can help," replied Ariella.

She quickly went to get April who was willing to help, but unsure of what the situation would be like.

"Are you ready?" Dr. Swann gently asked Vala when they were prepared.

"I'm a little nervous, but I trust you and your abilities. You'd better start, I'm ready."

Dr. Swann began preparing the sedation, and then he paused as a look of frustration came over his face.

"What's wrong?" asked Ariella.

"It's..." Dr. Swann let out a sigh of frustration. "My eyes are not fully healed. I can't do this."

Ariella gave a look of pity, and then determination. "Let me help. Just tell me what to do."

Dr. Swann was hesitant. Though she had done some work with her parents, she was by no means a trained surgeon. But there was no other choice.

"Alright," he said reluctantly. "That seems to be our only option."

Ariella administered the sedation and Vala began to fall asleep. Once they were prepared, Dr. Swann began giving out orders for the other ladies and watched Ariella closely as she followed his directions in performing the tasks he could not do himself. As they continued, April, unaccustomed to this circumstance, began feeling a bit sick and nauseous. Then it seemed as if her ears were blocked and all sounds were muffled. Her vision was slightly blurred and she felt a very slight loss of sense or numbness in her skin. Very slowly, these losses of senses grew and she began to lose coordination. She realized she was slowly fainting, but struggled with herself and feeling helpless, began to silently pray. Slowly, she regained all her senses and was back to normal but still felt sick. It had not taken long to recover and Dr. Swann and Ariella seemed to have hardly noticed her. At times it was a little difficult, but April was able to pull herself through. Meanwhile, the ride had recently grown rough and suddenly, Corin burst through the door.

"Stay out!" insisted Ariella.

"I have a problem, and I'm a bit short of hands," replied Corin.

He wouldn't move until he got what he needed. With an expression of slight annoyance, mostly at the situation they were in, Ariella sighed, quickly washed up, and joined Corin outside.

"The ship's been damaged. I need to fix it or we're in trouble. I need someone to pilot the ship and someone to help me with repairs."

"Are we on autopilot right now?" asked Ariella.

"No, I have Cosmo and Seren in the cockpit doing what they can."

"I'll help you with repairs then."

"Are you sure you can handle it?"

"You know me."

"Well then, let's get started. We will have to replace some parts, I just hope we'll have all the pieces."

Corin, with Ariella assisting him, began repairs. Sometimes he would ask her to give him a certain tool, she knew all the tools, or a part which often he would have to describe to her because she was unfamiliar with them. Other times they would both have to work together placing, holding, or removing parts. Then they ran into some difficulty.

"I need Cosmo to help with this part, he's the only one small enough to do it from inside the ship and he's very knowledgeable about repairs," said Corin.

"So I'll have to go take over flying," said Ariella.

"Yes," replied Corin.

Ariella sent Cosmo to Corin and took over flying. From what she found in the cockpit, she thought she might be the better pilot in the given situation anyway. They were still not out of danger and Ariella did her best to keep away from the pursuers. When Corin and Cosmo had finally finished the repairs, they returned to pilot the ship and Ariella quickly returned to the medical chamber. She found that the baby had been saved and Vala would be fine. Dr. Swann gave his new son to Ariella to care for while he finished with Vala. Ariella wrapped the baby in multiple layers and monitored him closely. When Dr. Swann finally finished with Vala, he left April to watch her while he went to see Ariella and the baby.

"So far no complications," said Ariella as Dr. Swann approached, "What will you name him?"

"We thought of Fabian, but under the circumstances of his birth perhaps that might change. We'll ask Vala when she wakes up."

"You know, before I had no interest in babies at all. Children a little… maybe, but not babies. I think maybe you and Vala might have changed that a little… just maybe," said Ariella.

"Well I'm glad if we did," replied Dr. Swann.

Then Corin approached, looking rather weary.

"You look like you've been through a rough job," said Ariella.

"So do you," Corin replied.

"What's the status, Captain?" Ariella continued.

"We're going smooth at the moment, but we're not out of danger; there's more to be expected I'm afraid." Then Corin smiled. "Ha, I must say you make quite a scene holding that baby. Who would have thought it? I thought it would take something more to get you to show even a slight interest."

Ariella smiled a little underneath a look of annoyance. "Well don't just stand there with that look on your face, I'm sure you have somewhere to be," she said, teasing a bit but also hinting at some resentment towards Corin's comment, "Or maybe you'd like to try holding him. Now that would be a sight to see."

"Oh, no. Like you said, I have somewhere to be," said Corin, turning to leave.

Ariella laughed. "I think I just scared him off."

Vala soon awoke but was very tired as the effects of the sedation were still wearing off.

"How are you?" asked Dr. Swann, standing beside her.

"Tired. Was it successful?"

"Yes, you suffered more harm than your son, so you're both fine."

"So it's a boy?"

"Yes, and we decided to wait for you to wake up to give him his name. Would you like to see him?"

"Of course."

Dr. Swann took the child and brought him to Vala.

"I'm reminded of Sunshine," said Vala. Then she continued. "I hear of a strange girl and I am reminded of her. Sometimes I wonder if she's come back. We've been living a rough life, everything seems to get worse all the time; but right now, something good has come in the midst of it all. Our son will be a comfort, he should have a significant name."

They took some time to consider names and eventually decided on Nehemiah Fabian Swann. Suddenly, Ariella rushed to the cockpit.

"Corin! We've been so busy with evading the enemy and delivering the baby that we've neglected Amara! She's contacted me; we have to go back!"

Corin sighed. "It will be difficult."

"We have to do it!"

"Of course we do," he sighed. "Well then, here we go." He turned around to go back to where they had started.

As they progressed, they noticed that most of the enemy ships were gone; they had left the area. Down on the planet's surface, it seemed Amara had defeated

Flames

Vanhi. They had continued their battle in one of the abandoned enemy stations and they had fought hard and bitterly. A fire had started during the fight and through the circumstances, as well as Amara's doing, Vanhi was pinned under a fallen piece of the building, too heavy for him to lift. He was caught; defeated.

"Many say you are too dangerous to be left alive. You deserve death, after the many lives you've taken," said Amara.

"Then what will it be? Can you really bring yourself to strike me down? Or will you leave me to burn?" Vanhi replied.

Amara stood still, she didn't know what to do. Compassion began to well up in her. She couldn't kill him by her own hand with her own weapon. Perhaps it would be the more merciful thing to do rather than let him burn, but she couldn't bring herself to do it. She had an urge to try to help him get free, but the flames were so close now, she didn't know how. Her eyes welled up with tears.

"I loved you Shaan, I never thought it would come to this. How could you do it? You've killed so many, and all because of me."

Vanhi was silent, he gazed up at Amara who still did not move as the flames came closer. For a moment, he felt some conviction over what he had done. The flames drew nearer and still Amara did not move. Then Vanhi realized what his fate would be and what Amara's would be if she did not move.

"Kaiya, run! Leave!"

She hesitated and looked back at him with tears in her eyes and indecision, sadness, and pity. She didn't know what she wanted to do.

"Save yourself! Go!"

Finally, Amara ran, grieving all the way. What should she have done? She wondered. Did she make the right choice? He certainly deserved it, but how could she leave anyone to suffer such a fate? She should have killed him quickly with her sword, but she couldn't have brought herself to do it. She felt terrible and suddenly remembered what Ariella had said. She finally made up her mind to contact the others and waited alone for them to arrive. While waiting, she saw another ship land in the distance and sat quietly until Corin finally landed the ship and she walked on board. She was very low in spirits. She was sad and weary and burdened.

"Were you successful? What's wrong?" asked Ariella as Amara came aboard.

"Please just leave me alone," said Amara, walking off.

Ariella was troubled. "Let's get out of here," she said, sitting down in the cockpit next to Corin.

Corin took off back into space.

"I asked Amara if she was successful. She didn't say, but she was very upset," said Ariella.

"Well, she's lost her people, that's enough to make just about anyone upset," replied Corin.

"I guess you're right, but I wish she'd talk to someone."

Eventually, Amara wandered out to go see Vala and learned all that had happened while she dueled Vanhi.

"You don't seem your normal self," commented Vala.

"I'm not, I'm not at all," Amara replied.

"What is it? I heard you wouldn't tell anyone."

"I don't know who to tell, or if I want to tell anyone."

"Tell me," said Vala.

Amara said nothing.

"Amara, what is it?" asked Vala again.

Amara gave in. "Did they tell you what my mission was? Who I battled?"

"Yes."

"He was the one I told you about, the one I left many years ago. The one I loved and escaped from. He slaughtered my people and my friends! How could he do that? I hate him! I let him burn... and yet, I couldn't bring myself to slay him with my own hand, I couldn't! It's like... there was something there... a trace of compassion or love that would not allow me to do it. I also thought I saw the slightest trace of regret on his face. I almost wanted to save him, but I didn't. Did I do the right thing to leave him there to suffer and die? He did deserve it though."

Amara was distraught and uncertain with herself.

"I'm so sorry. I doubt I could have done any better than you if I were in the same position."

The two sat in silence for a while before Amara left to be by herself once more, but not before she had the chance to see Vala's second child.

The Return Home

Before long, they were forced off their path home by a fleet of ships belonging to Casimir and ended up a long way from Aldura, and low on fuel and supplies. It was then that they encountered a friendly fleet which was carrying mostly supplies, but also people who wanted to follow the example of Aldura and leave Casimir's union. Some of the passengers even hoped to emigrate to Aldura. Being low on fuel with no other place to go, the senator and the others were welcomed to stay on one of the cruisers until the fleet made its way to Aldura. During the trip, Ariella and her companions offered to help the crew and made the ship a temporary home. It was onboard one of these ships where Vala went through her healing process. Dr. Swann found work to do in the medical bay and when Vala was well enough, she sometimes assisted him with simple tasks, in addition to other odd jobs. After running around the galaxy in danger for such a long time, they finally had some peace.

When they finally arrived home, they were in for a surprise. Casimir's army and fleet had just moved in against Aldura. As the small fleet approached the planet, there were already enemy ships nearby and a battle in space had just commenced. At the sight of war, the small fleet's admiral made the decision to leave but at the request of Ariella and Corin, along with some of the braver emigrants and freedom fighters who still felt Aldura was the place they needed to be, a smaller ship was deployed to risk taking them past the battle to the planet's surface. As the small cruiser began making its way past the battle to the planet, it was hit and damaged by a smaller outlying attack ship. Inside the small space vessel, after all their defenses were down, they felt a small jolt.

"I'll never forget that feeling," said Ariella, "we're being boarded."

"We'd better set up some barricades, it looks like we're going to have a fight. Amara, get everyone prepared for a battle, I'm going to see if I can help the captain try to get us free." replied Corin.

He began to analyze the situation while the others prepared to defend and take shelter. With the grappling cables in place, the enemies soon began extending tunnels for boarding and began to cut through the sides of the ship to enter. When the

The Return Home

soldiers finally broke through, Ariella and Corin stayed near the bridge and fought side-by-side. Fighting broke out everywhere, even in the small medical bay where everyone was evacuated as soon as possible. At the bridge, Ariella, Corin, and the others with them were pushed back while Amara and April were defending in the corridors near the medical bay. Most of the crew members continued fighting off the invaders while Corin called for Amara's assistance.

"I'm going out to cut the grapple cables, cover me," said Corin as he prepared a torch to cut through the cables.

"I got it," she replied.

"Is there anything I can do?" asked Ariella, coming to see how Corin was getting along.

"You can seal up the holes the invaders cut. When I remove the cables and we get out of here, the boarding tunnels are going to rip away and expose the holes to space," Corin replied.

As Corin, Amara and Ariella did their work, the passengers who were brave enough to volunteer themselves continued to fight until they won back the ship. When Corin finished cutting the cables, Amara assisted Ariella in sealing the last of the holes while Corin made his way back to the bridge. He talked his way into gaining control of the helm, as the ship's captain was inexperienced with war. As soon as the holes were sealed up, he took the controls and tactfully guided the ship down to the atmosphere but not without substantial damage from the continuing battle that had left the ship almost un-maneuverable and beyond repair, forcing the captain to order everyone to evacuate. As the ship was being evacuated, Vala and Dr. Swann wanted to make sure everyone else was safely off before they got off themselves and quickly went to work helping the others evacuate. Through the chaos of the evacuation, April ran into Vala.

"Aren't you coming?" April asked.

"We will, but we want to make sure everyone else is safely off first. Are you going?"

"Well, I'm supposed to."

"Then would you mind taking Fabian with you?"

"Of course I'll take him, just be sure you get off in time to take him back," said April, a bit concerned. Nevertheless, she took Vala's child.

"Thank you, and don't worry," replied Vala. She and Dr. Swann stayed behind to help until no one could be found on board.

The ship, which was now hovering in place after being abandoned by its crew, began to fall apart. Dr. Swann took Vala's hand.

"Come on, let's go while there's still time," he said, quickly leading Vala through the wreckage of the ship.

They made their way as fast as they could towards their last chance of escape when the ship jolted as if

The Return Home

it was hit and collapsed some more. As they tried to escape, the passage was smashed behind them and almost on top of them. As they fell with the rubble, Dr. Swann's leg was caught in the wreckage. Vala stopped to help him.

"Go, just go now! Nehemiah needs you; I won't have you die here!"

"Oh, don't use that on me! I'm not leaving without you; we're both going to get out alive," protested Vala.

She began to try to free Galen when the ship was hit again and began to collapse more. Both Vala and Galen were buried in the rubble. When the debris had settled, Vala's left arm was in pain. She used her right arm to clear some of the wreckage away and then winced and groaned in pain.

"What's wrong?" asked Dr. Swann.

"My arm, I think it's fractured," Vala replied.

She regained herself and proceeded to once again try to free Galen from the rubble that trapped him. She began using her right arm, but one arm was not enough to move the large piece that pinned down Galen's leg.

"Don't hurt yourself more," he said, but Vala would not give up. She began lifting the piece again, this time with both hands, as she cried out in pain.

"Get out! Get out quick!" she gasped.

Galen quickly pulled himself forward to safety and Vala dropped the heavy load she had been lifting and sat down, gasping and wincing. The pain was so great that she couldn't control the tears that began to flow from her eyes.

"Why did you do that? You know it only made you worse!" exclaimed Galen.

Vala was now weeping because the pain was so great.

"No one else was around to get you out; I had to do it," she replied, with tears still flowing.

Galen managed to seat himself next to Vala and took her in his arms. "Go on and cry; it will make you feel better," he said, and she did so.

He began gently examining her arm and found it was broken after lifting the wreckage; it was quite obvious. He then proceeded to make her a slint and sling using fabric he ripped from his clothing and pieces of the wreakage.

When Vala was feeling a bit better, she asked: "What about your leg? Come on doctor, tell me, and don't lie."

Galen hesitated. "Well," he began examining it, "...I think it's broken too."

Vala got up and began to search through the debris from the ship. Using a suitable piece of rubble she found, and strips of fabric from her skirt, she helped Galen make a splint. They sat still, Vala leaning against Galen, unable to move as they were surrounded by debris, and both were injured.

The Return Home

"Have you noticed it's getting harder to breathe?" Vala asked.

"Yes, I suppose it's the oxygen supply," Galen replied.

"Or an opening in the ship," Vala said. They sat in silence for a while as the oxygen slowly drained.

"How are you feeling?" asked Galen, after a while.

Vala looked a little better, but her looks could always be deceiving. She was silent.

"I'd rather not think about it," she replied.

"Of course. I can see it in your eyes: the pain; the pain and weight of many years. Too much for one so young."

"Do I still look young? I don't feel it. Though I suppose it really hasn't been long since all this started. It's hard to believe we've only been married a few years now, and have two children. It feels like the years have gone by so quickly and we've endured so much pain, sorrows, and difficulties with hardly any rest. Sometimes it seems I was meant to suffer. If this is the end, I have no fear of it. I won't try to escape it."

"Don't give up hope, where's that fire inside you? The one that keeps you going, keeps you fighting? The one that just freed me from the rubble? That's one of the things I've always liked about you, one of the things that everyone likes about you."

"I suppose it's gone... put out by weariness and despair."

"Well hold on, we are going to survive this and when we get free, we'll stay home and stay out of these situations and conflicts. We'll leave that to the politicians and soldiers while we live a normal life."

After that, they ceased talking, it was now very difficult to breathe. Just when they felt ready to pass out, they heard more rumbling and suddenly, the ship jerked and began to stall. It began moving and falling down to Aldura's surface, and they now felt sure they would perish in the crash. Galen held Vala in his arms again and shielded her from whatever might fall on top of them. The ship fell down to Aldura's surface and crashed while Ariella watched fearfully. She insisted a search party be sent to look for her friends; she was sure they were in the ship that had crashed.

Vala opened her eyes. It was a miracle that they had survived. Nevertheless, they were still trapped. The rich Alduran air began seeping through and they were able to breathe again. Then she noticed the pain in her arm again, the crash had made it no better. She and Galen sat silently, side-by-side, once again as they took in the air. When she had breathed enough, Vala spoke.

"We survived…but we're still trapped."

She was silent again but slowly became her normal self. She got up and felt around the sides of the ship where they were trapped.

"There's got to be a way out of here," she said.

The Return Home

Finally, she climbed the pile of debris, using only her good arm.

"Be careful," said Galen. She began clearing some of the rubble away and suddenly saw sunlight, the light of a new morning. The sun was rising.

"We're free," she sighed with a smile as she cleared a way out and gazed upon the sunlight.

Just then, the rescue team reached them, and not too soon. The pain in Vala's arm grew so much that she passed out just as the rescue team reached her.

Vala woke up two mornings later. Everything was fresh and rain-washed, and the smell of starflowers flowed through the window. It was a wonderful atmosphere to wake up to. She could feel the air and smell the scents, she knew where she was: Florina. She was glad to be on Aldura where they had the technology to decrease the time it would take for her and Galen to heal. She was also glad to be reunited with her friends and small family.

"Why are we in the country? It's nice and I'm certainly glad to be here, but this is not a normal hospital," Vala said to Ariella who was sitting at her bedside when she awoke.

"No...it's not... " Ariella replied thoughtfully.

"Something's wrong, I see it in your face. Tell me what's going on," said Vala.

Ariella turned to face Vala, she was grave. "Verona has been taken. By Casimir."

"Oh! So what is the plan? I assume we're going to fight?"

"Yes, we are going to take the city back," replied Ariella in her usual down-to-business manner.

"I should have expected nothing less," replied Vala with her fighting spirit revived, "How will we do it?"

"There are already a lot of Aldurans gathered here, preparing to invade, as well as some unexpected help. Casimir's armies have been spreading to other cities as well, and they have control over many of the roads. The country has proved more difficult for him to take, however. Some of the cities have been able to withstand invasion as well because many of the inhabitants are armed. I think Casimir's finding it harder to take us than he hoped, but we believe he still has other weapons he has yet to unleash. After what happened on Kirah, we know what he's capable of. If it is too difficult to take us by force then he will use his other weapons without a doubt. We must be prepared to use our latest science and technology and whatever intelligence we've gained on Casimir's ways. Unfortunately, a lot of research and records, mostly on defense and weaponry and top secret projects, have been destroyed. Whether it was legal or not, the queen wished for them to be destroyed when Casimir took over so that he could not have our secrets and technology. I think the scientists have all been smuggled to safety, but we don't know for sure. As long as they're not in enemy hands, they'll be working against Casimir."

"It must have been horrible. What about the queen? What's become of her?"

"As far as we know, she is being held captive in the capitol. Casimir may try to use her to help in his conquest, but I know she won't give in to him. She's much tougher than she seems, and she would rather die than be used against Aldura in any way. I think even now she may have secrets about her that Casimir is unaware of."

"Where's Aldura's army? Aren't they fighting?"

"Before Casimir invaded, he had the army drugged but we don't know how. Now they are all being held captive but where, we don't know."

Vala sat silently as she processed the news that Ariella had delivered to her, then Ariella departed but promised to return to see Vala soon.

Sometime later, after Ariella had left, a very young lady who was hooded stepped into Vala's room. She didn't even look full-grown.

"Who are you? I've seen you before, you seem to follow me," said Vala, looking her over.

"I thought it was about time I revealed myself to you," replied the girl.

She threw back her hood. Underneath, she wore black, and her hair was red and trimmed above her shoulders. She seemed to be shrouded in mystery and solemnity. She was stern, and weighted by responsibility, and the experiences of both past and future events.

"You look very familiar," said Vala.

"I'm known as Squimba."

Vala lit up inside with a certain hopefulness. "But that's not your real name," she said.

"No, it's not."

"Your real name is Sunny; Sunshine. You were raised in another time by foster parents, but you were born Sunny Swann and by the standard universal dating system, you're not quite two years old yet!"

"Yes! But I'm fourteen now."

Tears came to Vala's eyes and Sunny rushed over and the two embraced tightly.

"I've missed you so much. You've grown so much too," said Vala.

"I'm glad to meet you too, since I don't remember the last time we were together. I always wondered what my real parents were like and how they lived. When I was growing up, I was allowed to come back to this time every year for my birthday. I was able to see my real family every year as they grew and changed, but they did not see me. I've seen your future, but I won't speak of it." Then Sunny laughed just a little and smiled. "Speaking of ages, you look so young; maybe even young enough to be my sister."

Vala smiled. "Yes, but I'm still your mother."

The Return Home

    They spoke some more with each other before Vala took Sunny to see her brother and her father and their family was briefly reunited.

    Meanwhile, the band of Alduran fighters and their allies had been steadily growing. After a few months, they decided it was time to take back the capital. Aldura's allies in space and on other planets were not able to help them, they were on their own. A scout came bringing news that their location had been revealed to the enemy and they decided it was time to evacuate the area and go through the more uninhabited regions to get to the capital as unnoticed as possible. During the journey, they would also take out some of the enemy parties that roamed the country. As they began the journey, they loaded up with small packs and only the supplies they would need. They were to travel lightly and swiftly. Many in the party were archers and the majority of the archers were under Sunny's command, though where they came from no one knew. With the invasion going on, it was harder to get good weapons. Each archer differed in their choice of bow and equipment color, as well as their style of shooting. Those with brightly colored equipment had to re-fletch with duller colored veins and cover the rest of the equipment with mud or dark strips of fabric. Some archers shot instinctively with simple bows while others shot with recurves with extra equipment to help improve accuracy such as sights and stabilizers, and yet others shot with compound bows – which were usually the most preferred for killing with, though using bows as weapons was not pleasant for most of their wielders. Some archers kept their bows unstrung while others kept theirs ready. Because the recurve bows could be quite a burden to carry, especially the ones with all the extra equipment, the archers who used them typically carried them over their shoulders, often holding the stabilizer or limb over their shoulder or the stabilizer over one shoulder and a bow limb over the other. They began by hiking through the country and as they continued on their way, they eventually came to a small forest. As they were passing through, a scout returned to the main group and reported that there were enemies heading towards them. The group took cover in the trees and silently waited for their enemies to approach. The archers followed the command of Sunny and waited to draw and fire their bows until the troop of invaders passed right by them. The enemy was ambushed by surprise and had difficulty seeing their attackers. For some of the Alduran archers, it was difficult to use their precious sporting and pleasure equipment as weapons against the enemy soldiers, but they used special points designed to guarantee quick deaths, even if the arrow was shot poorly. With this surprise ambush, it didn't take long to defeat the enemy troop. One soldier remained, however, and being defenseless, surrendered and begged for mercy. Being the commander of the archers, Sunny approached him.

The Return Home

She stood above him, cold and hard, as he was on his knees begging for his life to be spared.

"You're one of Casimir Blade's soldiers, yet you do not fight to the death like most of them," said Sunny.

"I have proudly served him, but I don't want to die, please," he replied.

"What would your lord say if he heard you? Your kind have brought nothing but death and despair to this galaxy; and destruction and darkness with little hope to mine. All you warriors do is kill and destroy. A prisoner will only be a burden, and that's the last thing we need," she replied with little emotion and no compassion. She raised a weapon to kill him.

"Sunny, aren't you going to give more consideration to what you're doing?" asked Vala, speaking up.

Sunny looked back at her mother but did not lay down her weapon. She turned to face the soldier again, fear was in his eyes.

"Sunny..." continued Vala.

Sunny paused again, then threw the weapon onto the ground and walked away, sullen and slightly bitter. Vala followed her as she left the others.

"Were you taught to be merciless and hard?" she asked.

"Why did you do that in front of everyone? I'm their commander, I should decide what to do with our prisoners, not you," said Sunny.

"Are you always so quick to take a life? You've proven you're a good warrior, but did you learn justice? I can't believe a fourteen-year-old girl would be put in charge of this operation, let alone taught to be so unfeeling. Don't you at least have someone to advise you?"

Sunny cooled down and seemed to be sad. "I did..." she was hesitant. "He might have advised me to let the prisoner live. He's gone though. He's always watched over me, and he's always been there for me; but then when you were found to be alive after the crash, he said I wasn't his responsibility anymore and that I should go meet you. He's gone to do some other business. He told me to connect with you and my father...and to get counsel from you."

"He sounds like a wise adviser," said Vala.

"And I wasn't trained to be merciless, at least not in that way. It's just...my life...sometimes it's difficult. The time I came from is a dark place and the rulers and soldiers show little mercy. I've witnessed horrible things Casimir and his successors have done, including a murder he did himself. One that I cannot forget, one that makes me sad and worried all the time. A murder of someone I love. I dislike them all: all of Casimir's soldiers, servants, and the others involved in his conquest and rule, and those who came after him. I grew up in dark hard times, experiencing dark hard things. I have little love and mercy in me for a great part of the galaxy," said Sunny.

"I don't know what to say," said Vala, "but I'm sorry. And I've been told that you are going to fix all that."

"Yes, but I don't see how. I always had someone working alongside me and guiding me. And now he's gone."

"Well, I have faith you'll know what to do when the time is right. And you still have your training and now you have us," said Vala.

As the days passed, the troop continued on, and bonds began to form between the members. As they moved closer to Verona, the scenery and terrain began to change; the next region they passed through had many mounds and hills with scattered groves of trees. The sand was a natural clay color and green grass and wildflowers grew in the fields and on the hills. As they approached this beautiful region, scouts reported that there were enemies nearby. Sunny and the archers decided they could rid the area of the enemies and began hunting them down. They shot uphill and downhill, through trees or across water or ditches, and they shot both from long and close ranges, all from hiding places, which made it difficult for Casimir's soldiers to locate and attack them. The battle lasted a few days but in the end, that region was once again in Aldura's hands. At least for now. As they continued the journey through the newly liberated area, Vala admired the view and enjoyed the slightly breezy weather.

After several more days, they ran into another small enemy band. The band was quickly defeated but in the process, Ariella was hit by a dart. The dart contained a deadly virus and as time passed, she had difficulty keeping up with the rest of the troop as she succumbed to the virus. After examinations and analysis, Dr. Swann smiled a bit.

"Good news?" asked Vala.

"No, my smiling really isn't appropriate for her situation at all," he said.

"Then why did you do it?" asked Vala.

Dr. Swann smiled again. "Because it's the same one that brought us together. I may not have met you if it didn't exist. But now on a more serious note, I don't have anything here that can cure her, our supplies are very limited. It's also contagious, which means those of us who have been immunized are the only ones who we can be sure are safe around her."

"We could make a vaccine for the others who may wish to use one," said Sunny, stepping up.

"We could..." started Dr. Swann, thoughtfully.

"I have equipment here we can use to produce a vaccine," said Sunny.

She took some of her equipment out of the pack she carried. The pack had many tools, equipment, and supplies from the future and on Sunny's belt and slung over her shoulders, were various futuristic weapons and devices. Together she and Dr. Swann worked

The Return Home

to manufacture a vaccine that was administered to whoever wished to receive it.

"What about Ariella? Is there hope for her? Is there anything I can do for her other than to care for her?" asked Vala.

By now Ariella had grown much worse and didn't seem to be getting any better. Dr. Swann thought for a moment.

"Well... you have memory cells in your immune system that can quickly and more efficiently fight off the infection. If we could give her some of your memory cells...it could work if her immune system doesn't kill them off. Sunny, what equipment do you have for that?"

Sunny took a kit that could be used for the desired purpose out of her pack. Together, she and Dr. Swann successfully transferred some of Vala's memory cells to Ariella. Though she got even more sick from the procedure, the transfer seemed to work for Ariella, and she soon recovered and began to improve every day after.

"I think this situation, me being infected by one of Casimir's own men, proves my suspicions that he really is the one behind that virus outbreak that happened at the capital. I'm sure he manufactured it to help in his scheme for getting rid of the president," commented Ariella.

After a few more days, they came upon a camp. It was an enemy camp; a small one, but there were many horses there, all tied up.

"It appears they've captured or taken the horses and are transporting them somewhere," said Amara.

"What do you all say to freeing the horses? They could also provide good transport," said Ariella.

The party agreed wholeheartedly, and they set off to free the horses and take some for themselves. The task was very easy, there were only a few soldiers to guard and herd the horses. Only a few of the horses had saddles and bridles but that didn't stop the Aldurans from riding them. They could control the horses with just their natural aids as long as the horses were trained. They took the horses and traveled on, now swifter than they had been while traveling on foot.

"There's a base with supplies and transports not too far from here. We'll stop there before we head to the capital," said Sunny.

They continued on, the horses making the journey easier, until they finally came upon the base. There they were able to resupply and stock up on ammunition and weapons. They also received news about an evil agent of Casimir's who went around destroying and terrorizing. The latest scout reports said that he was currently residing in the palace at the capital. They remained at the base a few days to rest and prepare for battle while more Aldurans gathered to join them on their quest to regain Verona.

The Return Home

Once they were ready, they set off with their supplies, weapons, transports, and other war machines they had acquired at the base. Now that they were prepared, they marched on down the final stretch.

When they finally reached the capital, they found it was barricaded and heavily guarded. No one could easily get in or out. The militia of Aldurans took cover in front of the city, hoping they had not been spotted, but almost positive they had been. They remained silent but were prepared to make an attack. As they prepared to break the silence, an armored man walked out. He was alone. He was unpleasant to look at and a few of the Aldurans in the newly formed militia recognized him as the one who had led attacks on the innocent and defenseless. Dr. Swann recognized him too, he had killed Camilea and detonated the enemy base in the desert that would have killed him if it had not been for Vala. How had this enemy survived the blast?

"Perhaps we can come to an agreement and avoid more bloodshed. I will negotiate on The Lord President Casimir Blade's behalf. Is there anyone in your group who can represent you?" started Casimir's man.

Ariella stepped forward. "I will represent them. I am their galactic senator, or was until Casimir's tyranny."

"Ah, the famous, or should I say infamous, former Senator Callista. You will do perfectly," replied the spokesman for Casimir.

"What do you have to say to us?" continued Ariella.

The representative for Casimir began. "As you see, I have complete authority over this city. Everyone must obey my every wish and command, or they receive punishment, including," he snickered, "your precious queen. Yes, she is in my hands now. Oh, imagine the things I do to her. That's not all, I spread fear throughout this whole region in ways that could ruin and destroy the people; though I must say you are a very tough people to subdue. I have a proposition for you. Give up your fighting and give in to our sovereign, unavoidable rule now and we will give you equal treatment with the rest of our commonwealth citizens- now that's an honor. Give us your weapons and we will give you peace. You also managed to hide or destroy all your advanced technology and your research data. We would have it recovered or replaced and in our hands to use for the better good of the union."

Ariella turned to those behind her, some looked worried.

"If I may," began Dr. Swann in a low voice to Ariella, "this spokesman cannot be trusted. He is very crafty and he murdered my sister after making it appear he would spare her."

Ariella spoke so that those near her could hear, "Casimir and those under him all cannot be trusted, they lie; and don't fear for the queen, she's much tougher than she appears." She turned to confront the representative once more. "And what if we refuse? You should know we won't give in."

"You will all suffer, and you will be destroyed. Your planet has rockets of massive firepower programmed to hit it at just the press of a button. I share the ability and authority along with The Lord President Blade to detonate the surface of this whole planet, and it would be my pleasure to do so after I've taken what spoils I wish. Casimir Blade also has a second deal for you, Senator Callista. Become his wife and your friends will be spared and your planet will no longer be under threat of destruction but will be allowed to live with some honor. I will remind you again about Aldura's current situation, how its people and its queen are made to suffer, and how it is in danger of existing no more. I warn you not to attack or the suffering of your people will worsen."

Ariella stood still, contemplating the situation. It looked as if she might give in to at least one of the enemy's deals. She walked closer to Casimir's representative.

"You are cruel and heartless, and a dishonest liar as well," she said and suddenly, he fell dead as Ariella pushed a small weapon up her sleeve. "Let that be an example to you all!" she said in a raised voice facing the captive city. "You can tell Casimir that I'm coming and that he can never take Aldura for his own! Be warned! Be afraid! Because we're coming in there to take back what is ours!" she cried.

Her bold statement was effective and some of the greener enemy soldiers began to fear. Ariella turned back to the militia with a cold, stern expression. She was very resolute.

"What did you just do?" asked one of the Aldurans.

"I started a battle for liberation. Now, let's go reclaim Verona and then Aldura," Ariella replied.

The Battle for Aldura

The Aldurans were ready to reclaim their own, but Sunny stood back with a fearful, worried look. The Alduran militia began their attack and swiftly pushed their way past the enemy blockade and fought their way into the city. Once they were in the city, they were joined by some of the captives who still had weapons they had hidden, as well as resistance fighters who had been hiding in the city's underground. As they all began to show themselves and work together, the number of Aldurans fighting to reclaim their city grew. The enemies were startled by the Aldurans' success and a few began to despair as the Aldurans fought boldly.

"Amara, we have to get to the enemy headquarters that are set up in the palace and find where our captive soldiers are being held. We won't last long when the enemy sends reinforcements," said Ariella, as the battle continued. Amara agreed and Corin, who would not part from Ariella, also agreed to go. The three began making their way to the palace. Ariella suddenly had a thought, perhaps a gut feeling, that she may need the information that Dr. Swann had obtained from the exploded desert base. She looked around for him and saw him just up ahead on her path to the palace. The three of them caught up with him and Ariella asked him to join them. As the Aldurans began to triumph, Casimir's soldiers received an order from the ships above to don their masks. They swiftly obeyed and their confidence doubled. Ariella noticed this sudden move.

"I think we're in trouble, we have to get to the palace fast!"

They did their best to move quickly, but it was difficult to fight their way through. When the soldiers of Casimir had prepared themselves, gas was released all through the city and it quickly took its effect. The Aldurans slowly began to lose hope and they developed an irrational fear and despair. Casimir's army began reclaiming the city and controlled it once again. All those who had breathed in the fumes had no hope; all but Ariella, and Amara to a small degree, seemed to be affected by it.

"We can't go on, there's no hope. They've won," Corin lamented in desperation.

"Yes, it's too risky, let's go give ourselves up now and we'll be spared," put in Dr. Swann.

Amara was silently struggling with her feelings.

"No!" exclaimed Ariella, "There is hope, I will not let our planet be taken in to submission. You're cowards! Now are you going to follow me or abandon me?"

Corin was hesitant, but he couldn't abandon Ariella. "Well, I don't want to do this, we'll surely die, but I'll go with you," he complained.

Ariella looked at Dr. Swann.

"I think I should go back and find Vala," he said and turned to leave.

Ariella pulled him back. "There was a secret you learned at that base in the desert; I was told I may need to know it for what I am about to do. Tell it to me before you go."

"I-I don't know, I can't think...I can't remember," replied the doctor.

Ariella was moved to the point of frustration. "You can remember! And I won't let you go until you've told me! You're just being influenced by that gas of Casimir's, you of all people should know this! You're a doctor, I expect you to be better than this! Come on, tell me. You can remember."

Dr. Swann struggled hard, then managed to bring it back to memory. "Rebel," he said.

"Rebel?" replied Ariella.

"Rebel. That's all I was told," said Dr. Swann.

Ariella had expected more and wondered if he was really was telling her all she needed to know.

"I remember, I remember clearly. That was all. Now I have to go find Vala," said Dr. Swann, and he quickly departed.

"Well, it's the three of us then," said Ariella, and she led the others to the palace.

She knew what she had to do, she had agreed to take on this assignment when the possibility of it had been discussed with her in her meeting with Sunny all the way back in the cold snowy village after their crash-landing. She had been deemed the best person to carry out this task and she took it, knowing all along what she might have to deal with when they reached Aldura. With the fighting settling down, the enemy soldiers' minds were on other things and so Ariella, Corin, and Amara were able to move with greater speed until they made their way stealthily into the palace. When they ran into guards, Corin was not much help. He was too frightened at first but eventually warmed up to defending Ariella as they had more encounters with the enemy guards. When they reached the headquarters, they fought to gain it for themselves and used some of Aldura's most secret tactical weapons Ariella carried with her to rid the enemy headquarters of its occupants.

"Amara, find where Aldura's soldiers are being held and see if you can free them," said Ariella as she began searching for something.

Amara did as she was bidden and found that the soldiers were being held nearby. She departed to go free them and left Corin and Ariella to carry out their mission.

"Here it is, the main gas dispenser," said Ariella.

She took out a capsule she had kept with her at all times since she had left the snowy village where she met with Sunny and Marcel many months ago. It was an antidote for the gas, very similar to the one that had been used on Vala. She replaced the empty vial from the attack with her antidote vial and activated the dispenser. She realized the gas couldn't get into the room she and Corin were in and saved the last bit of liquid in the capsule. She drew the remaining antidote into a syringe with a needle, she needed Corin in his normal state of mind. She drew near him with the syringe in one hand.

"What's that for?" he asked.

"You," replied Ariella.

Corin backed away fearfully.

"Corin, I know you don't like needles, but you've never been afraid of them like this. I'm only trying to help you. This will make you feel better and more confident. I need you, your normal self."

Corin didn't comply. Ariella tried to give him the injection but he evaded her. Now she would have to do it the hard way. She would have to be quick. She thought of her mother working with fearful horses. She feigned putting the syringe off to the side and quietly concealed it in her clothes. She waited a bit and casually neared Corin in a charming manner. She took his hand and then quickly pulled out the syringe and injected his arm as he cried out in shock. While Corin recovered, Ariella rushed to the enemy computer console and began to sign into the system. By getting into the system, she could shut down enemy communications and various devices, ships, and vehicles. She had gained all the information she needed from her stay on the icy and sandy neutral planet. She tried to get into the system, but the password had been changed. The one she had learned was no longer valid. She tried the word Dr. Swann had given her and everything she knew to do but still did not succede. Finally, frustrated and not knowing what to do, she sat down. She had never suffered a defeat such as this before and began contemplating what to do. As she sat down, Corin finally revived. Turning back to his regular self, he stepped in.

"What's the problem?" he asked. Ariella looked up and seeing him, jumped up and rushed back to the console with a revived hope.

"I can't get into this system, the password's been changed," she said.

Corin tried all the tricks he had learned in his past life to bypass or change the password but with no success.

"I wish Cosmo were here, he might know what to do. Unfortunately, he's hiding somewhere," he said. He paused and thought for a moment. "I suppose I could hack in," he said as he took the controls.

As Corin went to work, the room suddenly fell under attack again. Casimir's soldiers were trying to take their headquarters back.

"They're getting through! I'll try to hold them off!" exclaimed Ariella as she readied herself and stood guard.

They continued in their current states until Corin finally accomplished his goal.

"I'm in!" he exclaimed.

Ariella rushed over to see. "Good! Shut down all the systems before they break through," she responded.

Just as she had finished speaking, the enemy broke through the doors and rushed in. Ariella fired at them and did her best to hold them back while Corin quickly shut off all systems. Once he finished, he joined Ariella in the firestorm.

"I think we've done everything we need to do here," he said.

Ariella didn't answer, she was busy firing back at the enemy. Then they heard a large blast just outside the room they were defending. As the smoke cleared, Ariella cautiously looked out to the hall while Corin finished off the remaining soldiers in the room. She saw that all the soldiers just outside had fallen dead or unconscious, yet their surroundings remained undamaged. Then a dark figure emerged out of the smoke the explosion had created and drew near. Ariella held her weapon ready. As the figure approached, it looked smaller than Ariella had expected; then she recognized who it was.

"What are you doing here?" she asked.

"We're in danger! I may need your help!" exclaimed Sunny gravely as she rushed into the room with Ariella and Corin.

She went to the main computer and began frantically looking for something.

"What's going on?" asked Corin.

"I was able to delay the detonation of the explosives meant to destroy this planet, but nothing more. Casimir or anyone else with the controls will soon be able to detonate them again unless I do something. And Ariella, they're coming for you two."

"They won't take us," Ariella replied.

Sunny continued. "Casimir has a hidden network within this network, I'm trying to find it." She searched all over the computer until finally, she found the secret access. "Here it is. We need a password. One wrong answer and the computer will self-destruct as a safeguard. Any ideas?" asked Sunny.

The three began to think for a while.

"What about Rebel?" asked Ariella.

"Rebel?" asked Corin.

"Are you sure?" asked Sunny.

"Dr. Swann learned it from the secret enemy base in the desert. He was given one word: Rebel." replied Ariella, she thought it over some more. "Of course, it makes sense. Corin and Ariella Rebel, and they're coming for us. We're Casimir's obsession it seems, why would he not use Rebel as the password?"

"Well then, here it goes. Nevertheless, I would advise you to take cover," said Sunny.

She entered the word and to her relief, was accepted into the system.

"Now we have to find how the explosives are controlled and shut them down for good, unless...I'll change their course! They will be released at the invading ships rather than at us!"

Sunny tried to access the wireless controls to the explosives but was denied. "It says to now insert the thorn's blood. What in the universe is thorn's blood?" questioned Sunny, very baffled.

They all took some time to ponder the words and determine what they meant. Sunny continued to try to find a way around it and both she and Corin used all their computer knowledge to try to hack or get past some other way but they could not. Ariella continued to think to herself. She pondered it over and over, then realized what it meant.

"Agh Casimir, you're so obsessed. The blood of the thorn in Casimir's side, the one that interfered with his plans! That's you Corin!"

Corin didn't know what to say and was rather stunned.

"I'm sorry Corin, but I'm going to have to stick you with a needle again. If I can find what I need," continued Ariella.

"You don't have to look for anything, I have this," said Sunny, taking a small blood-collecting tool out of the pack she typically kept with her.

Ariella took it and drew a sample of Corin's blood quickly and easily. She passed the tool to Sunny who took out the small container of blood. Sunny studied the computer some more and found a thin slot.

"I think it goes in here," she said.

She studied the slot some more, then drew out a knife, dipped the blade in the blood, and stuck it into the slot. The computer analyzed it and to their relief, granted them access.

"Casimir, what has become of you? You're mind has become so sick," said Ariella.

Sunny changed the course of the rockets.

"The rockets' course has been changed, now we fire them," said Sunny triumphantly.

She gave the command for the rockets to fire and they shot off from their secret location and went towards the enemy ships.

"I'm sure they'll be confused; I have to go now," said Sunny and she quickly departed.

Ariella and Coin left as well to join the battle. When they appeared outside, the battle didn't seem to be going as well as their mission had. All of the enemy soldiers in the area, as well as reinforcements from the ships above, had been summoned to Aldura's capitol where the battle was taking place as soon as they noticed there was trouble with their communications system. Now the palace grounds and Verona were overrun with the enemy and there appeared to be little hope of overcoming them. During the battle, the queen had escaped her captors and began making her way to safety, but had not been able to avoid the battle. She was now caught in the fight herself. When Ariella rushed outdoors, the first thing she saw was the queen, fighting desperately with all her loyal guards fallen beside her. She thought of Vala, April, Corin, Amara, and Captain Camara when she saw the fallen protectors. Where was Amara? Then horror seized her as Queen Jasmine Selina was shot before her eyes, making her escape. Ariella rushed to her as she slowly fell. Just as Queen Selina was about to hit the ground, Ariella caught her in her arms. The queen looked up at her with some relief through her fading eyes and managed a smile.

"Go get them, bring us victory; you're Aldura's hope and leader," she said as she collapsed and drifted away.

Ariella grew in all sorts of emotions as she laid down her fallen sovereign and then jumped up and fought fiercely as she was fired upon. The Aldurans were losing the battle, but she would fight hard and make the enemy, especially Casimir, pay dearly. When there seemed to be little hope, the thundering of many hooves was heard in the distance. Ariella looked up and saw a vast mounted army approach with foot soldiers and war machines in its wake. The soldiers' armor and weapons, and the tack and armor of the polished horses, shone brightly. At their head was the commander of Aldura's army and Amara who had gathered them all. Ariella smiled and the Aldurans trapped in the deathly battle cheered. The cavalry rushed into the city, followed by the rest of the army. With their high-tech weapons that had been secretly preserved, the army overcame the enemy. Unfortunately, they had come a moment too late for Ariella, and the last thing she saw was Aldrua's cavalry charging towards the city as she began to collapse on the battlefield...

Over the course of time, in other places on Aldura and in the galaxy, Casimir's armies were defeated until there was little left of them. When the battle for Aldura was won, the dead were taken to be honored and buried; there was victory but also loss. The city, and soon the planet, mourned the loss of their queen. Ariella too, was found by Corin on the battlefield, with no signs of life. Corin was distraught as he checked her for signs of life. He could find no pulse. The two women were placed in caskets full of flowers and taken into the palace before an official memorial could be held for them. The people mourned them both and said they were too young and too beautiful to have died in such a way. Vala was the most grieved of all, other than Corin, for the loss of Ariella. She retreated to within herself, much like she had done when she lost her friends and family years ago, and blamed herself for Ariella's death. She would sit or stand alone. She would not rest, eat, or accept comfort, not even from Dr. Swann. Corin felt much the same as Vala but processed the grief differently than her. He would accept others' offers for comfort whereas Vala denied it. Corin was sitting silently in the room where the two bodies were being kept when Dr. Swann strolled silently in.

"I can't believe she's gone this time. She's always had some trick up her sleeve, often literally. She's always been able to avoid death, why not this time? I should never have left her out of my sight. One moment was all it took," said Corin.

"Why not indeed. Vala is very upset, she's laying way too much blame on herself. I can barely speak to her," replied Dr. Swann. Then he said to himself in a thoughtful tone, "Why not?" As he thought, he perked up just a bit. "Corin, was there anything in her hand, anything hidden in her clothing?"

"Why?"

"Because what if she did survive?"

"But they said there are no life signs, she's dead. I think you of all people could see that for yourself."

"But was there?"

"I didn't see anything in her hands, no."

"But you didn't check pockets or sleeves?"

"No, why would I?"

"Well one thing I've learned is that you never underestimate Ariella Callista Rebel," replied Dr. Swann and he approached Ariella and began searching her.

Corin stood back, watching the doctor with some disbelief. Dr. Swann rolled up the end of one of Ariella's sleeves.

"Oh, yes! Here it is! She does have a trick up her sleeve. Go get a medical team to help, fast!"

"Why?"

"She may not be dead yet!"

Corin was astonished and it took him a few seconds to recover from the shock and fully understand the situation before he rushed out to get help. While Corin left, Dr. Swann briefly made his way to Queen Selina, he wanted to get a closer look at her wound. He examined it closely. It was just as he thought, the wound itself was not necessarily fatal. Corin returned with the requested help and Dr. Swann began ordering them around in order to revive Ariella.

"Corin," he said, and held up some form of a tiny syringe, "search the queen for something like this, her wound doesn't look fatal."

Corin searched and found one and soon both Ariella and Queen Selina were revived. Ariella was startled at first when she awoke. She opened her eyes suddenly and looked around.

"What... am I doing in a casket?!" she asked.

"We... thought...you were dead," answered Corin.

"Thought I was dead? You were going to bury me alive?!" she responded.

"Well, you didn't tell me or anyone that you might use that... what was it?" replied Corin, turning to Dr. Swann for the answer to his question.

"It's a confidential drug that makes its user appear dead and exhibit no life signs. I'm surprised you weren't told about it," Dr. Swann replied to Corin.

"I am. Ariella, as head of your security, and husband not to mention, I should have known this; you should have told me."

"Well, I guess I just never got around to mentioning it. I guess I should have," replied Ariella, though she seemed to care less at the moment.

"Why did you use it? And why didn't you tell anyone?"

"It was a spontaneous decision in the moment. No one was around me, we were loosing the battle, and I wanted to avoid ending up in the hands of

Casimir and his men at all costs. Perhaps I didn't think things through."

When Vala heard the news, she joyfully rushed over. She entered the room where Ariella and Queen Selina had been placed. When she saw Ariella, she ran to her and embraced her tightly.

"I'm so glad to see you alive and well! I thought I had failed, that I'd lost you!" she exclaimed joyfully and relieved.

"She might really have died if it had not been for your husband. She would have been buried or died from lack of the right attention required for the drug she and the queen both used; which, Ariella, was not a wise thing to do without letting anyone know. He discovered their secret and revived them right away. Galen, I owe you my thanks," said Corin.

"Oh, you're so wonderful! And brilliant!" exclaimed Vala, jumping into Galen's arms, throwing hers around him, and kissing him. Galen was startled, but glad.

"I love you so much!" Vala exclaimed cheerfully.

"Well, it's good to see you in high spirits again," said Galen with a smile.

"Corin, can I speak to you a minute?" he asked.

Dr. Swann took Corin off to the side. "In a thorough examination of your wife, I found something else."

"What?" asked Corin, trying not to look worried.

"If you listen close enough in the right spot, you'll hear a second heartbeat."

Corin looked a little confused.

"In other words, she's pregnant," said Dr. Swann. Corin was stunned.

"What! For how long?"

"I would guess about a month. Do you want to listen?" replied Dr. Swann.

Corin still looked as if he couldn't believe it. They returned to the others, and Ariella in particular. Dr. Swann handed a stethoscope to Corin with a bit of a smile.

"What's going on?" asked Ariella.

"Just stay where you are," said Dr. Swann as he guided Corin's hand.

"What is it?" Ariella asked again.

"Shh," replied Corin. He listened, a faint smile appeared on his face and then he handed Dr. Swann his stethoscope back.

"It's true," said Corin, smiling.

"Will one of you tell me what's going on?" asked Ariella.

"I think you have something to tell us; of course, it's up to you. I'm sure you've at least suspected something if not known for sure for a few weeks now, doctor's daughter," answered Dr. Swann.

The others in the room looked at Ariella, Dr. Swann, and Corin for answers with baffled or suspenseful looks.

"I... don't know what to say, I never thought it would happen quite so soon; or at all. Oh, look at your faces, I suppose I might as well tell you. I'm going to have a baby, mine and Corin's."

Everyone joyfully congratulated Ariella and Corin while Ariella managed not to smile much. Right now, she had mixed feelings and as long as she wasn't involved in political speaking, she really didn't want to attract anyone's attention. She wanted her private life to stay private. During the commotion, Vala approached Dr. Swann.

"I'm sorry I ignored you and everyone else when I thought Ariella was dead. I just felt like I had failed in my job of protecting her. I should have been there with her. Besides, she was a close friend," she said.

"I forgive you. You should remember though, that Ariella does not currently hold an office and there is no obligation for you to protect her the way you used to. Besides, our son needed your protection more; I think you did the right thing," he replied.

Vala slightly nodded. "You're right. She is a good friend though. Is there anything I can do to make it up to you?" continued Vala.

"Well...you can let me take you out some night, after all the victory celebrations have finished. It will be just you and me, enjoying a quiet evening," replied Dr. Swann with a smile.

Vala lightly laughed and agreed to it.

The Battle for Aldura

Sunny spent the rest of the day silent and lurking in the shadows.

"You don't say much. Why are you hiding?" asked Dr. Swann when everyone had left the room.

"I prefer to go unnoticed. I'm not supposed to be here, I'm out of my time. I suppose it's just a habit to keep my distance and speak little, I'm afraid of letting the future out, though it's history to me. I know what would have happened in the battle we've won, and I know what it did to the future. You weren't supposed to win this battle, everything should have ended with it and Casimir should have won. The rockets were supposed to destroy much of the surface and population of Aldura and Ariella would have been taken as his captive, and I won't speak of what could have happened after that. From here on, you were supposed to weaken as a civilization until the entire planet was completely wiped out in a mysterious way. Casimir's successors kept the whole thing shrouded in mystery. We have no idea how it happened except that it started here with this battle. But now history's changed. Casimir is part of a bigger scheme and much of their work still remains hidden throughout the past. That's why I've been sent here: to make sure Casimir and his network are defeated and his weapons destroyed. I cannot leave until I am sure this evil will not happen. From here on, I don't know what the future holds and I cannot leave until Casimir is defeated. For the first time, I don't know entirely what to do. No one could foresee what would happen after the battle for Aldura was won. Now it's up to me to decide what to do next."

Dr. Swann was rather surprised at what Sunny told him.

"Well, you're not the only one who wants Casimir defeated, we all want to figure out what to do next, and you're not the only one who needs to decide what to do, we all have a role to play in that decision. I don't think it will be too hard, seeing that Casimir lost just about everything," he said.

"Maybe not to defeat him, but there are still more mysteries at work," said Sunny gravely.

Tears of the Past

A few days after the battle, the capture of Casimir was discussed. No one knew exactly where he was but it was a fact that he and his personal ship had survived. As days passed, the issue of how to deal with Casimir Blade and his scattered armies grew into a large debate and it appeared there would be no resolution for a while. While the discussion of tracking down Casimir continued, Ariella, Corin, Vala, Dr. Swann, Amara, April, and Sunny all gathered together privately to share their own opinions and talk about what they would do next since they planned to soon part and go their separate ways. Verona was still not entirely secure, there were soldiers and secret agents still roaming around, though they were no longer in control of the city. A secret, secure place to talk was essential. With the help of Corin and Amara, Ariella selected the location. The next day, all seven of them gathered at the location to have a private discussion of their own. Little did they know, however, that Ariella, Corin, and Amara had been followed the day before. As they began, they were quietly and quickly ambushed and knocked out. Amara put up a fight, as she had sensed the intruders, but could not avoid the massive fire of tranquilizing ammunition that was shot at the party. When they were all passed out, they were smuggled to a small hidden transport; their captors were some of Casimir Blade's remaining soldiers and agents. When they arrived, the captives were all searched thoroughly, especially Ariella and Sunny, before they were finally brought before Casimir on his remaining space vessel.

"We meet again; and again, I have you captive," said Casimir triumphantly as they were taken before him.

"Casimir Blade, you never cease to give up; even after such a massive defeat. Do you not think we will escape again?" responded Ariella.

"Last time you used me to escape; that was clever and bold of you. But I will make sure that it does not happen again. You will all be locked up but still kept in my sight. And I know what your female guard and pilot is. Such a great and dangerous threat. That is why I have my ally, Vanhi."

Vanhi stepped out of the shadows to show himself. Amara gasped silently.

"You're alive!" she exclaimed, with some relief.

"When you left me to burn, I was saved...by my Lord Casimir. It's obvious he cares for me more than you do," replied Vanhi.

Amara almost cried at the memory. "I'm sorry," she said in a low voice, unable to bring up any other words in her mind to say.

"Lock them up, but keep these three out. I have need of them," commanded Casimir, motioning to Amara, Vala, and Sunny.

His orders were carried out at once. Casimir approached Sunny who held a stern, cold expression on her face.

"This one's the dangerous one, she carries many secrets. There's one in particular, her darkest secret, that I desire. Something that will allow me to change my fate and the fate of many others."

He reached and snapped a chain from her neck. Sunny's jaw dropped; she was stunned.

"How do you know of this?" she asked.

Casimir smiled. "I am resourceful," he replied.

Sunny remembered a scene from the past. In her mind, it all connected, all with this one necklace Casimir had stolen from her. Her emotions got the better of her.

"Don't use it! Please don't use it!" she cried out fearfully and desperately.

"Put her with the others," said Casimir.

Sunny was locked up with the rest as she began to cry and Dr. Swann held her to comfort her. "I shouldn't have taken it, I should have refused it," she said as she wept. She would say no more, however.

Casimir turned to Vala. "Just look at everyone. Consider all that has happened in the last few years, specifically my downfall. And who's to blame? You. Many of these events happened because of you. Because of you, I have been brought to ruin! Now, I will have my revenge! If you could re-live your life again, would you still make the same choices? If you could, would you tell yourself to take another path? To choose differently in certain life choices?"

Casimir fingered the necklace he stole from Sunny as he asked Vala these questions. As Vala got a closer look at Sunny's mysterious necklace, it suddenly seemed remotely familiar. She was silent, then spoke.

"No, I would not!"

"Well then, maybe I can convince you otherwise. Vanhi, start with her! She's the one who's the most dangerous around here!" Casimir pointed to Amara.

Vanhi did not move.

"Well, go on! Destroy her!" commanded Casimir again.

"Sir, she's a Kalipyrah. I cannot honorably oppose or kill her while she remains bound and defenseless," replied Vanhi.

Casimir was annoyed and rather angry, but he didn't want to get into an argument so he obliged Vahni.

"Very well, lose her and give her a blade."

Casimir's orders were followed and Vanhi and Amara began a dual. As they battled, Vanhi and Amara did not look the same. They began to look tired, tired of fighting, and each one was burdened with their own internal battles.

"You're not the same as you were when we last met," said Amara.

"Neither are you," Vanhi replied.

Amara continued. "I was supposed to kill you that last time but I'm glad you're still alive, even though I despise you for what you did. I left you because...I just couldn't bear to kill you myself, but I couldn't let you go free either."

"So you just left? Just like that other time long ago, you left."

"I didn't know what else to do."

"What about the first time, before you despised me?"

"If you wanted something from me, you should have said something. I thought you had given up on me, which would have been the right thing to do under our laws. I felt it would be best if I just left, left the place in which I struggled, no matter how much I still loved it. I felt I was doing us both a favor. But now most of those feelings I once had for you are gone after what you did, murderer."

They carried on, but their minds were bent on other things rather than their battle so eventually, they just stopped.

"What are you doing? Destroy her!" demanded Casimir.

"No more, I'm tired of it. I will not strike her down like I did the others."

Guilt had been building up in Vanhi and he could no longer fight.

"But she's an enemy! She left you to burn!" replied Casimir.

"No," Vanhi responded.

"Well then, if this is the way it's going to be… restrain them both!"

Vanhi and Amara both reacted before Casimir could get his words out but they were heavily fired upon by stun weapons using a low concentration to stun them just enough so that they would only be out for a few minutes - just enough to restrain them. Once Vanhi and Amara were securely restrained, Casimir spoke again.

"If you refuse to obey me, then you will suffer your punishment!" He took a whip with many thongs that had little pieces of metal on the tips and began to use it on Vanhi as Amara watched in fear.

As she watched, in some ways she thought Vanhi deserved this punishment; this was the life he chose to live and the master he chose to serve, and yet, she could not let it go on. In her heart she had already begun to forgive him. He truly seemed to be sorry and broken. He had given himself over to serve Casimir but now seemed to regret his choice and was now facing the consequences. He was beyond help...help from anyone but her. Finally, she made up her mind and would not let it happen any longer. She broke loose with all her might and fury and ran between Casimir and Vanhi, though she was still bound and weak.

"Stop this! That's enough!" she cried.

"Get out of my way or you will receive his punishment!" replied Casimir.

"I will not," protested Amara.

"Then you shall suffer too; but I'm warning you, you will regret this."

Amara still did not move and stared Casimir in the face with her terrible gaze. Casimir proceeded to continue, but first dipped the ends of the whip in a liquid poison. He began to lash Amara who refused to move as Vanhi crawled off to the side. As Casimir whipped Amara, she cried out in intense pain as the whip ripped the clothes and flesh off her back. The others stood by either watching in horror or looking away, feeling powerless to do anything about it. Vanhi watched as his hatred melted away and his guilt grew. He was the cause of this. He deserved this lashing more than anyone else but this beautiful, young, innocent woman had taken it for him.

"Enough!" he cried, jumping up.

His wrath grew and he moved between Amara and Casimir who backed away. Vanhi bent to Amara's side. She was weary, in pain, and the poison was beginning its effect on her. She appeared to not have much life left. Casimir was not finished, however. He pulled himself together.

"See all the pain," he said to Vala as he strolled over to the other captives.

"I will make you suffer for all that you cost me! You had to get involved, and not only that, you dragged your husband and daughter into this too. You brought them and yourself together and you all took steps that brought me to my ruin. Well, do you regret it now?"

He took a small knife from his garments and stabbed Dr. Swann. Vala shrieked and Ariella helped the doctor keep pressure on the wound.

"They will all die here, but you could do something about it. You could change it by letting all this never happen. Take this, and it will take you back in time to where you want," he held up the necklace, "convince yourself not to make those certain choices. I will go along, of course, to make sure you don't play any tricks. What do you say?"

Vala was silent, thinking it all over. All her worst fears were coming true. She could save all her friends and family if she changed her choices. She was tempted to take up his offer, but then began to ask herself how it would effect the rest of the galaxy around her. Right now, Casimir was near destruction and Aldura was safe. They had suffered so much to defeat Casimir and get to this place, what if choosing to change her past changed that? She knew what her answer would be. Dark as her past was, she was not going to put the galaxy at risk and change it, especially if it was Casimir's idea. Then she erupted in fierce anger.

"No!" she rushed at Casimir, aiming for his knife.

Then Vanhi, upset over Amara and having revived some strength, also rushed at him from the other direction despite his pain and weakness.

"Soldiers! To me!" cried Casimir. A few soldiers quickly made their way to Casimir's side. They all quickly joined hands with him and each other.

"This isn't the end yet, Vala Swann, Vala Stella! If I can't have my revenge here, I will have it elsewhere. Perhaps I can still persuade you in another time, or," he smiled, "kill you!"

He hit the center of the necklace and disappeared with his soldiers.

"No! Nooo!" cried Sunny and she burst into tears again.

Vala mused over what just happened. Then, she put it all together. Casimir had gone back in time to seek revenge on her. She realized now what was about to happen and she too began to weep.

Vanhi returned again to Amara. "I'm so sorry, I'm sorry for everything. I can see why you have the right to be angry at me, I deserve death. I'm sorry."

"I forgive you Shaan," Amara replied weakly. She smiled amidst the pain and death that were taking her while Vanhi held her in his arms and began to weep.

"Why is everyone so upset? What's going on?" asked April, somewhat confused over why Vala and Sunny were so grieved, as were some of the others. "Casimir's gone with his soldiers, there's no one left in this room. Vala, why don't you just hurry up and free us so we can get out of here?"

Everyone else suddenly turned to look at April. Their surprised faces showed that they had not given thought to what she had just suggested.

"Well someone had to think of it, it's quite obvious," she replied.

"April Rain, you never lose your head no matter how dark or desperate the situation. I'm glad to have you around," said Ariella.

Vanhi pointed Vala in the direction of a spare key and she took it and freed the rest. Vanhi carried Amara who was fading away and Vala took one of Dr. Swann's arms.

"I'm taking you to Doctor Mirella," said Vala, reviving from her sadness.

"Please not her, I can take care of myself," objected the doctor, a little sarcastically.

"I'm doing it whether you like it or not. I think you should have the help of another doctor, you can't do it well on your own," Vala replied.

They found a transport and made their way back to Verona.

The necklace took Casimir to just the time he wished to get to: a time in Vala's past. He ordered the soldiers who had come with him to hunt down Vala and her family and all her close friends and their families and take them quietly to the secluded spot he had chosen. Casimir had done his research. He knew who they were and where they lived, and it didn't take long for his soldiers to gather them all. The soldiers were equipped with specialized weapons and defenses that would allow them to carry out their tasks with little resistance.

"I have you now, Vala Stella. Watch, and see my revenge," said Casimir when all his victims had been assembled.

He had his mask on and a thick cloud of gas surrounded him which instilled fear in his victims and partially hid him. He ordered his soldiers to slay them all, all except for Vala, and the bitter act was carried out.

"Perhaps I should kill you too," said Casimir, towering over the young, cowering redhead.

She was only fifteen years old. Then behind him, a ship appeared, and it was no ordinary ship. It could become invisible, as it was in this case. Out stepped a man, though Vala was too frightened of Casimir to notice. He stabbed the guards who stood behind Casimir and then came up behind Casimir himself, catching him by surprise.

"Whoever you are, you will not stop me!" Casimir declared and lunged towards Vala who was very frightened.

The man quickly restrained Casimir, took his weapon, and bound him. Realizing his defeat, Casimir tried one last desperate action. "May this scene always haunt you in the future. This is my revenge for your doings, all that you cost me. Maybe you will even think twice next time you have the chance to start a strong relationship, hated child!" As soon as Casimir spoke his words, the man pulled him away, out of the smoke, and into the ship that had brought him here.

Casimir was taken inside the ship and bound securely.

"Now then, what should I do with you Casimir Blade?"

He stepped close to Casimir who had hate in his eyes. Then Casimir gave a mischievous smile.

"Nothing." He drove a small but deadly blade into his captor while a young stowaway, a girl only twelve years old with red hair cut short, watched silently and grieved. As the man began to collapse, he smashed the necklace Casimir wore. The damage made it forever unusable, but it also brought Casimir back to his own time, to his own ship, and he found that all his prisoners, Vanhi included, had escaped; but he was not finished yet.

The stowaway girl on the ship, which was a time ship, crawled out of her hiding place and knelt beside the man who Casimir had stabbed.

"Marcel," she said gently with tears streaming out.

"Sunny, why are you here? It's dangerous."

"I wanted to see what you do and where you go every time you leave," she replied.

"You've seen too much," he said and smiled up at her and gently fondled her. "Don't be sad, you will see me many more times in the future. Do me one last favor and get yourself home. You know how to fly this ship; I've shown you how. Go home and carry on. Don't ever give up."

He collapsed and appeared to have breathed his last. Young Sunny cried over him and then started up the ship and navigated her way home.

Back on Aldura, in the present time, Amara, Vanhi, and Dr. Swann were taken to the nearest hospital in Verona once they landed. It was the same hospital Dr. Mirella worked at. When they arrived, Dr. Mirella, being the first available, put her attention towards Amara first and Dr. Swann shot Vala a brief triumphant look. She just smiled a bit and shrugged in response. She wasn't surprised though, the patients in the most critical condition always came first on Aldura. Dr. Swann tried his best to treat himself, but in the end, had some help and Vanhi too, was looked after. As they recovered, the shadow of Casimir's existence still remained, and they feared he was up to something even now in his defeat. On a quiet day, while Casimir's victims were still recovering, Ariella and Corin went for a walk together along a country road just outside of the city. With no warning, they were both knocked on their heads and fell down with a sudden loss of consciousness.

When Corin awoke, it was dark outside, and he found himself in Dr. Swann and Vala's Alduran cottage. Vala walked in.

"You're awake," she said.

"Where's Ariella?" asked Corin. Vala had a rather grave look.

"I was hoping you might have an idea," she replied.

"Well then I have to find her," said Corin, getting up.

Vala put up her hand in a 'stop' gesture. "Not so fast," she said, "Sit down."

Corin reluctantly did as told.

"Galen, he's awake but is in a hurry to go search for Ariella!" she called out.

Dr. Swann came from another room with some of his instruments.

"Please let me go, I have to find her," said Corin.

"I'd prefer that you stay here for a while so we can make sure you're all right. We can send someone else after her," answered Dr. Swann, checking Corin over.

"I will not stay! She could be in danger, especially if... if Casimir has her. I bet he's still up to mischief. If he's taken her, he's going to get it from me!"

"Stay just a little longer," protested Dr. Swann, "you've witnessed how dangerous it is trying to go up against him."

"No, I'd rather not. I just hope she has one of her secret devises with her - wait, her tracker! Vala, do you still have your detector?"

"Yes, yes I do," she replied.

"Go get it!" urged Corin.

Vala reluctantly went to where she kept all her things from her past life as a handmaid and found the detector. She took it out and brought it to Corin. He took it and quickly searched for Ariella's signal.

"I found it! But it's not coming from Aldura, it's... that's weird... it's coming from some sort of man-made asteroid nearby," said Corin.

"So, you're going there then?" asked Vala.

"Yes, right now," he replied.

"Well then, I'm going too," said Vala.

"You're what?" questioned Dr. Swann.

"My friend is out there, and I don't want Corin going by himself. I'm going," Vala replied.

"Dr. Swann would have gone with her this time but he was in no condition with his wound still recovering. Is there anything I can say or do to change your mind?" he said, concerned for her safety.

"No," Vala replied.

"I didn't think so. You know, every time you run off after her, something happens and then you lament your life. But you still continue to do it."

"I...know...but I can never rest as long as our enemy is out there and my friend is in danger."

"Then be careful, please. Make it a short trip, I don't want this to be the last time we see each other. I can't believe I'm letting you go," said Dr. Swann.

Vala and Galen embraced each other and then Vala departed and followed Corin. As they walked down the street to Corin's ship, Sunny noticed them.

"Where are you going?" she asked.

"Sunny, I'd rather you go home," said Vala.

"To which home? I still haven't moved into this time era yet and won't until I'm sure Casimir Blade is defeated entirely; and I have no way of getting back to my future home," she said.

"Don't get smart with me. We're going to find Ariella. It could be dangerous, why don't you go and help your father," said Vala.

Sunny was conflicted. Her mother wished for her to stay and she knew she was supposed follow orders; but she felt she was perfectly capable of going on a dangerous trip and wanted to go with, so she hesitated. Then Corin told her to wait a moment as he drew Vala aside.

"There's clearly something special about her and if we are going to find ourselves facing Casimir, she may be useful. Besides, she can't rest until she's accomplished what she came here for."

Vala was hesitant. "Alright, I'll let her come. Sunny, you can come with us. I'll let your father know you're coming," she said.

They walked off together and boarded Corin's ship, then took off and followed Ariella's signal.

Ariella awoke to find herself in chains and in a strange place. It looked empty. Then, she saw him: her rival and enemy.

"You've come around," he said, turning to her.

"Come close enough and I will kill you," said Ariella with a bold challenging expression.

"Kill me? How?" asked Casimir, amused.

"Why don't you come find out?" replied Ariella.

Casimir laughed. "You are very spirited and fearless. You never play nice, do you? Here, at last, I have you as a trophy, I think having your stubborn, spirited attitude around will be very amusing. I still have plans and more secrets for taking back all I have worked to obtain. I still have the capability to destroy those who stand in my way. Soon I will have my power back and in the destruction I pour out, your husband will die, and you will finally be free to become my wife. You've managed to slip out of my grip so many times before but now I have you, with no friends to help you escape, and I will make sure you do not escape again."

"Try what you will, you will never win. I will make sure of that. I will fight you and continue to fight you until I emerge victorious."

"It's true, you are very tough to subdue. You submit to no one except those whom you choose to submit to. Your head is hard, and it makes me wonder... is your brain damaged in any way? Because that gas that was released in the last battle for Aldura was supposed to affect EVERYONE; but it didn't, did it? It had no effect on you, at least no visible effect. You must really be tough indeed, but it will be my lifelong pleasure to finally break you and make even you obey my wishes. Many years ago, I was close to having you, but then he showed up and took you: that snooping, lonely fortune hunter and his pet."

Ariella broke in, "well, having me captured certainly wasn't going to win me over to your side if that's what you thought."

"Oh, but it wasn't supposed to be like that. Those ships and soldiers bore an unknown emblem and colors for a reason, though all my soldiers and fleets would soon bear them as well. They were supposed to be an unknown faction and that's what everyone thought at first. They were supposed to capture you and I was supposed to save you and thus gain your trust and approval of me. But he had to make his escape and find you first. Not only did he know too much, he also stole you from me and made off."

"You talk as if you and I had been engaged, which we certainly were not. I was only using you by pretending to consider your proposal. I never intended to accept; it was just business. I made a choice. I could have left Corin... but I didn't, I couldn't," replied Ariella.

They maintained silence for a while and then Casimir spoke again.

"I would have finally gotten rid of him. There was some poison hidden in your flat. It was intended for your husband, who wasn't your husband at the time. I knew your plans. I knew he was going to be alone that night. He was supposed to poison himself and then die quietly with no one around. But that maid of yours had to go and take the poison herself in front of others, which resulted in a marriage that brought that girl into the universe, who brought about my ruin. Oh yes, you and your friends are the ones who destroyed most of what I had. You all are to blame for my ruin! From now on I will show absolutely no mercy. The next time I come across any of your friends or that man you married, there will be no more show. I will kill them right away!"

Casimir finally had his say and left Ariella while he went to work on another one of his schemes.

The following day, Casimir appeared to Ariella again.

"I missed your company working yesterday, but now my weapons of destruction are complete. Watch and see the galaxy submit to my rule or be destroyed," he said as he approached Ariella who remained silent. "Don't you have something to say?" asked Casimir.

"I do!" said a voice approaching. "Stop where you are! Don't touch her!"

Ariella lit up; it was Corin. He had come to rescue her.

"You again, always spoiling my plans," said Casimir.

Corin stepped over to Ariella. "Here, get yourself free," he said, handing her a pin.

"Never mind that," said Ariella, holding up her hands which were now free of the chains.

Corin was astonished "How did you..." then he smiled. "I love you."

Ariella rushed to his side and uncharacteristically clung to him tightly like a desperate princess who had just been saved.

"It took hours to get free, you're late," she said, but she was very glad and relieved to see him and would not let go.

"I have you now!" continued Corin, addressing Casimir. "If you make an offensive move in any way, I will shoot!"

Casimir slowly backed a few steps.

"That's far enough! Now stay where you are!" demanded Corin.

"Very well, I'll stay, I won't make an offensive move... just this!"

Casimir suddenly shot up out of reach to the surface of the asteroid on an elevator platform that was hidden and normally appeared to be just part of the floor.

"He's escaped again!" exclaimed Ariella.

"Don't worry, Vala and Sunny are up there, they'll take care of him," replied Corin.

"I'm so glad and relieved that you came. I was frightened, really frightened. I didn't know what would happen. I didn't show Casimir any fear of course, but I was still desperate. You see, I need you. I'm so happy to have you in my life."

She was still clinging to Corin where right now, she felt safest. Then she spoke up with urgency in her voice "Casimir is still up to something."

"I saw some rockets on a platform nearby, I'm sure they're his," said Corin.

"Well then, what are we waiting for?" continued Ariella.

Corin smiled a bit. "Nothing, let's go."

He and Ariella rushed out together and took Corin's ship over to the platform where they busied themselves by deactivating and taking apart the rockets.

Vala and Sunny reached the surface of the asteroid where one last rocket of Casimir's was kept. As they approached it, they saw Casimir who had just reached the surface himself.

"Well met again, mother and daughter. Prepare to die, I show you no mercy this time," he said.

"It's over Blade, surrender now or be destroyed," said Sunny, pointing a small firearm at him.

"This rocket is a special one, that's why it's here. If you shoot me, I will signal the rocket to launch as I fall."

"But you can't be trusted, you may launch it anyway whether I shoot you or not. Just know that you will not get away; not this time," replied Sunny.

"I will not be defeated by a girl and if you should bring me down, that planet Aldura will fall with me," replied Casimir.

Sunny glared at Casimir. Then Vala's face became grave and sad as she came to realize their situation. Unless he was bluffing, which she doubted this time, it was inevitable that destruction was going to happen regardless of whether they moved against Casimir or not. Either Aldura was going to be destroyed, or the rocket, and if the rocket was destroyed, everyone on the asteroid would be too. She looked Sunny in the eyes who turned to face her. Sunny read Vala's expression and gravely nodded as Vala took out her weapon, there was no other choice. She took out her communicator and contacted Galen. Galen acknowledged her right away and with a sad but loving expression, she gave him her message.

"I'm sorry. I love you," she said through a few tears.

Then she quickly pulled the trigger of her weapon which was aimed at Casimir's rocket. The blast was so powerful that the whole asteroid burst into pieces and was no more. Ariella and Corin watched from the nearby platform in shock and then sorrow when they realized Vala and Sunny had been in the middle of the explosion.

"Such a great, horrible price for the defeat of Casimir Blade. Why did it have to be Vala and her young daughter?" cried Ariella.

Dr. Swann was heartbroken after he contacted Corin to learn the truth. Once he heard the news, he made his way to the platform in space and to Corin's ship as soon as he could. When he arrived, he joined Corin and Ariella in their search for the bodies, if they were still intact.

After some searching, Corin, Ariella, and Dr. Swann found the bodies of Vala and Sunny, which appeared to be quite well-preserved despite the explosion. Surprisingly, their respirators and space suits also remained intact. They took the two corpses and carried them into Corin's ship. Casimir's body was also found and was more broken than Vala's and Sunny's. Despite the others wanting to leave Casimir, Ariella insisted they take his body too. She felt uncomfortable leaving it out there alone. The bodies were taken and laid in Corin's ship, and the respirators were removed. As Dr. Swann laid Vala down, he thought he noticed weak vital signs. He examined her closer with little hope but to his relief, found that she was still alive but in a coma resulting from a concussion. Sunny was alive too, but also comatose. Even when Vala had shot the rocket, Sunny still had a surprise that saved them. She had used a shield from the future just in time to save her and Vala from death. Casimir too, was found to be alive but was also unconscious and his injuries were more severe and numerous than Vala's and Sunny's.

"He can die for all I care, the galaxy's suffered enough because of him," said Corin.

Dr. Swann replied. "He is responsible for the war and deaths and sufferings of many; and he is very dangerous and crafty, but we must still show compassion towards him in his current state, and I will do my job to heal him."

The three victims were taken to the hospital as fast as they could be and once they arrived, Dr. Swann insisted on treating his wife. In the end, they were all cured, though it would take them some time to recover, especially Casimir who was always kept under heavy guard. As Sunny was brought to the hospital, a young man came to find out how she was doing, and when she was finally conscious, he went to see her.

"Marcel, you came back," said Sunny in a delighted voice.

"I decided it was about time I came to check on you. I heard what happened, I'm glad to see you alive," he said. Then he continued. "How have things been?" he asked Sunny.

"Well, not everything turned out as I expected. It was different. But Aldura is such a beautiful, free place. I wonder how the rest of time has been affected," she replied.

"Well, you'll soon be able to see," said Marcel, hiding any kind of expression. "I'm glad you like it here since from now on you'll have to live here."

"I still feel out of place."

"You won't for long, though you'll always have memories of the future and of Aldura's past that you really should be too young to remember."

"What about you? Will I see you again?" asked Sunny, remembering what she saw about three years ago in her timeline.

"You will. I'm going to stay in this time, though I will take some trips, until I'm called for another task."

"Have you met my parents? Do they know who you are?" asked Sunny.

"I did. I just saw your mother today now that she's awake, and you know me. You know that I don't tell anyone my life's story, but I did tell them what I thought they should know."

"Do you think my foster family has changed?" Sunny suddenly asked.

"Well, you'll be able to find that out yourself once you're healed and ready for travel. I think you'll find not everything has changed. You do know what lies before you on that trip?"

"Yes...goodbye. Forever I suppose?"

Marcel sighed. "As far as I know, yes. There will be no more time traveling except for certain circumstances."

"How can I be made to do this? To be raised in one time with one family and then suddenly be taken to another time and another family? It's like living one life and dying, and then living a second new and different life. Can't you take me for visits?"

"I'm afraid not."

"Then how can I go on?"

"I'll help you; I'll be there for you. You can share all your memories and thoughts of your past with me."

Sunny took Marcel's hand.

"It's always a pleasure to be your friend and to watch over you," said Marcel.

As far as Sunny could remember, Marcel had always been around. He had guided her, taught her, and looked out for her. He was different from the others. He traveled to many places, places she knew not where. Sometimes he would appear young and other times older, but never as young as her. He was mysterious and exciting, and she loved him as a brother, a friend, and now, perhaps as something more.

Amara had recovered well, though she would bear the scars she received for the rest of her life, as would Vanhi.

"You know you've done an act that condemns you to death by our laws," said Amara to Vanhi.

"I know. And I'll pay the price, whatever it is," he replied.

"And you also know that though I am an Alduran citizen, I am also still a Kairahn and as a soldier and keeper of the Kairahn laws, it is my duty to keep you in custody until, though it's rather unlikely, I come across enough of the right Kairahns to carry out your sentence and likely...your execution," she said with difficulty speaking the last words.

"Amara, you hold to the rules to the end. But I suppose it's not an easy thing to do sometimes. I honor you in that you stay strong where I fell short." He paused, "But I know the laws too. It sounds like you're going to have to keep me in your sight for who knows how long."

"Yes...I guess it does. Perhaps we got our wish after all," said Amara, a small smile forming on her face.

"Well, that will make it easier for both of us, since I have no desire to part from you," finished Vanhi.

Aldura was finally safe and Casimir was defeated. The war was coming to an end, though the Galactic Union had much cleaning up to do. Thankfully, Aldura was now independent and had less work to be involved in. Ariella and her friends were safe, though the years of war had taken a toll on them. Now that they were confident their planet was safe, it was time for them to step down and take a break, but for some of them it wasn't as easy as they anticipated. This had been their life and all they knew for so long. No one else around them could fully understand what they had been through. They received honor and recognition, but they had paid a high price. They had broken bodies and broken lives that might never be fully restored.

When Vala and Sunny were healed, the queen wished to host a dance in their honor. Both mother and daughter refused to be recognized, however. Vala felt uncomfortable being the special guest, being publicly highlighted in front of others, especially when there were more people who deserved the recognition than just her. Sunny would not go at all. To the queen's invitation, she responded, "All you know is that I'm a mysterious girl who showed up in a time of great need. I only share my identity with those who need to know and with respect, Queen Selina, you do not need to know who I am; just that the fate of your planet, and the galaxy, has changed and for the better."

So a victory dance was held and per Vala's wish, she was not publicly highlighted but instead, all the victors were celebrated. The dance hall was beautifully decorated, and the guests wore many colorful and beautifully designed clothes, many of which included fresh flowers. As the night went on, a masked couple suddenly appeared to join the dancing. It was Sunny and Marcel. Sunny had decided to join after all but wanted to stay secret, as did Marcel, so they arrived late with beautiful intricate masks. Sunny was not wearing black this time; she was wearing a beautiful yellow ballgown that was finely decorated, and Marcel was dressed to match her. Some guessed who they might be while others had no idea. Only Dr. Swann, Vala, and the other four knew who the couple behind the masks really were. About halfway through the night, Dr. Swann requested a song to dance with Vala. The rest of the dancers stood back as he led Vala to the center of the floor with a smile on his face.

"Please, not like this," whispered Vala, blushing a bit.

"Come on, show them your skill. You're special, this dance is for you, and if you're not going to let anyone else honor you then I will; and don't think you're going to get out of this," replied Dr. Swann, giving Vala a cunning smile.

Vala smiled and blushed some more. "No," she lightly and quietly laughed with slight embarrassment, knowing she was not going to get out of it.

She buried her face in her husband's shoulder as if to hide while they began to dance and everyone else circled around them in a jam circle fashion and finally joined in towards the end of the song. When the night was finally drawing to its close, Sunny and Marcel decided it was time to leave. They would depart from the current time in the morning and told Vala and Dr. Swann of their plans. Before they left, however, Dr. Swann wished to share one last dance with his daughter before they were separated again for many years. So, Sunny danced her last dance with her father and then departed to prepare for the morning with Marcel to escort her.

The next morning, Sunny and Marcel prepared to leave. They were accompanied by Dr. Swann and Vala and went to Verona's main harbor on the sea where ships brought goods from across Aldura's oceans. A small ship would take Marcel and Sunny to a secret island where Marcel's time ship was kept hidden. As they stood at the harbor, they said their last goodbyes.

"I suppose we'll have to wait a long time," said Vala.

"About thirteen years," said Marcel, "Though for us it will just be a trip to say goodbye to Sunny's foster family and then we'll come back here, just as we are now," he continued.

"It's such a long time. I wish we could just keep her," said Vala.

"I think things will work out best if she lives as a fifteen-year-old in the time that she's really supposed to be fifteen," Marcel replied.

"I suppose so, but still..." replied Vala.

The ship was finally ready for boarding and Sunny hugged her parents goodbye and stepped aboard with Marcel, then the ship began to sail off.

"That's the second time I've watched him take her away, only this time I'll have to wait much longer for her to return," said Vala as she and Dr. Swann stood together, watching the ship sail off.

They stayed there until they could see the ship no more.

"Well, we still have a son to care for," Vala said, and they finally left the harbor to return home. They had a new life to return to. A life of peace and rest.

Epilogue

Some time after the victory ball, Ariella stopped by to see Vala. She and Corin were preparing to transition into a new life as well as Galen and Vala and the others, but had not yet thought about what it would look like. This was the first time in years they seemed to have the luxury to dream about it.

"How are you doing after all this? Honestly?" asked Ariella. "Now that you're free to settle down and do something different with your life?"

Vala pondered her answer before giving it. "Honestly... I don't know. It's hard to believe it's all over. Every time I think it is, something else happens and I end up running back into the battlefield. I'm grateful for rest and a home and a family, but I'm still a little afraid. And... time has passed, and good things have come... but I'm still wrestling with the pain of loss. I lost my family and childhood friends, I lost my first child – at least, I'll have to go many years without her – I almost lost my husband a few times, and I've been pretty beat up myself. I don't know if all of the wounds will ever fully heal."

Ariella looked at her with empathy. She had experienced loss as well, but nothing compared to Vala. "I'm so sorry. I really am. I wish there was something more I could do. If only I had insisted you stay out of my battles long ago."

"Don't blame yourself. You had no idea what would happen, and remember, you gave me a choice. I didn't have to do what I did," Vala paused and seemed to be meditating on something. "I feel like I'm responsible for destroying my family's lives, even Galen's."

"Vala..." Ariella began but then stopped.

She didn't know what she could say to truly make Vala feel better. Vala needed something more, something deeper than what comfort Ariella could offer. She needed something that could go into the depths of her soul and comfort her...or, a new heart. Then suddenly, she remembered hers' and Corin's experience in the Garden.

"Vala, why don't we take a trip to the Garden?"

"The Garden?" asked Vala.

It was certainly a relaxing place, but it was quite far.

Epilogue

"Well, that sounds like a nice idea. It would be a good place to visit for a mini vacation...do you want to plan a trip there?"

"I'm saying we should get up and go now."

"Right now?"

"Yes. Remember that miraculous healing of Corin's mind?"

"Yes, I do," said Vala.

"Well, maybe you'll be able to experience something like that."

Vala thought about it. That would be nice, but could something like that really happen to her? After all she'd been through, it seemed unlikely that she would ever be able to find complete healing.

"Well, maybe it can work on some things I'm dealing with, but I don't think I can ever be healed of my past – it's already happened."

"Well, anything is better than nothing. And what's the harm in trying? The least you'll get out of it is a trip to a place of peace and rest."

"Alright," Vala agreed.

"Great. I'll arrange something with Corin and we can go when you're ready. Invite Galen to come too... in fact, I think Amara and April should come," said Ariella. Vala went inside to talk to Dr. Swann about the visit while Ariella returned to her family's home in Verona to speak to Corin and to get in touch with Amara and April and invite them to come as well.

The next day, Corin landed the ship carrying the former senator of Aldura and all her companions, with Vahni who was to stay with Amara, at the entrance to the Garden. They exited the ship and stood at the entrance, taking in the wonderful atmosphere.

"Come on," said Ariella, beckoning the others to follow as she passed through the Garden's entrance, Corin closely following her.

The others slowly began to walk after her, a little skeptical, but full of awe over the place. Ariella guided them to the center of the Garden as they continued to look all around, taking in the heavenly sights and sounds. It was too perfect to be real, and yet they couldn't deny it was. They approached the spring and Ariella walked right up to it. There was no one there, but she looked around in expectancy.

"What are you looking for?" asked April.

"There was a healer who appeared to us last time, in this same place," replied Ariella.

The others exchanged confused looks.

"I don't know where you are, I don't know your real name, but please come, we need you, Healer," said Ariella.

She paused and disappointment began to creep on her face when she saw that nothing seemed to be happening. Then, a gentle breeze blew into the clearing from the place they had entered from. They all turned around to look and there was the man, the same man who Corin and Ariella had seen last time.

Epilogue

He approached them in shining white robes, if they could even be described as robes. It was as if he was clothed in light.

"You asked for my help," he said.

"Yes," said Ariella.

The man paused and stood in front of them, looking each one in the eye with his gentle, loving, and fiery gaze. "I'm glad you're here," he said, with a warm, compassionate smile. Then he strolled over to Vala.

"Vala Stella, now Vala Swann, you're the reason you are all here. Your friend wanted you to find rest and healing." He took her hand and led her a few steps from the others. "Dear Vala, you've experienced so much pain throughout your life with little rest and seemingly little reward for it. It's more than you should ever have had to face at your age. But know that you will receive a rich reward and you will find rest and peace in this new season of life."

Vala looked at him as a few tears trickled from her eyes. He continued to speak to her

"You are harboring pain in your soul and you've believed it can never be healed. It has caused you to stay in bondage and it steals your joy. You do not have to stay in bondage, I'm here to help you break free. You are holding bitterness against the one who caused so much of your pain, and you are holding bitterness against yourself. Will you release the one who hurt you?"

Vala suddenly looked up at him, almost offended. "Will I what? You're asking me to release him? After everything he did? It was wrong of him, and I'm sure he knows it. He doesn't deserve forgiveness so why should I give it to him?"

The man maintained his calm, gentle expression, but the fire in his eyes seemed to grow a little. It was the face of love; just pure love. "I didn't say he deserved it, but are you going to let what he did to you keep you in bondage or do you want to release yourself from everything he did to you, and from the debt he owes you? Do you choose to hold on to it and let his debts against you continue to torment you or do you want to let go and be free of it all forever? And no doubt you owe debts to others as well. Do you want your debts to be paid and forgotten?"

Vala paused to consider those words. She felt something bubbling up, a conviction to release Casimir, despite what he had done. It didn't make sense, but she felt compelled to forgive. She wrestled with her thoughts a little and then spoke out. "I forgive Casimir for all he's done to me, and I release him from any pain and bitterness in my heart."

The man looked at her with a compassionate smile. "Now what about yourself? You've been holding guilt and unforgiveness for yourself too."

Vala paused again. She had trouble wrapping her head around his question. Forgive herself? That didn't sound like a very humble thing to do. He spoke again.

Epilogue

"Do you release yourself from all the harm you've caused, or believed you've caused?"

Once again, Vala fought the idea of forgiving, but she gave in. "Vala Swann, I forgive you for everything you've done that might have hurt me and others," she said.

Then the man took her hands and suddenly, she felt a warm peace rise up inside her heart. The pain and bitterness was breaking off. Then joy and lightness began to replace it and she began to laugh out loud in pure joy. The man touched her heart and all the traces of sorrow and bitterness completely dissipated. It felt as if her old heart had vanished and a brand new, light one had replaced it. She was overcome by joy and freedom. She could also feel warmth around her leg and arm that had been broken during her previous adventures. She could feel bones, tendons, ligaments, and muscles moving back into perfect alignment and her limbs felt brand new. It was all too wonderful to be real, and yet the change was clear. She began to cry but this time, it was not tears of sadness, it was tears of relief. The man released her and she sat on the soft green ground, weeping and laughing at the same time. Then the man stepped over to Amara and Vahni and took both of their hands.

"You have done well to forgive each other, and your relationship is already being healed as a result," he said. "In the end, you were faithful to each other despite the sacrifices you've had to make and I honor that. Would you like your bodies to be whole once again?"

They stared at him, but after witnessing Vala's healing, they believed it could happen to them too. Amara nodded. The man touched their shoulders. They both felt a warm peace and then a cooling sensation crept over their old wounds. Amara felt it on her back where she had scars from the poisoned whip and Vahni felt it wherever he had received not just whip lashes, but also where he had been burned by the fire after his first battle with Amara. Their skin was being made new right before their eyes.

The man continued on. "You were both treated unfairly in your youth. You did well to not allow your feelings to control your actions, but you were denied the space to express and discuss your emotions in a healthy way. You were pushed into an emotionless life which is not how you were designed to live and it has caused you much pain and confusion. I want to free you from that too." He touched their heads and it was as if a fresh breeze and many colors blew into their hearts and minds. They felt joy and peace, comfort, and so many emotions bubbled up and these emotions felt deep and real. Amara and Vahni began to weep as their emotions and pain from the past were healed and made new. The world around them looked more colorful than it ever had before.

"And one more thing," said the man, turning to face them, "that unique gift you were born with: it's

Epilogue

not a curse that needs to be locked away in the dark. It's not an accident that you were born that way. It was given to you for a reason, and I want to invite you to explore how it can be used for good. If you should ever need help, just ask and you will find it."

Then the man continued on to Dr. Swann. "Galen, you got pulled into many battles and a lifestyle you never wished for, and never dreamed you'd have. But you remained faithful and supportive of your wife and your friends. You've also experienced much loss and grief, and you've had to support your wife in her moments of pain, often not receiving any support yourself. You've had to walk through so much and yet, perhaps, you've received the least amount of honor and recognition of anyone here. For that, you will also receive rest and a huge reward along with your wife." He paused and looked into Galen's eyes. "Your eyes, too, have never been the same since your injury, but you've been afraid to acknowledge it. You've been worried about what might happen to you and your life. You've been concerned that they may get worse. I say to you that they will not get worse, and you will no longer have to live with that fear." He placed his hand over Galen's eyes and when he removed it, Galen could see better than he ever had in his life. His vision was crystal clear.

The man continued. "April," He said, coming to face her. You may feel that no one sees you or recognizes your value. You may not have walked through some of the same sufferings that the others have, but that doesn't make you less valuable. You played an integral part in the success of every mission you were a part of. You were the constant, optimistic one who kept everyone together when their worlds were falling apart. Like your name, you were the refreshing rain in a dry desert. You have seen much for a young person, but you don't have to lose your joy over any of it. I bless you to live a free, joy-filled life with no limits." After he spoke, her heart grew light and cheery and she began to smile and laugh.

"Corin," said the man, moving to Corin. "You have remained strong, and you will continue to have strength. You will receive rest and peace too. I know there is more in your heart as well. More burdens from the past. You may have lost your mother at an early age and did not receive everything that you needed from your father, but know that you are loved and that you are valuable. You are not just trash from the streets, you are not the low-life spawn of a pirate, you are a prince among men."

Finally, the man stopped at Ariella. "Ariella Callista Rebel. You possess a cold heart because others did not always treat you well. You felt as though you had to fight for your safety and significance. You have been harboring some bitterness in your soul. Do you forgive all those who hurt you and tried to take advantage of you?"

Epilogue

Ariella wrestled with the idea of forgiveness. Her proud heart did not want to yield. But she couldn't deny that amazing things had happened to the others when they chose to forgive. "Help me to forgive," she finally said. The man touched her heart and suddenly, she felt it – a genuine forgiveness grew in her heart. "I forgive them," she said. "I release them from all the harm they caused me."

He touched her again and a wonderful warm feeling came over her. It was a release from pressure and a new softness in her heart. "Be free to enjoy your relationships to the full," he said.

Ariella began to melt to the ground, crying, as a beautiful, wonderful transformation took place inside her. The pain and the hardness were leaving her. The world suddenly seemed brighter, and more beautiful, and still. She lay down in the grass and lay for some time, soaking in the atmosphere of the garden around her.

When their hearts and minds were full, they left the Garden and returned to Verona, in a joyful, hopeful state. Just a day later, Queen Selina requested that Dr. Swann and Vala come to see her at the palace.

"We all want to thank you for all you've done in this war and for Aldura's freedom and safety," she began. "A special committee has decided they want to gift you with the ownership of Capitol Haven, and it would be staffed by the palace since there's no way you can keep up the whole place on your own. I know it's not something you will lightly accept, but we want you to have it. Think about what else you could do with it besides living there. Imagine how your child, or children, would enjoy growing up there."

Vala was taken aback, Capitol Haven was a three-story historical mansion from one of Aldura's golden eras that for years had been unused before it came into the hands of the Alduran government. Even so, it was still little used and was more of a historical site.

"You know I couldn't do it," replied Vala.

"Well, please don't give up on it so soon. Think about it, maybe your mind will change," replied the queen.

When Casimir was finally healed, a trial was held for him at the union's capitol. Even Steelar-Romlin took part in the trial, for he had defied their authority with his acts. Representatives from many planets gathered to decide what to do with Casimir. Ariella was chosen to represent Aldura since no one knew better than her or experienced much more than she of Casimir's acts. After much discussion, the decision of whether to execute Casimir or imprison him for life came down to Ariella: the one who had not yet decided. Her decision would affect the outcome of the trial. Most were sure she would choose to have his life terminated after all she had been through. She took a while to think it over and discuss it with the people she represented and finally came to a decision. He would be imprisoned

Epilogue

for life on Steelar-Romlin. Her choice surprised many, and none more than Casimir himself. When she was asked why she made her choice, she answered, "He is clearly guilty and the choices he made are deserving of death. However, there may be a story behind how he became who he is, and I think he should be given an opportunity to find restoration for his brokenness. And quite simply, I've released him from all the harm he's done to me. He owes me nothing."

After some thought and some persuasion from those closest to her, with Galen agreeing to whatever decision she chose to make, Vala finally agreed she would accept the gift of Capitol Haven. She reasoned that it would be a wonderful place for guests to enjoy and for her children to grow up in; and so she and Dr. Swann became the new owners of Capitol Haven. They settled down in Verona with their son, and Dr. Swann chose to work in the emergency department of Verona's largest hospital, the same one where Dr. Mirella worked. Capitol Haven was a large house. Through the main entrance, it had a vestibule with closets for guest's coats and accessories on the left. On the right of the entrance, there was a door to the large ballroom, and straight ahead was a hall with two large columns of a rare, polished stone, and stairs on either side. The hall opened to three hallways, one that went straight back, one that went left, and one that went right. There was also a second set of double doors that opened to the ballroom from the hall. The ballroom had large windows on one side, an area with counters where refreshments could be served, and a bandstand for live performances. In addition to the ballroom, the right side of the house on the ground level held a library, a lounge, and a conservatory. The left side had a spa with an indoor pool, a large public dining room, a kitchen, and even a small theatre with a small stage that could be used for performances. The hallway that went straight back passed by utility and storage rooms and went out to the back where there was a porch with columns, a deck, a large pool with a fountain, and some sand with tropical trees from Florina. In the back on the left side was also an outdoor kitchen and a small, heated pool, a garden and garage, and a path that led to a glass and marble ice skating rink. From the second story inside and up the stairs, they could look down at the hall below. On the second floor, there was a large, more public parlor. There was also a recreation and game room, a music room, and a private sitting room. Through several hallways, a gym, art and sewing room, study room, office, private dining, and breakfast rooms, and guest rooms could be accessed. The third story included another open area, the master bedroom, six other private rooms, one of which was used as a playroom, and a small indoor archery range. On the back of the house outside, the third and second stories had columned porches with tables, chairs, and benches. On the third story, on the front, there was also a large

Epilogue

open veranda with no cover. From the second story, a waterfall fell down into the pool which had lights in the floor that would light up at night. The indoor pool and outdoor pool were connected by an underwater passage that went under the house. In the back on the right side of the house, there was a large garden with various plants, a little colonnade with vines growing on it, benches, chairs and tables, a fountain, and a waterfall. Next to the garden, there was a gazebo and a covered patio with a fire pit. On the side next to the covered patio, there was a larger open patio. The house also included many acres of land, an open riding arena, a covered riding arena with jumps, a barn, a pasture, and various paddocks. There was also an outdoor archery range, a cross-country course, and a field archery course. Dr. Swann and Vala were very generous with their estate and money, and were also very smart with it, choosing not to spend it on lavish things. They enjoyed giving money to those who needed it and found that they always had more than they needed themselves. After the gift of the house, because of their continued service to the community, they were awarded the honorary title of Lord and Lady of Capitol Haven.

As time passed, they had four more daughters: Lynn, who looked like her mother, Ella and Auralia who both had brown hair, and Clair who had dark hair like her brother and father. Although they spent most of their time at Capitol Haven, they would often visit a smaller home they owned in Florina. Ariella's and Corin's first child was a beautiful blonde, blue eyed girl who grew to look very much like her mother. She was named Mariah. After her, two boys - Colt and Rian - were born and last came another girl, Marie, who looked similar to her sister but kept her hair in curls. After Mariah was born, Ariella and Corin took a break from their normal life to try doing something new. They were encouraged to pursue dancing and ice dancing competitively and finally agreed to do it. It was a refreshing break for the two of them and with constant training, they danced so well that they were invited to compete for Aldura at various inter-galactic events. After this break, however, Ariella continued her political career as an Alduran ambassador, but only for a few years before deciding to run for offices within Aldura. Eventually, she would serve as the queen of Aldura for two terms. Even afterward, she was still active in politics and would occasionally travel the galaxy. Corin continued to act as Ariella's head of security while also taking on the responsibilities of a husband and father. April too, continued her role as Ariella's handmaid and bodyguard. Amara and Vahni settled down on Aldura and were both granted high-level positions in Aldura's military and police force. Amara and Vanhi eventually were married and had a family of their own and Amara, like Vala and Ariella, chose to keep her children at home and teach them herself. It was something very appealing to her given

Epilogue

the experience of her childhood. Vala would not be able to continue her career as Ariella's handmaid and guard as she once had; her responsibilities now lay with her family and Capitol Haven. In some ways, she was sad and missed the job she had grown to love, but she had a wonderful life and continued to keep a strong relationship with Ariella. The Swann and Rebel families remained close, and their children became very close friends with each other. Vala chose to teach her children at home, herself, and even Dr. Swann contributed to their learning of science and mathematics. Vala also enjoyed helping the community and various organizations with her time and money and she would frequently host events at Capitol Haven. She always made sure her children were well-mannered and were educated in the highest standards of Alduran court etiquette. She taught them to work hard, enjoy life, and to never take their position at Capitol Haven for granted.

As life continued, Sunny's fifteenth birthday finally came and passed by. Vala and Dr. Swann began to anticipate her return. Finally, at the end of the year, Marcel and Sunny returned. They were still the same as they had been when they left. They hadn't changed a bit while everyone and everything else had gone through years of change. Sunny felt a bit out of place now that things had changed and she had five siblings. Her parents were very glad to have her back, however, and Aldura was a wonderful, pleasant place to live. Despite her young age, Sunny was able to work in some of Aldura's best labs. Even though much research had been lost in order to keep Casimir from obtaining it, many copies of the data had been stored in secret places. Some of the information and research that was lost was regained with Sunny and Marcel's knowledge. With both Sunny and Marcel's minds at work in Aldura's labs, there were many advances in technology; though Marcel and Sunny held back some of their knowledge so it would not be discovered outside of its time.

    And so Sunny lived with her parents at Capitol Haven and worked in a lab or two with Marcel. Marcel was pleasant and well-liked by everyone, but he was still shrouded in mystery. He never told anyone about his past or where he came from. Always, Sunny worked with the pleasure of Marcel's company. He had constantly guided her and befriended her, and she had grown to love him but at the same time, she always carried a sad weight over what she had witnessed in her past and Marcel's future. He knew she was bothered by something but could get nothing out of her. It was mysterious for him because Sunny would always tell him everything that was on her mind. If anyone asked Vala and Dr. Swann who Sunny was, they would say that she was their long-lost daughter who, under the circumstances of the beginning of Casimir's rise, had been lost but was now recently found. Some thought she looked like the mysterious girl who had appeared in the times of war, the one called Squimba, but they could never be sure since she had always been either masked, hooded, or kept out of close sight. On Sunny's eighteenth birthday, her parents hosted a ball in celebration. Sunny was beautiful in her yellow dress and seemed quite happy during the celebration, dancing many songs with Marcel. After the party and the days following, Marcel seemed to have something on his mind and Sunny wondered about it. When he came to visit Capitol Haven one evening, as was his weekly custom, Sunny drew him off to the side and into the garden before he left. She wanted to find out what was going on.

"You're hiding something, I know it," she said.

"There's no hiding from you, Sunny. I didn't tell you because I know what you'll do but I see there's no way out of it. I know you won't let me leave until you've heard what you want from me."

"No, I won't," responded Sunny.

"I'm going to leave; on another one of those missions assigned for me."

"So you're leaving? Again?"

"Yes, I must. I'm going tomorrow evening."

"What about me?"

"You know you can't come, you belong here now. Your work in this time business is finished."

"But I'm not a child anymore, you can't tell me what I can't do with my life."

"Sunny, you know how this works. Age and experience make no difference. Even I have to follow orders regarding time travel, it's not something I can just do on my own whim."

"So you'll just leave me? Will you ever come back?"

"I can't say for certain where I'll end up, but I do hope to return here when my task is finished."

"Please do…what is your task?" asked Sunny suddenly, with worry building up.

"Somewhere out there in time is a mother with her first child. That child is you, and she needs to be taken to the future before it is too late."

Sunny relaxed a bit. Then Marcel continued.

"Then after she is safely delivered, I will go to save her mother's life."

Tension rose in Sunny. "When she's only fifteen years old?" she asked.

"Yes."

"Then don't go, please don't go!"

"I have to, or Casimir Blade's rule returns; and you may never exist."

"Then take someone with you, let me go!"

"You know I can't do that. Why are you saying this? Why are you so worried?"

"I…I was there when you saved my mother. You…" she began to weep,"…you died."

Marcel looked at her with a bit of surprise. "I see. Is that what's been bothering you all these years?"

Epilogue

"It is."

"How did you witness this?"

Sunny would not answer. "Please don't go," she said.

"But I have to go, you know I must; and if I'm going to die, then that's how it will have to be."

"So you won't change your mind?"

"No."

"Then...beware of the knife, even when you have Casimir captured and bound, beware of the knife. I want to go with you."

"I won't let you come. If there's danger for me, there's danger for you."

"So this is the last I'll ever see of you?"

"If what you say is true, perhaps it is."

Sunny began bawling. Marcel held her to try and comfort her.

"I can see you tomorrow before I leave if you would like. If there's anything you want me to do for you, I'll do it. As long as it's within my rules."

Sunny knew what she wanted besides being able to go with Marcel, but she didn't know how to begin or whether Marcel would wish to give it to her.

"You've been around me for a long time, you usually know what I'm feeling. I suspect you know somewhat of how much I like you...how I feel about you."

"Well, I know you definitely like me, I would say I'm probably your closest friend."

"Yes, you are right about that but…you're more than my closest friend. Would you say the same about yourself? Is there a reason you stayed here in this time with me?"

Marcel considered the question. Why had he stayed with Sunny? "Well…I suppose I enjoyed your company…I've always enjoyed watching over you and sharing in your growth and in your life. I could share more with you and relate more to you than I could with most others and you always confided in me. I suppose I enjoy being around you more than others because you have more in common with me than just about anyone else."

"And that's it? Because…like you said, you're my closest friend. You're special to me, very special. I've never known exactly how you feel about me but I've always looked up to you, admired you,…and… loved you. Since you're leaving, going to your death, I'll never see you again. If I could ask for one thing from you before you leave, it would be this: to have your heart and to let me be your wife, even if it is just for a day."

Marcel did not expect this request and it took him a moment to ponder it. He had never given much thought to his future, only to the present because of his involvement with time travel. Marriage, or any lasting relationship for that matter, was not something he had ever given much consideration. With his way of life, it would have been difficult. Sunny was different

Epilogue

though, she already knew what his life was like and had experienced it for herself. They were close friends, and she was no longer a child. Why had he stayed on Aldura when she moved there? It was for her. In fact, much of his life had become about her and when she was sent to Aldura, he hadn't wanted to live life without her. He had always believed he was watching her and teaching her out of obligation, but really, it had been more of a choice than a command. The more he thought it over, the more he realized that he did in fact love her and that's what had kept him on Aldura with her. Sunny waited in suspense as he pondered his answer. Marcel continued,

"It's a crazy idea, seeing as I may be headed to my doom in a day…but you are right, I do love you too. You're the reason I'm here on Aldura and not somewhere else. But there is one thing I am concerned about: could you bear the loss if I don't return?"

"I'll have to bear it regardless. I would rather spend one day fully yours than just to have known you as a friend and to regret that decision."

"Sunny, you are the love of my life, and this decision makes me happy. I will accept your request, but first allow me to ask you properly," he said with a smile. "Of course, I would like to get your parents' approval, so, on that condition, will you marry me Ms. Swann?"

Sunny accepted him with joy and relief, but also with the bitterness of his future in the back of her mind. Together they went back inside the house and up to the second floor where most of the family's more private rooms were. They entered the smaller sitting room that was colored red, brown, and green with a wood floor, ceiling, and trim. The girls were off in other rooms while the rest of the family was in the small parlor. Vala was getting ready to sleep and Dr. Swann was browsing over some medical research. Sunny and Marcel entered the room.

"We have something we want to ask you," said Sunny to her parents.

She turned to glance at her brother - often called by his middle name - who was quietly minding his own business in the far corner, and decided it was okay for him to stay. Vala and Dr. Swann gave Sunny and Marcel their full attention. Sunny explained to them what Marcel was about to do, their relationship and current situation, and that they wanted to get married right away. Vala gave her wholehearted approval, she had seen it coming for years and wasn't as surprised as Sunny and Marcel would have thought. Dr. Swann seemed to be pondering something however.

"Marcel, it's been wonderful getting to know you over the last few years. It has become more and more obvious that you two are a good fit but your history is still unknown. You are still a mystery Marcel, and I don't feel right about giving my approval unless you can tell me who you really are."

Epilogue

"Well... it's my deepest secret... but I will tell you if I must, only please don't tell anyone else; it's a secret that should remain a secret. The truth is...I don't exist; in a way at least. I know it's a mystery and seems impossible, but it's true. There is no record of my birth, I don't have a birthday, I wasn't born at any particular time, and my parents cannot be found. When my mother was pregnant with me, she and my father were involved in the secret agency that built the time ship I travel in. They had built a time ship and though it had been tested with artificial intelligence, it had never been used by living beings. My parents volunteered to take the time ship on its first run but when they did, they discovered it had some defects and they could not land it. They were trapped flying through time with no hope of returning. My mother gave birth to me aboard the time ship they were trapped on. One day, the ship malfunctioned further, it was breaking apart. My father would not leave the ship because he was afraid it might crash and do damage if it was left uncontrolled. My mother would not leave him to pilot the ship for possibly the rest of his life alone, and so they both stayed. They wanted me to have a better future so my mother laid me down in safety and fastened a necklace around my neck. It was very ancient and its history was shrouded in mystery, it had the power of time travel. She also placed with me all the logs from their journey. She used the necklace to send me back into the time she wished for me to go to and so I ended up in a time just before the one I took Sunny to those many years ago. I was found with the logs and the ship's creators learned who I was and how the time ship had malfunctioned. The information that was found with me helped with the building of the second time ship. There I was raised and ever since, have worked for that same secret agency whose main goal was, and is, to keep Casimir and the menace that grew in his shadow from coming to power and destroying everything. It's the same agency your daughter was part of. We typically only monitor the past, present, and future and not get involved but this event they felt they must change. Several members worked on building a second time ship and then it was given to me so I could travel between times doing what I must to ensure Casimir's defeat. They decided to leave the ship in my care and let me keep it because it could be a dangerous thing to keep around. They thought it best if only one person possessed it. That is what I do, I travel through time. It's the only life I've lived."

Dr. Swann and Vala were amazed at Marcel's answer but it seemed to satisfy Dr. Swann. They agreed to support the marriage of Sunny and Marcel however they could and the four briefly discussed the matter and made some plans before they would part their ways.

Epilogue

"You're getting married now then? How are you going to be able to do it at this time of night?" asked Vala.

It was late and the courthouses were closed, but the Swann family knew someone who could help make the union official and legal. Marcel and Sunny prepared to leave, they wanted to waste no time.

"We'll go with you," said Vala, quickly preparing herself. Then she paused, as a thought dawned over her. She knew where Marcel was going and there was something he might need.

"Marcel, wait," she said. She ran to her room and rummaged through a box of jewelry. Then she found it – her engagement ring. She returned downstairs and handed it to Marcel. "I think you will need this. There's someone who's going to need a lot of convincing that you're genuine and safe."

The rest of the family was gathered and the girls swiftly ran out to the garden to collect a few flowers for Sunny, and so they were married late that night. Afterwards, Sunny parted ways with her family and went with Marcel to his small home and they took the next day off to enjoy each other. This was Marcel's last day before he would depart. At the end of the day, during the last two hours of sunlight, they went to a beach near the harbor. As soon as it was dark, Marcel would leave and go where Sunny could not. The sunset was a beautiful and sad sight. When it finally set, a ship anchored nearby to take Marcel to the island.

Marcel and Sunny gave their final and emotional goodbyes and Marcel boarded the ship, never to return. Sunny cried as she stood alone in the dark, watching the ship sail away. When she could see it no more, she returned back to the main harbor and then to Capitol Haven, in sorrow. She went to the garden where she had just been the night before and sat down and wept. She stayed this way for a while until her father came upon her in the dark. He sat down with her and comforted her. Few words were spoken between them, but they both understood each other. For the next several days, Sunny stayed in her room in a miserable state. She began to grow sick and would not eat and hardly drank until Dr. Swann insisted she take in more nourishment or he would use IV fluids on her. She seemed to have no desire to live until finally, she grew so sick that she was in a desperate situation and near death. Dr. Swann cared for Sunny and Vala acted as her nurse until both her health and her spirits, to some extent, finally revived. During Sunny's sickness, Dr. Swann had discovered that she was with child and when Sunny was told, she was comforted and regained the desire to live. Once she had recovered, Sunny got to work with her problem-solving mind. She spent many long hours, which turned into a few years, working away on a project - something that had never been done before. Marcel had taught her how to operate his time ship and showed her many of the parts and how it worked. She had journaled

Epilogue

everything she learned about the time ship, as well as many calculations and plans. She was going to use her records to build a time ship of her own. Finally, after a few years of labor, her ship was completed and tested. Sunny packed some of her weapons and gear from long ago and loaded them onto her ship. She told her family her plans and departed, leaving her little daughter Lilly, who had been born at home, with her family. She was going to save Marcel. When she arrived, Casimir had already been taken inside Marcel's ship. Sunny landed out of sight and stealthily crept into Marcel's time ship without being seen by anyone. She arrived just in time to see Marcel already dying while her younger self was bending over him. *Move kid, I don't want to spoil your memories since they're what brought me here, but we're running out of time!* she thought to herself. Finally, the younger Sunny silently walked away now that Marcel was certainly dead. As soon as the younger Sunny was out of sight, Sunny rushed over to Marcel. She examined him and found that there was still a small bit of life left in him. He opened his eyes briefly and weakly and saw her bending over him, then he closed them again.

"I'm here, I won't let you die," said Sunny.

She quickly rushed him out and into her own time ship just as the other one departed. She did all she could for Marcel and then brought him back to her home and to the hospital in Verona at a time when she knew Dr. Swann would be there, the day after she left. She quickly brought Marcel in and he received treatment immediately. The next day, Sunny brought little Lilly to see her father for the first time and he was delighted.

"I saved you," said Sunny with a smile.

"So you have... It's funny, I sort of watched you grow up right before my eyes in one day. I took you as a girl to help convince your mother to make her choice and gave you that necklace, the one Casimir somehow got his hands on. Then I took you in my arms when you were just a baby, I'm sure you don't remember that. I saw you as a stowaway and then, just for a brief second, I saw you as you are now."

Sunny lightly laughed. "It seems like I'm your life's work."

"I can agree." He paused. "It appears I've missed a few years since I left. You've changed - a little - but you're still the same Sunny. I see you've let your hair grow out too."

"There wasn't much to see other than your daughter growing. You haven't changed a bit, and now I've caught up to you by a few years."

When Marcel was well enough, he and his family returned to their home on Aldura.

"Sunny, where did you take my time ship?" asked Marcel when he realized what Sunny had done to rescue him.

Sunny remembered back to when she was twelve.

Epilogue

"I-please don't be too upset with me, I was just a girl; frightened, and sad. When I landed back in the proper time, you were gone... I wrecked it and I'm sure it's beyond repair. I'm sorry, I can pay you back with the one I built though."

Marcel didn't know what to say, there were certainly other things she could have done with it. Then he laughed.

"Oh well, I don't suppose we should go back and help you save it. I'll share your new one with you. It's not as nice as mine of course, but after I work on it, it will be the best time ship yet," he said, half teasing, "You didn't destroy your plans and calculations for it I hope."

"No, they're around somewhere. Why do you ask?"

"Because my parents and your foster parents - before they took you - discovered them and were able to make the time ship you destroyed based on those plans. I was able to help with the project."

"Well, I'm glad you ended up with the time ship and taught me about how it worked, or I would have never drawn those plans," said Sunny. "Wait...so you're saying the only reason your time ship exists is because my time ship was built?" she asked.

"Yes...and your time ship was built only because my time ship was built, and it was based on your plans!" replied Marcel.

They both laughed in wonder.

"So our time ships exist because of each other!" exclaimed Marcel.

"Yes! But which one came first?" replied Sunny.

They both gave each other a look and then laughed again. So Marcel modified and improved Sunny's time ship as another year passed. Shortly after the completion of the ship, Marcel began to grow restless and decided he couldn't stay in one time and place, he felt like he was out of place; he knew too much of the future and had experienced it as well. He had come from the stars and that's where he desired to return. Having experienced much of the same life Marcel had experienced, Sunny agreed to travel somewhere new. They lived out the remainder of the year on Aldura and when the new year came about, they loaded up into the time ship which had been converted into a comfortable abode, and began to live their life traveling through many different times and places. What better way to teach Lilly about history, geography, and culture than to actually experience it? thought Sunny. They could go anywhere, but only to observe and experience, not to interfere with timelines. Besides, Marcel's parents were still out there and now that he was relieved of his duties and had more freedom, he couldn't rest until he did his best to locate them and save them. So they left and lived their life traveling through space and time, but would always return to visit Sunny's family.

Epilogue

Back on Aldura, Vala and Galen's son, Fabian, grew up to enjoy the quiet country life and became a writer and storyteller, working with many different types of media. Their second daughter, Lynn, grew to live life to the fullest and loved to get excitement out of it. She enjoyed riding horses and became a great rider in her younger days as did her second youngest sister. When it came time to choose a career path, she decided to follow the same path as her father and became a doctor and a scientist which came from her love of science and desire to help people. The third daughter enjoyed gymnastics and dance, including ice dancing. Vala and Ariella maintained a close friendship and Ariella enjoyed teaching Ella, the third daughter, all she knew about dancing and passed on her passion for it. Ella became so talented that she, just like Ariella, eventually earned the reputation of being one of the best dancers in the galaxy. She also became a well-known artist and fashion designer when she was no longer physically able to keep up with rigorous competitive dancing. Auralia, the fourth daughter, enjoyed many activities and hobbies, all of which Aldurans were famous for, but had a special passion for horses and archery. She was a top rider in various disciplines, but also excellent in archery and horseback archery. After some years of competing in her favorite sports, she became a veterinarian and coached archery and horse riding later in life, as well as serving as a representative in Aldura's house for a term. Clair, the last child, loved flowers and horticulture. She too enjoyed archery but also liked to raise and show chickens and rabbits. When it came to education, she decided to go into plant and animal sciences. Ariella's oldest daughter became quite popular. She began as a fashion model and went on to beauty contests. Unlike her mother, who never cared for such things, Mariah went all the way to the galactic level and competed in the Galactic Beauty Pageant. She won and was from then on known as the most beautiful and talented young lady in the galaxy. From there, Mariah was involved in popular galactic entertainment and was widely known. She was also tough and spirited like her parents; she loved to ride horses and became a very good rider, even for an Alduran and as a youth, competed in equestrian competitions. Her sister enjoyed sports and fitness as well as several other common Alduran activities. She was fun and pleasant and went on to study sports medicine. The oldest of the brothers, Colt, loved adventure and was fascinated with weapons as a boy. Eventually, he took a role serving on Aldura's police force and then moved into some secret operations. His brother Rian enjoyed working with horses on the ranch and became a horse trainer and growing up, he and his older sister would often spend lots of time working with their horses and taking them on adventures in Florina's rural farm region. He also developed a talent and passion for

Epilogue

making music. Although they lived at Capitol Haven, Galen and Vala often liked to take time to travel with their family to Florina and stay at a smaller house they owned. Ariella and Corin too would take their family when they could, to stay in Florina, Ariella's beloved homeland; it was where they preferred to live when Ariella was not needed at the capital. It became a wonderful life on Aldura.